TELEPORT 1

JOSHUA T. CALVERT

PROLOGUE

The drill ship looked like a gray, salt-eaten garbage dump. Two hundred and fifty-five meters long and forty-two meters wide, it was an ugly colossus formed of steel, dirt, and the monetary dreams of wealthy executives on another continent who wanted nothing to do with the dirty work that made them so much money. There was so much metal protruding from its hull it resembled a dense forest. It made your eyes blur as it dominated all but the actual drilling rig, a one hundred-meter-tower of spindly struts, atop which sprouted two yellow-painted fingers containing numerous probes and the arm-thick bolts of the rig's safety system.

The *Deep Sea Explorer*, as it was called, trudged leisurely through the mouth of Lake Maracaibo accompanied by a fleet of smaller barges and supply ships. They passed the town that gave the lake its name, whose houses overgrew the left bank like spotty mushrooms.

From the stern of the main ship leading the small fleet, Anders Larsson felt the passage through the strait was a rape of the place's natural beauty. The bluish green water stood out against the long Major Rafael Urdaneta Bridge, a silver line connecting the two shores in the background. It had opened only a few hours ago with great fanfare.

The thousands of inhabitants of Maracaibo had come to witness the spectacle of their passing. Not because the leisurely procession was particularly handsome—no, the people's dreams overrode its lack of beauty. The *Deep Sea Explorer* meant prosperity for the whole region. At least, that was what the Venezuelan government had been trying to assure them for months.

But that was not why Anders was here. He had come to oversee the drilling effort and ensure that schedules were met, not deal with the political lies that had guaranteed his employer was contracted.

In truth, it was not his usual employer at all but an art enterprise, a diplomatic Frankenstein. A year ago, prospectors from Shell had discovered a new oil reservoir under the lake, which was already a rich source of black gold. The first samples were taken by engineers from Russia's Bashneft. No doubt it was due to the close ties between the Russian and Venezuelan governments that this *incident*, as the EU Commission president had called it, had occurred. Eventually, an agreement that all sides could live with had been reached, unhappily but greedily.

A European-Russian company was formed to exploit the new oil source. That the data was hardly clear enough to be so contentious in advance of drilling had apparently interested no one. Anders, however, knew that the huge cavity under the seabed—because the lake was not actually a lake at all but an inlet of the Gulf of Venezuela—could also be a bubble of compacted gas. Not an ideal proposition.

"Why are you making such a face?" Alexei Yevchenkov asked. Yevchenkov, the Russian chief engineer, stood next to him, his elbows on the railing. He eyed the ugly pile of ships marked by the dirt of their work, lit a cigarette, and inhaled with a hiss.

"Smoking is a bad habit, but for someone who works in the petroleum sector, it's practically suicidal."

Yevchenkov waved it off. "Ah, I don't see any oil yet, and I have reason to celebrate."

"Like what?" Anders raised a brow.

"It's warm!" The Russian put the cigarette between his lips and spread his arms. "Tropical temperatures, fresh sea air, a new project with good pay! What more could you want?"

"To confirm what we think we've found."

"Don't be so doom and gloom. My compatriots found the black broth, so it's there."

"The entire lake bottom is full of oil, but a reservoir like what we think we've found sounds almost too good, if you ask me," Anders replied glumly.

"Think positive. The fleet is here. Tomorrow night we can start drilling the first well." Yevchenkovv's rolling accent somehow matched the rugged appearance of the ships leisurely pursuing them. "Then we'll stand here and watch our contracts turn to gold."

Anders shook his head. "No, we're not going to stand here."

"I don't know what you're going to do, but I don't have anything to do until the day after tomorrow…"

He interrupted his Russian colleague. "Did you read anything about this place before you got on the plane?"

"Yes. The weather data and how high the Andes are that frame the lake."

Anders stifled a frustrated sigh.

"Oh, come on!" Yevchenkovv rolled his eyes. "All right

then, why won't we stand here?"

"Because this is place has the most lightning per square kilometer in the world. There are violent thunderstorms just about every night.

"The lake is a warm celsius. The high foothills of the Andes, which you like so much, hold the moisture that evaporates during the day in the geological basin. At night, the slopes of the mountains cool much faster than the warm air above the lake. Now, at the height of summer, up to one hundred lightning bolts per square kilometer have been recorded—per night. Five oil production facilities catch fire or are destroyed every year. Shoreline deaths occur weekly, and the discharges kill entire herds of livestock." Anders nodded as saw his colleague grow pale. "So, the high salary that you're so happy about has the proverbial *catch*."

They remained silent until they arrived at their destination ten hours later.

Anders ate in the small mess hall, reviewed final checks and reports from his staff, and signed off on the plan for the initial drilling.

The inland sea was only thirty-five meters deep at its deepest point, making a drillship like the *Deep Sea Explorer*, which could drill to fourteen thousand meters, overkill. Still, this was not his easiest project. The presumed proven oil reservoir was over nine thousand meters deep. The bottom was riddled with tiny veins of seawater, perfect conductors for the electrical discharges that boiled over the lake every night. On top of that, there was the danger of not being able to drill a direct channel, instead they'd have to fight fractures in the sediment over and over again. Apart from that, he could already envision a disaster similar to BP's in the Gulf of Mexico approaching after the first lightning cascades set fire to an improperly sealed pipeline.

At 11 p.m. local time, he was standing on the bridge of the *Dolphin*, the only reasonably comfortable ship in their sweatshop fleet, that housed management, and thus he and Yevchenkov as project managers. Together, they stood on the bridge and watched the *Deep Sea Explorer*, now just a conglomerate of lights in the darkness, surrounded by the nearby escort ships holding their positions like smaller outgrowths. From a kilometer away, the colossus in their midst almost looked like a still image, creating many reflections on the rippled surface of the lake when not moving restlessly back and forth.

"*Que trae desgracia,*" said one of the Venezuelan engineers near the captain, who was disinterestedly sipping a coffee.

"What is he saying?" Anders wanted to know.

"Something about bad luck," Yevchenkov replied shrugging. "But don't worry, they're all superstitious here."

"Because of the lightning, I suppose."

"Yes. Read a guidebook. Locals think the center of the lake is cursed, partly because of lightning. Supposedly, a lot of fishermen have disappeared here."

"Disappeared?"

"Sunk, I don't know." The Russian shrugged again.

"Well then..." Anders put his radio to his mouth. "All right, get started. Constant pressure checks. I don't want the valves loaded above ninety percent. Got it?"

He received confirmation from his chief engineer aboard the drill ship and hummed with satisfaction. Red lights started rotating above the rig, a sign the project had finally begun.

The predicted thunderstorm arrived half an hour later, announcing itself with a deep rumble of thunder that rolled in from the mouth of the inland sea. Half an hour after that,

Anders was one of the few still awake and following the events on the *Deep Sea Explorer* by binocular and radio.

The storm reached them and enveloped the entire fleet with dense rain, boneshaking thunder, and so many flashes of lightning that he had to keep blinking to get rid of the flickering afterimages. At times, the entire horizon lit up, and he thought he saw dozens of discharges at once forming jagged blurs between the masses of smothering black clouds and the whipped-up sea.

It was an eerie sight that made the hairs on the back of his neck stand on end.

Just a thunderstorm, he thought. He urging himself to be calm.

But the next flashes of lightning struck the surface of the water next to the drill ship, causing white spray to leap up in several places at once. In their light, the ships looked bizarre, like nightmarish shadows of angular metal and sharp blades. And if these impacts had frightened him, it soon got worse.

Second by second, more massive electrical pulses crashed into the water. They seemed to move concentrically toward the *Deep Sea Explorer*. Anders spotted irregularities on the dancing waves and jerked back from his binoculars. He was startled when he realized they were merely dead fish.

Over his radio, he intercepted the first panicked calls from security technicians on the drill ship, their initial worried queries now manifesting. Someone was taken to the infirmary. It was hard to make out because so many employees were calling in the confusion, some in different languages.

"Meyer! Come in!" he yelled angrily on his safety engineer's channel.

"Larsson? All hell is breaking loose here! We've had two impacts. They didn't do any structural damage, but several workers got burned and the Venezuelans are totally freaking out. They want to evacuate!" His German co-workers voice was scratchy with static.

"Have they gone crazy? Threaten immediate dismissal! I don't care! They're just flashes!"

"I'm trying to do that, but..."

"Meyer, what's wrong?"

"Um, we've got something weird on the ground sensors here. There's a lot of energy building up."

"In what form?"

"Electricity."

"Down there?"

"Yeah. Also, the drill head has registered some magnetic anomaly. It's pulling almost five degrees to the left."

"Impossible!"

"Larsson, I'm telling you, this says—"

The connection broke.

Anders kept hitting the Send button and yelling into the microphone but got no response. He looked up through the bridge windows. At first, there was just a feeling that something was happening, though he didn't see any change. Then the lights on the *Deep Sea Explorer* shook and danced. The steel colossus shook as if it were standing on a vibrating plate. Suddenly something happened that he saw with his eyes, but his brain could not make sense of. The ship was squeezed like a soda can, the hull wrinkled and cracked, compressed until it was the size of a semi truck, and buffeted by the inland sea tides rushing in. The escort fleet was moved, pulled downward several meters and toward the flotilla's destroyed center, as if invisible hands were tugging at them from the depths.

"What's happening?" Larsson shouted, not expecting an answer.

The entire *Dolphin* bridge crew froze until the captain started yelling wild orders in Italian.

The horizon of destruction before Anders's slowly veered away as their ship was pulled to port and the engines engaged with a loud roar. "Where is my ship?"

The compressed mountain of sheet metal left a mighty whirlpool as it sank into the water, whipped up the concentrated lightning striking exactly where a ship, over two hundred and fifty meters long, had been moments ago.

The night seemed especially dark and the thunder deafening as the *Deep Sea Explorer* disappeared and the fleet fled hopelessly.

Anders breathed heavily. His heart was pounding like a steam hammer in his chest, and cold sweat stood on his forehead.

"Mr. Larsson?" The voice was slurred and he hurriedly looked around. He was lying in his bunk on the *Dolphin*, looking into the boxy face of an unshaven man. *Yevchenkov.* "They're here."

"I'll... I'll be right there," he said to his colleague. He struggled out of the wet sheets and stepped into the shower, letting the rain of tingling drops run down his face.

The images of the dream slowly rolled off him like stubborn dirt. The last week had been pure hell. Not only had all the local employees and suppliers pulled out, but many of the European and Russian employees refused to fulfill their contracts—not that Anders had any idea about how they would do that anyway.

Experts from the Russian/European conglomerate had

flown in but never arrived at the lake. They were special diplomatic envoys with their respective EU and Kremlin advisory staffs and displayed such a strangely cool manner that they could only be intelligence officers. They had questioned him, Yevchenkov and the bridge crew for days before the first warships had arrived. First the USS *Brixton,* a Navy cruiser, then the Russian's *Kuzneszov,* until six ships from each of the two nations reached the center of the lake three days ago. They were assured it was merely a joint maneuver following an invitation from the Venezuelan president, as if the US and Russia would ever conduct combined operations. Since then, the water shook continuously and the number of dead fish on the surface had increased.

Anders dried off, got dressed, and picked up his luggage, which he had packed the night before and placed next to the door.

On the quarterdeck, the helicopter that would take them to the international airport was already warmed up. Yevchenkov and the captain of the *Dolphin* were already sitting in the passenger cabin and wearing their thick headphones to protect their ears from the noise. Anders began to sweat again despite the gale-force winds. He ducked under the rotors to join them.

On his seat was a folder held closed with a rubber band. He picked it up before he sat down and pushed his suitcase under the seat with his heels.

"It's a cease-and-desist," Yevchenkov said over the radio.

"A cease-and-desist letter? For what?" Anders asked as he fumbled the mouthpiece to his lips and clumsily removed the rubber band. "Two hundred pages?"

"Yes. Your people and my people obviously don't want us to talk about this crazy thing."

"But... *two hundred* pages?"

The helicopter took off as if in slow motion, wobbling slightly.

"They pre-dated the military exercise by a week. Supposedly, there was an accident with a nuclear submarine under our drilling fleet. Some sort of secret maneuver that caused the rig to blow up," the Russian explained then pursed his lips.

"Such a..." Anders waved it off. "It doesn't matter. With two hundred pages, I'm sure they've covered everything even remotely related to Venezuela to silence us in court."

"And break us financially," Yevchenkov added.

The helicopter banked in a long arc, past the tightly clumped fleet of American and Russian warships arrayed in an almost perfect circle. Two supply ships, thick hulks of gray steel, were in their midst. From their decks, huge cranes supported steel cables that descended into the blue waves. The cruisers and destroyers in the vicinity began to darken the sky with smoke launchers, obscuring the site from prying eyes in orbit or aircraft skirting the no-fly zone.

Anders managed to catch a glimpse of an oval shadow being lifted from the depths by the cranes. At first, he thought of a giant whale, but the shape was too uniform, too perfect, even if the edges were anything but clear and blurred by the water effects.

"What is that?" he whispered, not needing to ask to know this mysterious shadow was located exactly where the *Deep Sea Explorer* had sunk a week ago.

"That must be the wreck!" opined Yevchenkov, leaning over the armrest of his seat, but the smoke was already so thick their view remained locked out.

That was not the wreck, Anders thought.

1

James pretended to read the mission briefing but held the documents in front of him so he could hide his smartphone from the two State Department officers. The flight from Washington to Mombasa took forever but sleep was out of the question. He was far too nervous for that. This mission was too delicate to even take a quiet minute. So, he bred little pixel chickens, planted new fields, and laid tiny streams to nurture his digital farm.

The game was a useful distraction, not because he was worried about blowing the assignment, but because of the special conditions it entailed. He had waited for this opportunity for three years and the time had finally come: the right assignment at the right time. Now he eagerly waited for a text. He'd been checking for a total of twenty hours and thirty-one minutes—and for good measure, his email, too. Nothing. No answer.

"Mr. Hamilton?"

He looked up at one of the two flight attendants dressed in blue and white uniforms providing service on the small

Learjet. Her smile was flawless as she offered him a perfectly folded hot cloth on a tray.

"Thank you."

He carefully picked it up and wiped his hands, and when no one was looking his face as well.

The Foreign Service Officers, Carl Vega and Mitch Blake, were two feisty Washington civil servants with big bellies and thinning hair. They shifted in their seats and woke out of the half-sleep that had befuddled them for the past few hours and allowed James to get some rest.

Vega cleared his throat noisily and said in a groggy voice, "Good morning."

"Good morning," James replied.

"We landing soon?"

"They're about to serve breakfast. Maybe an hour."

"Didn't you sleep at all?" Vega rubbed his eyes and smoothed his shirt.

"No need."

"This thing is really important, Mr. Hamilton. Vincent Debongo is a key informant for the CIA and—"

"I really need to interrogate him to know what he might have revealed. I get it. Besides, his father is an extremely wealthy industrialist in Kenya." James tapped the folder and flipped it shut, letting the smartphone fall into his lap as he did so, concealed by the table. "I went through everything."

In truth, he hadn't read a single line of the CIA report, certain there was nothing unexpected there.

"Good, then you also know that—"

"Vincent Debongo is an undercover agent with Boko Haram. Your eyes and ears in one of the worst terrorist organizations in the world. Those were the secretary of state's words, weren't they?"

"Exactly." Vega raised his hands in surrender "All right."

"You have to trust me. I'm the best at my job."

"That's what we've been told," Vega responded, nodding and smiling as he got his own hot towel.

The jet touched down at Moi International Airport at 9 a.m. local time and slowly taxied to the small private terminal where a host of intelligence officers checked their IDs and special documents and bombarded them with a huge arsenal of stamps, before loading them into a large Volkswagen SUV with tinted windows, one of three vehicles waiting for them. The soldiers accompanying them wore baggy uniforms and held Kalashnikovs with scuffed wooden elements. James had been to Africa enough times to know these guys were tough and probably better trained than they looked.

Their small convoy raced over the dusty streets of the smoggy city, breaking all traffic rules and not caring about red lights. More than once, James thought they were going to crash and was happy he had buckled up. Blake, the other Officer, was turning white and looked as if he wanted to throw up.

It got better once they left the city and were traveling west over endless dirt roads. He had never been to Kenya before, which had disappointed him the last three years, and he had imagined it differently. The land near the great deltas and inland seas surrounding this juggernaut of a city was surprisingly green and well-watered. There were banana plantations and cassava fields as far as the eye could see.

The sun blazed down on them. It was so hot that he felt it through the roof of the SUV, although the air conditioning was running at full blast. It was probably just his imagination. Still, he was sweating where his back and buttocks touched the faux leather of the back seat.

Each kilometer they traveled west, the landscape became drier and more barren. Green fields were replaced by brown ones. Old farm machinery no longer functioned, so instead hundreds of men and women with cloths on their heads rammed simple tools into the earth to plow or harvest the meager crops. Leaves were replaced by withered branches and grasses and eventually by light sand. Their motorcade, speeding madly, kicked up huge clouds of dust behind them, which looked like a storm front in the rearview mirror, shifting northward on the light southerly wind, enveloping the field workers and settling on their few crops.

It was like looking at a real-life metaphor showing him how the world worked. Some drove through the countryside in luxurious cars, their soft bodies wafted by the cool of an air conditioner, while others tried to wrest food from the earth by the simplest of means and were smothered by the dirt of others in the process.

The world in one sentence, he thought and chewed on his lower lip as the shadowy figures in the dust slowly became recognizable again. *I wonder if they are even bothered by it anymore? Or do they just keep working and take it?*

"Are you all right?" Vega asked, worried. His shirt was already sweated through where it was stretched across the rolls of flab. "You look restless."

"Don't worry; the deal will work out."

"What makes you so sure?"

James shrugged. "I have experience, and your boss requested the best, right?"

Blake turned around in the passenger seat and looked like he was about to say something, but James just raised a hand.

"Look, both of you. It just occurred to me how strange it is to be here."

"What do you mean?" Vega frowned.

"The CIA is making a deal with Kenyan intelligence, whose acronym I don't even know. These people here"—he pointed out the window, even though there were no more fields to be seen—"work their whole lives to make a dollar a day. They have calluses on their hands, aching backs, and one of their five children will starve to death next year. How much money do we have available, huh?"

"About twenty million US dollars," Vega replied not understanding it was a rhetorical question.

"I wonder what you could do with that money instead of playing a game that has only created chaos for a hundred years."

"You mean we should give the money to the people? So they can have more food only to have Boko Haram slaughter them a few months from now?"

"Come on, you don't believe that, do you? The CIA just wants to get their hands on your informant to protect our people. If it hadn't been for the attack on our embassy in Mombasa, we wouldn't have lifted a finger. How long do you think it would take to eliminate these terrorists if we really wanted to?"

"It's not our place to judge," Blake grumbled, turning around. "You're here because you know Vincent Debongo personally."

"I don't need a motivational speech. And I only spoke to him for fifteen minutes two months ago at an embassy reception in Cape Town where he was a guest with his father. That's hardly a special connection."

"The Agency needs you to be as motivated as possible to

do your best. And so does the Ministry. We don't need to worry about anything else."

"Of course, we don't. So, let's get our rich son out of there and make the world a better place," James snorted and looked out the window, ending the conversation. By now, there was little to interest the eye except various shades of brown and the mountains, which looked like they were covered in rust. They were rugged and jagged while possessing a raw beauty that radiated something untouched, authentic, just like this entire continent, which he was never sure whether to love or hate. He had enough reasons to do both wholeheartedly, that much was certain.

Rukanga, their destination and agreed meeting place, was, Wikipedia assured him, a village, but the CIA's brief had been much more realistic: There were perhaps a dozen huts with corrugated iron roofs and rough wooden walls that appeared to date back to colonial times. There were never more than two huts in one place, and the few gnarled trees barely concealed the neighboring houses, which were a few hundred meters away.

Their convoy stopped in front of a particularly long one-story building with "Moi High School Kasigau" written above the entrance, then stopped with a screech of tires. It took a minute for the cloud of dust catch up with them and pass; then their driver turned to him.

"We are here," he said. He had a strong accent and a serious face.

"All right, then. I guess it's my turn now," James said, nodding. He prepared to get out.

"Wait a minute. What about your bag?" Vega asked, pointing to the small briefcase in the footwell.

"Is this his first time?" James asked Blake. He shook his head, exited.

He slammed the door behind him, and silence fell until a hot wind blew withered baobab leaves around his feet. The school was surrounded by rust brown dust clouds formed by tiny breezes and appeared abandoned, but he knew better. He walked along the short gravel path to the front door, avoiding the urge to look around for his escort. He recognized the need, that basic instinct, wanting to call his tribe for support, help, or even simple closeness. But the task at hand had to work without all that.

That was his job.

He knocked on the dry wood. He felt its rough grain against his knuckles. A Kenyan man in a forest camouflage uniform opened the door and pressed the muzzle of a pistol against his forehead. The metal was cold, making it feel absurdly comfortable.

"I am unarmed," he said and swallowed.

The knowledge that death was, as of now, a potential outcome for the day, hit him in his core and electrified him from the soles of his feet to the tips of his hair. There was no more room for sorrow or worry, only breathing, arrow quick thoughts, and the assimilation of every smell, no matter how tiny. Every one of his senses resonated and was focused, as if someone had turned an intensity knob past maximum.

"Step forward, *tumba!*" the man hissed, dragging him inside by his shoulder before scowling at the SUVs and slamming the door shut. They stood in a dimly lit room, a huge classroom, the only one in this supposed "high school." Four more gunmen stood or sat around two desks, their rifles shouldered. The whites of their eyes shone in their ebony faces, like predators at dusk.

James was roughly searched for weapons, but he had nothing on him except his smartphone. One of the terrorists took it and removed the battery before putting both in his pocket. He then pulled a black burlap sack out of his backpack and put it over James's head. The world abruptly went black and he nearly tripped as he was grabbed roughly from behind and shoved forward. Someone pushed something pointed into his back that his imagination and experience made into the muzzle of a Kalashnikov. The bag smelled of a mixture of dust and sweat, and a hint of cinnamon that confused him. Door hinges squeaked, barely audible, but the unpleasant sound did not escape James's brain which was running in overdrive, nor did the wind blowing across a loose piece of varnish on the door through which he was pushed. He was put into a car that smelled of leather faded by the sun. The air became suddenly stuffy as soon as the doors were closed. The engine howled.

He felt no fear, at least no more than he was used to in situations like this. He was experienced enough to know how this worked, and there was nothing unusual happening yet. Since he would be nothing but trouble for them anyway, he could relax, and he did, in his own way. He enjoyed the heightened senses, the metallic taste in his mouth as if he had taken too many painkillers. Nothing mattered more than the sounds around him, the feel of the seat under his buttocks and against his back, of being carried and not having to do anything. Freed from monotonous thoughts about unimportant things that had nothing to do with real life, he relished the here and now, inhaling and exhaling, perceiving one moment and the next—and all at the same time. Simple and intuitive, his body took care of all that automatically. It needed no intervention, just his presence.

The drive lasted a about two or three hours, although it was impossible to estimate since it seemed to him like an eternity, but at the same time as long as it took to snap one's fingers. Their vehicle stopped, ending the endless hum of the engine and the scratching and cracking of the gravel in the wheel wells. Doors opened, phrases were exchanged in the local language, then he was dragged out into the scorching heat and the ubiquitous screeching concert of locusts.

The bag was ripped from his head and the glare of the blazing sun poured down on him like a laser. He groaned and squeezed his eyes shut, blinked repeatedly against the pain in his eyes until he could make out the outlines of five figures, one of which was smaller than the others. He gradually realized the figure was not smaller but tied sitting in a chair. Two heavily armed men in dark camouflage clothing stood to the man's right and left, their faces emotionless.

A sixth man entered his field of vision from one side. He was unarmed and wore a Muslim prayer cap on his head. Although it was hard to be certain, James did not believe he held any religious beliefs.

"Good afternoon," he said, straightening and trying to regain some dignity. In doing so, he assumed a stiff formal posture.

"You're Mr. Schmidt?" the man, possibly the leader, asked.

"You can call me that. I'm sure you know how that works."

"Good. I am Shahir. We can negotiate now."

James looked at Vincent Debongo. He was a stocky young man with a calculating look and soft mouth. He was wearing a dirty pinstripe suit and was bound to a simple chair with duct tape. They were standing in the middle of rough, semi-desert surrounded by rocky hills a few hundred yards away. The sun beat down mercilessly on them and he broke out in a sweat.

"Are you all right, Mr. Debongo?" he asked calmly.

The young man nodded.

"Have you been subjected to psychological or physical violence?"

"No."

"Have you been injected with potentially dangerous substances or had your health compromised in any way in the long term?"

"No."

"Good, then we can start the negotiation."

Shahir got straight to the point. "We want fifty million US dollars."

His African accent, which danced up and down, had sounded somewhat like a sputtering engine, making it seem bizarrely menacing. Quite fitting for someone who had probably amputated more limbs and slaughtered more children than depicted in your average American horror movie. It was easy to forget who you were dealing with when it was just two people having a normal conversation, but James did not.

"That kind of money doesn't exist. Not for this."

Shahir motioned to one of his men, who drew a pistol and put it to Debongo's right temple.

"If you want to end the negotiation now, go ahead."

James swallowed with feigned nervousness, which he pretended to cover. "I'll tell you what will happen then: you will no longer have a hostage and I will no longer have a bargaining chip. After that, you have two options: You let me go and you've cost the American and Kenyan taxpayers some money. A big win for your *organization*? I don't think so. Or you can also shoot me—though I would not welcome that—and this will become the last ransom negotiation for Boko Haram. The CIA will think twice about ever spending any money on you or your people. You understand what I mean, don't you?"

Shahir gave him a long look, which James returned, before looking at the ground, as if intimidated, in keeping with his self-assigned role.

"I wouldn't be in favor of either option," he continued, presumably trying to fill the awkward silence. "If I'm successful, I might get a raise and keep my job and you'll have more money in your bank account. How does that sound to you?"

"Like a salesman's line," Shahir said but motioned again to his lackey, and he tucked the pistol back into its leg holster.

"I *am* a salesman. I sell the future. The future of Mr. Vincent Debongo here and a future for *you*." James clapped his hands and rubbed them together. "So, Mr. Debongo's father is willing to pay you ten million US dollars if you release his son now and return with me to the exchange point."

"Ten million?" Shahir's hand twitched, as if he wanted to gesture to his man.

"Wait. That's a lot of money. You can buy a lot of Kalashnikovs and matériel with that," James hurried to say, as if nervous, and wiped fresh sweat from his forehead with the back of his hand.

"Thirty million."

"I have a nephew; his name is Jeremy. For his fourth birthday, he really wanted the new knight's castle from Playmobil. You know Playmobil, right?" The terrorist leader scowled. "All right, so he wanted this castle, but he already had one. It was smaller and not quite as impressive as this new one he'd seen at the toy store, so he did what all kids his age do: he howled like a dog. But my sister was smart. She told him he could have it if he gave up his old castle in exchange. He couldn't have both of them."

"Get to the point, man, or I'll show you my *old* machete!" Shahir growled.

"So, uh..." James swallowed. "He was only four years old, but he understood and remembered it two years later when he was about to start school. He had his eye on a new satchel and my sister didn't want to buy him the new one because his old one was still good. He reminded her about the castle, and she realized that—"

"Thirty million!"

"Look, if they cough up thirty million now—which I don't have available—that's the last time you'll get a knight's castle from us. If you want a new satchel, we'll remember that you didn't want to give away your old castle, that you were a greedy boy."

"Are you calling me a damn kid, *Momba*?" the man roared, and his right hand went to the rusty machete hanging from his belt.

"He's telling you that you could get a new satchel in the future, too," Debongo said. He sounded exhausted but didn't look hurt or dehydrated.

Shahir eyed James closely and bared his teeth like a predator before exchanging a long look with his hostage and finally nodding.

"Twenty million."

"Fifteen. I have a reputation to uphold!"

"Eighteen!"

"All right, it's a deal."

James held out his hand, palm up, whereupon Shahir gestured to another of his men, who reached into his pocket and placed the smartphone and battery in James's hand. He quickly reassembled it and opened the only app on it. "I need the bank details."

Shahir held out his own phone to him on which the corresponding data could be seen. James initiated the transfer and waited until his counterpart's device emitted a loud chime after a few minutes of silence. Instead of smiling greedily as he had often seen the other party do, the Kenyan's expression barely changed.

"You can leave your cell phone on," he said and signaled to his men. Vincent Debongo and he had black bags placed over their heads and James was dragged to the chair and bound with duct tape to one of the legs.

He did not complain, he had expected something like this.

"Mr. Hamilton, I—" Debongo started.

"Don't," was all he said and they fell silent.

Through the sack of coarse cotton, his world was dark with many tiny twinkling stars in the firmament and a brooding heat that made sweat run in rivers under the fabric of his suit.

He soon fell into a kind of trance of thirst and exhaustion. He felt feverish, restless, while at the same time as if he had been injected with a sedative. The rise and fall of the screeching locusts that somehow managed to live in this barren land became more and more unpleasant, as if it was trying to crush him with its volume. Thus, he did not notice the sounds of approaching engines until they were so close that he could hear the squeak of their hydraulic brakes tormented by the omnipresent dust.

"That took a long time," he grumbled as one of the Kenyan soldiers pulled the sack off his head and another fought with the duct tape restraints. He kept his eyes closed until he and Debongo were completely freed. Only then did he blink, his eyes protesting again against the blinding light, and see Vega and Blake standing in front of him, fanning themselves with their hands.

"So?" Vega asked, sipping from a water bottle, which he handed to James after being glared at.

"Eighteen million," James replied breathlessly. He emptied the water in one go and made sure the hostage was taken care of as well.

"Eighteen? You're slipping."

"It was an extremely tough negotiation." He turned to Debongo. "Are you ready to go home?"

The young man nodded, visibly tired. "Yes. Thank you, Mister—"

"It's okay," James said, patting him on the shoulder. "We should get out of here now."

2

James glanced in the mirror and tried in vain to smooth the crow's feet at the corners of his eyes. The water droplets ran in beads across his skin. His face seemed to have aged in the last twenty-four hours. *He* seemed to have aged.

The door to the restroom opened and two men in fine suits came in, laughing, and only quieted when they saw him. They gave him quick nods, then went to the urinals and continued their conversation more quietly as they relieved themselves. James took one of the fresh towels from the basket between the sinks, dabbed his face and hands, and looked in the mirror one last time. His tanned skin still made him look younger than his slightly mottled gray temples did, and his neatly contoured three-day beard high-lighted his prominent chin. His short hair, with its shorn sides and slightly fuller top, seemed out of time, but he felt it made a statement. He turned away, satisfied.

In the hallway outside the restroom, he smoothed his tailored steel-gray suit and red shirt one last time and checked the lay of the wide white laces in his red All Stars.

Finally, he straightened the knot of his dark blue tie and walked into the reception area of the mansion. He had left his black briefcase under one of the two sinks.

Normally, this was the foyer of the city villa of the Debongos, one of Kenya's largest industrial families. The large double door, flanked by liveried servants, was reminiscent of the English Stuarts and led to a grandiose staircase, in front of which, until just moments before, the limousines of the invited guests had stopped every minute. Large columns lined the hall in front of the stairs leading to the right and left, leading to a terrace on the third floor, level with the golden chandeliers, where William Debongo stood in a traditional Kenyan robe, a prayer cap in the colors of his country on his head.

He belonged to the Muslim minority and was the only major industrialist to have emerged from it, only one reason everyone in the country knew his name. In addition, the understated folkloric tones of the musicians on the podium under the stairs had been composed by his daughter, who was a superstar throughout Africa and filled opera houses and concert halls worldwide. His eldest son, Justin Debongo, was a much sought-after heart surgeon with his own clinic in Nairobi.

Judging by the looks Debongo was giving him as they talked, one could only feel sorry for the middle child of the three, Vincent. According to various newspaper reports, he had dropped out of his studies in the US to become a soccer player but he had not found his way back to his promising form after tearing his cruciate ligament. Dressed in a plain suit, he stood between his father and older brother and seemed to do his best not to attract attention. But even from James's vantage point below, among the hundred invited guests in the foyer, James saw the angry gleam in his eyes, which shone like white brocade in his dark face.

"Mr. Hamilton," someone mumbled beside him, and he lowered his gaze from the terrace to Vega and Blake, who were edging past a couple patrons, martini glasses in hand, and walking toward him. Vega was chewing an olive and pointing the small wooden skewer at James. "I have to admit I was a little angry about staying an extra day because you want to bask in your success, but the drinks are really fantastic."

"And I hear there's about to be another buffet!" Blake added, adjusting the belt holding back his mighty belly. "I don't know who you called for that, but I'm not mad at you."

"I'm glad you're pleased," James replied curtly. He squinted up at the terrace again, but there were still only the three Debongos. So, he began to stand on his tiptoes and search among the guests for a familiar face.

"One thing I don't understand," Vega continued, sipping his drink, "no one knows what you did. Does that mean the food is *that* good?"

"I don't know, never ate here before."

"The little shit, Vincent," Blake said, snorting. "Just rescued yesterday, and today his father's already dragging him in front of the rich and famous of the city."

"Probably never really feared for him. More for his money," Vega said.

"He's only paying half of that, isn't he?" James asked.

"Yes, and now there's nine million less in his account. A businessman like him doesn't let that sit." Blake sounded certain. "He wants to leverage the loss somehow, and that's what he's doing here. The great man who got his son back, the one kid who was never destined for greatness, who will now be forever reminded of that."

"As the one who was kidnapped?" Vega asked.

"Yes."

"Doesn't sound very heroic," Vega said.

"It doesn't matter. People are all about stories. The story of the outstanding surgeon, the story of the musician and composer of the century, and the story of the good-for-nothing son kidnapped by Islamist terrorists who outgrew himself in captivity. What terrible things he must have experienced, yet here he is today, not even looking traumatized. I'm telling you, people just want a cool story. Hey, Hamilton, what's going on?"

"Huh?"

"Looking for someone?" Blake frowned and looked around.

"No. I just wanted to see how full it was," James replied, as the bright *clink* of a spoon on crystal sounded and the hushed conversations gradually died down. All eyes turned toward the terrace, where William Debongo was handing his champagne glass to a servant and resting his hands on the sandstone balustrade.

"Welcome, dear friends. I am very happy to welcome you all here today, and with my two sons, Justin and Vincent." Debongo's voice was such a rich baritone that it left no doubt the septuagenarian was an outstanding salesman.

Applause erupted.

He raised his hands, playing to the crowd as if none of this was necessary. "As you all know, hardly anyone wanted to believe that Boko Haram would become active in Kenya, even though we were warned about it for a long time. These terrorists are a plague now affecting much of Africa, and we cannot afford to continue looking the other way."

There were approving shouts along with renewed applause.

"I have therefore decided to take personal action to protect our land," Debongo continued. "Not with fire and sword, as these barbarians do; I don't want to repay hate with hate. I don't want them to be able to take root here in Kenya. Boko Haram means 'books are sin' in Nigerian 'Hausa,' many media outlets quote. But that's not entirely accurate. 'Haram' *does* come from Arabic and means sin or taboo, but 'Boko' in modern usage includes all non-Islamic or Western teachings. So, it could be translated as '*education is taboo*.'"

"Hmph," Blake said. "Boko Haram has been part of ISIL since 2015."

James ignored him and continued listening to Debongo.

"I am convinced that from their name we can derive the best weapon against them: education. We must ensure that our Muslim children, and the children of other religions who are at risk of conversion, receive the education they need to see through the madness and empty promises of these fanatics. That is why I am donating the same amount I spent to free my dear son Vincent from the clutches of his kidnappers to the Archaeologists for Kids Foundation, and I do so in Vincent's name!"

Vincent showed something like a smile as the guests applauded again. A few called his name. His mouth twitched but it quickly disappeared as his father continued.

"That's not all. My oldest son Justin"—Debongo pulled the chief physician next to him into the foreground—"has promised to add the same amount from his own pocket."

Now the applause became a roar. This time, the family man did not stop his guests and waited patiently until the enthusiasm had barely subsided.

"The head of the Archaeologists for Kids Foundation accepted my invitation and is here tonight to accept the check in person and tell us a little about her work." Debongo gestured to the crowd and waved someone over. James felt his hands tingle and his scalp itch. "Joana Bretoni, ladies and gentlemen!"

"Archaeologists for Kids?" snorted Vega beside him. "These do-gooders are always coming up with new shit, I'll give them that."

"Shut up!" James hissed at him without taking his eyes off the stairs. A slender woman in a nondescript cocktail dress and flowing black curls made her way up the right-hand staircase to polite applause.

"I would like to ask someone else to come up. Namely, the one who made my son's rescue possible. Special Envoy James Hamilton, whom I congratulated personally yesterday. Unfortunately, we will never know who completed the ransom negotiations on the ground because that, understandably, remains a secret, but Special Envoy Hamilton was instrumental in making it happen," Debongo explained, smiling broadly. "Please join us, Mr. Hamilton."

James tightened his jacket and left the two Foreign Service Officers staring openmouthed and took the other staircase. The guests parted and the finely dressed guests gave him friendly nods, some tapping him on the shoulder. He smiled shyly as he made his way up the stairs, careful not to keep glancing at the woman on the other side who had almost reached the terrace. He reached Debongo and shook hands, first with him, then Justin and Vincent before turning to Joana, who faced him, petrified, and only smiled again when they stopped looking at each other and turned to face the guests, who looked like a small sea of faces below them. The many servants with their trays moved between them like particles in a complex pattern, exchanging empty champagne glasses for full ones and removing napkins and used olive sticks.

"Ms.. Bretoni, would you please tell us how your organization plans to use the money?" Debongo asked, and she nodded gratefully.

"Of course, Mr. Debongo." She dropped an elegant curtsy before turning to James. He though she did masterful job of masking her displeasure. "And thank you, Mr. Hamilton, for suggesting us. The Foundation truly appreciates it." She turned back to the crowd. "As many of you know, we have been working in Kenya for three years. The Turkana Boy was found here, one of the oldest hominid fossils in history at over a million and a half years old. Your country has so much to tell us about the evolution and formation of humankind and we want to pass this knowledge about our anthropological origins to our children. 'Why would children of elementary school age interested in fossils and ancient stone formations?' you might ask. 'They'd rather sit at home and play with their PlayStation.'"

There was polite laughter.

"We have found that it is good for our children in particular to focus on simple things that promise no immediate reward, but eventually reveal amazing results after long, intense work. Just a few weeks ago, in Sibiloi National Park, we uncovered an ancient stone tomb. Over the past three months, a total of four school classes have participated in the excavation. Amazingly, they quickly learned how to use hammers, stone chisels, round brushes, and spatulas, but above all, to be careful, to pay attention to details, and to work as a team, to not get impatient or damage anything. When they saw the finished uncovered tomb and understood its significance, they wanted to know everything about it and how we could determine its age.

"This is the kind of curiosity for new things that we try to instill in children through our work. We will use this generous donation from the Debongos to start more such projects. We archaeologists dig around in the past while the world prefers to deal with the future. I understand that, but by pursuing our roots we may find answers to our current problems.

"Sumerian proto-cuneiform script was the first writing of mankind, more than three thousand years older than the Bible. In one of the oldest dated texts found in Mesopotamia, it was written: *Tiit lapan warkanum. Warkanum ullanumma ina pani aksu.* Translating directly is difficult, but it means, roughly, that life takes place before the future, and a future without a past means danger.

"This is why it is so important for us to teach our children about our past so that they do not fall prey to the empty promises of a bleak future. If the first people with their own writing understood that, so should we. Thank you."

Joana stepped back. Her cinnamon skin was beautiful and her face perfect. James sighed inwardly.

Debongo applauded with the guests, clearly pleased at the audience's enthusiasm. James stepped back and felt a tug on his left sleeve.

It was Vincent. He leaned toward him and whispered, "There is a door behind us, on one of the chairs is your briefcase."

"Thank you," he replied. He continued looking straight ahead. Debongo continued speaking and a moment later Hames felt another tug on his sleeve. He was about to snap at Vincent when, to his surprise, he was looking into Joana's face.

"Can we talk?" Her dark eyes glinted. He gulped.

"Of course." He allowed her to pull him toward a door a half dozen steps behind them. "Not there."

"Why not?"

"I think these are private rooms, from..."

She looked at him questioningly, then she shook her head, pushed down the latch, and stepped inside. The room's floor was made from thick wooden planks and the walls were decorated with European-style rugs depicting hunting scenes from the colonial era. On the far wall were several windows and a glass door that opened onto a huge terrace. There was a single table with six chairs in the middle, one of which held his black briefcase, which he deliberately ignored.

"Private rooms, huh?" Joana asked, walking over to the briefcase and picking it up.

"Not that—"

"I *know* this is yours. I gave it to you for the opening of the agency, remember?" She snorted and threw it at him. His heart sank, and he almost dropped it, but he managed to catch it at the last moment.

"No, I didn't. Why are you so angry?"

"I'm starting a project in Kenya to..." Joana ran her fingers through her thick black curls as if she wanted to pull them out, before lowering her hands and making a placating gesture. "What's this about, huh?"

"What?"

"Eighteen million dollars? That's the highest single donation we've ever received."

"So, that's... *good,* right?" he asked.

"Of course, that's good. But I asked you to stay out of my life, remember?"

"How could I forget?" he muttered, then sighed and raised his hands. "Look, I did you a favor, that's all. It doesn't mean anything."

She looked skeptically at him. "It doesn't mean anything?"

"All right, I'm happy I'm doing something nice for you, okay?"

"So?"

"And..." James hesitated. "I admit I wanted to see you, too."

"I knew it!" Joana growled, and started pacing. "And now you're going to ask me if things can go back to the way they were."

"No, that's not my intent," he lied.

"Oh, James Hamilton decided out of the blue to do the right thing and develop a conscience?" she said sarcastically.

"Joana, the agency thing was not what you always made it out to be."

"No? Then please explain to me what it was like then."

"I—"

"No!" She held her hands out as if to push him away using the Jedi trick. "I don't want to hear that again. If there's one thing you know how to do, it's sell twisted views. You'll end up making me believe you did all this for me!"

"The foundation is yours. You're making a lot of money and doing something good with it," he said, almost pleading. "It turned out well, didn't it?"

"It *destroyed* him, James! Destroyed! The agency was his life! I don't want it; I *never* wanted it."

He wanted to say something but instead bit his lower lip and squinted at the suitcase in his hand. In the silence,

Joana ran her hands through her hair again and paced in a circle a few times, sighing.

"I loved you, James. You're not a bad person; you just don't know how to be a good one, you know? Everything you touch, you touch out of greed, and then you break it. Life is not about getting *more*."

"I know," he replied, lowering his gaze. "But without you it's become less."

"No!" She glared at him, her voice quivering with anger, and raised her index finger. "You are not coming at me like that now, understand?"

He saw her tear up. Her trembling lips were full and beautiful. Her growing sadness filled him with compassion and ignited a spark of hope in his heart.

"I didn't mean to embarrass you."

"You did that, didn't you?" she asked in a soft voice. "You got young Vincent released. You're a ransom negotiator for the State Department, am I right?"

James nodded. That one nod was a vote of confidence in her favor, and she knew it. She could end his career, here and now, with a single phone call.

"That's good." Joana reached out to touch his cheek but pulled back as if she'd been burned. More seriously, she said, "It's good. Maybe you'll find your way after all."

"I did."

He tightened his grip on the suitcase when he heard a low hum in the background that quickly grew into a rattle. Maybe a helicopter flying overhead. "Can we just talk? I don't fly out until tomorrow morning. I have a little time. Please?"

Joana flinched as if he'd slapped her, but instead of yelling at him she seemed to struggle with herself. James thought his hope was about to be realized as she opened her mouth, but suddenly she frowned and looked at the glass door, which started rattling violently. The beat of the helicopter rotors were so loud that it hurt his ears. Before he could say anything, the door flew open in the artificial storm and cutlery and dishes, which he had taken no notice of before, were swept off the table.

"James?" Joana cried.

But he didn't respond. The briefcase fell out of his hand, either in fright or surprise or because of the sudden gusts of wind. It crashed into the wall behind them and opened. Countless $100 bills flew into the air, while those bundled together slid to the wooden floor. For a moment, he and his ex-fiancé just stood there, staring at the bills blowing around them like green and beige snowflakes. The look on her face was a mix of horror and disappointment that struck him in the heart.

"Joana, this—"

He tried to yell over the noise of the Army helicopter landing on the large terrace. Soldiers rushed through the side door and rushed toward them.

Joana said nothing as she stepped back as he reached for. His heart sank into the black hole that opened in his stomach.

"Mr. Hamilton!" The young soldier had a broad Texas accent. "I need you to come with me now, sir!"

When he didn't answer, the uniformed man gestured to his comrades and they grabbed him, right and left, and ran him onto the terrace and into the helicopter. James looked over his shoulder at Joana, who stood there staring after him like a ghost among the dancing banknotes—*his* dancing banknotes.

Damn it! he cursed before his mind abruptly realized what was happening to him. *What the hell is going on?*

3

"Who the hell are you?" James shouted into the headset he'd been given to protect his ears from the horrible noise of the rotors. They took off, and he felt like he was being torn away from Joana, whom he could no longer see through the window of the military helicopter.

There were two rows of seats facing each other, each with three seats. He sat in the middle of one seat, his back facing the cockpit. Across from him was an older officer with a star on his shoulder. They each had soldiers in simple camouflage uniforms and peaked caps sitting to the right and left of each other. Only now did he notice they were not armed.

"I'm Major Timothy Norton, US Army," the officer replied.

He had a boxy face that looked bony and portly at the same time, was of sturdy build—as far as the loose-cut uniform could suggest—and he eyed James with a piercing, analytical gaze.

He suddenly worried about the suitcase full of money

and carefully examined the serious faces of the soldiers sitting in the red light of the helicopter cabin with him with whom he sat in the red-lit helicopter cabin. He knew there was an Air Force base in the north part of the country, near the coast, Camp Simba, if he remembered correctly, but it was very small. Were they there to arrest him? But why the military? And how had they learned about his deal in the first place?

"Look, whatever you've been told, I think you should hear my side of the story first," James said carefully. He pushed his emotions down enough to breathe again and tried to stop thinking about Joana standing amid a million dollars flying around her like paper smeared with sin.

"I apologize for removing you so abruptly from the party, and without warning, but you were unavailable by phone."

"How did you even know I was in that room?"

"That's not important now. We are in contact with the Director of the CIA and the secretary of state. You've been loaned to us for a special assignment on an interim basis," Major Norton said.

"Special assignment? Where? Why?" James asked, confused.

"Army. We need you for a special project in Wyoming."

"I'm a civilian, not a soldier; I never have been."

"You will be managed as a civilian employee."

"For what, exactly? What kind of *project* is it?"

Rather than answering, Norton reached under his right leg and pulled out a folder, which he held out to James.

"Sign this," he said, his voice crackling in the radio.

"Two hundred and forty pages? I'll need a lot of time to read that."

"Just sign it."

"I do have a choice, don't I? After all, I am a citizen of the United States. Or is this a kidnapping after all?" James breathed an inward sigh of relief as it became increasingly clear the document was not an indictment, but an extremely detailed non-disclosure agreement, including waivers and cease-and-desist letters.

"Of course, you have a choice," Norton replied tersely.

"Next, you're going to tell me you can let me out right here?"

"No. Go ahead and read. We have a very long flight ahead of us."

"To Wyoming?"

"To the airport. We'll take an Air Force Learjet to Ramstein then New York, and from there to Francis E. Warren Air Force Base in Wyoming," the major explained. He pointed to the thick folder in James's hands. "So go ahead and read it. It better have your signature under it at the end, though."

"Or what?"

"Otherwise, you will never know why we extracted you from Mombasa under these circumstances."

"You're appealing to my curiosity?" James snorted. "You just ruined my career."

And probably my last chance to get Joana back, he thought indignantly. He would have liked to bury himself deep underground, to never again face the world and its damned weight.

"No, Mr. Hamilton. I just gave it a whole new boost. But I won't be able to explain that to you until you've signed that." Norton pointed again at the folder in James's hands.

The flight to the airport only took about ten minutes.

They landed on a small airstrip next to a maintenance hangar. They crouched under the rotor, and the major led him toward a fairly new looking G5 that was waiting for them. They were met by two men in muscle shirts and jeans who nodded to the officer, and followed them up the short, foldout staircase behind the cockpit. Inside, there were four pairs of leather chairs facing a central table, eight seats total. The ample luxury was expressed in the details if not so much in the directly visible furnishings. This was a politician's machine, that much was certain.

He had expected the major to sit directly opposite him, but instead, he left James sitting alone at the back near the toilets, so he actually had time to read what he was holding in his hands after the bumpy takeoff. Only now, as the turbines made a sonorous roar and they flew northwest over the night clouds of Kenya, did the absurdity of the situation he was in catch up with him. It was all so unreal that he thought he was dreaming.

First, the meeting with Joana, which he had been working toward and which had made him nervous for weeks. Then the conversation and the look she'd given him when the suitcase had opened, and the money had flown out. Then, a military helicopter and soldiers appearing in the middle of the whole horrible scene, dragging him out like the shocked victim of an accident.

Where was Joana now? Had she left the celebration? What was happening with Debongo? The sudden appearance of the helicopter wouldn't have gone unnoticed. Had he and his sons burst through the door after his disappearance?

Oh Joana, he thought, feeling all warmth leave his body. What if they connected the money to her? Had he gotten her into trouble again? Now there was no chance she would ever forgive him, that much he was sure he could say with certainty.

He couldn't concentrate for the first few hours of the flight. Again and again, he tried rummaging through the documents, but as soon as he read a paragraph and was ready to move on to the next, he had already forgotten he had read. His thoughts kept circling around Joana and the Debongo's, the suitcase with the money, the helicopter, and he kept thinking about locking himself in the bathroom and screaming to get rid of the pressure in his chest. He kept turning his smartphone back and forth in his hand. He wanted to dial her number but kept deciding against it. Even if it wasn't ripped immediately from his ear, what could he say to her that could possibly salvage the situation?

Only when he grew tired did fear, stress, and self-pity finally recede into the background. The avalanche of emotions subsided and gave way to deep exhaustion. The adrenaline had washed out of his veins, leaving a sour burn on his skin. He set the folder aside and closed his eyes.

When he woke up, they were on approach to Ramstein Air Force Base in Germany. They changed planes instead of just refueling, so in the pouring rain, they ran to a jet emblazoned with the Air Force crest. James used a uniform jacket Norton had given him and held it over him like an umbrella. He felt rather silly, as the old soldier looked upright and relaxed, as if he didn't mind the cold shower.

There were several officers on the new plane. They were flying back to the States and talking animatedly to each other. James and Norton sat up front in a kind of business class outfitted with larger seats that folded out all the way. There were two colonels in the section, but they immediately laid down and pulled sleeping masks over their eyes.

After taking off for New York, he finally read through the

documents one by one. Although he still felt miserable, his inner turmoil was no longer so extreme he couldn't think clearly. After almost six hours, he was finished. He went to Norton and slammed the folder with his forty-two signatures and one hundred and eighty initials onto the foldout table.

"There's nothing in there except that the project is called 'Hyperion.' However, I did have to sign that I would never mention the project. First rule of Fight Club and all, I get it," he said with his arms crossed and lowering his voice a bit. He dropped into the vacant seat next to Norton and tapped the folder with an outstretched index finger. The major eyed him calmly the whole time. "Basically, it's full of threats and lists of punishments should I violate any of it. Factually, I'm not allowed to talk about anything, except that I've been hired as part of a personnel reorganization of this '90th Missile Wing' for a minimum of one month and up to ten years. *Ten years!* You can't be serious."

"So, you agree?" Norton asked calmly, eyeing him coolly.

"I thought I just did."

"No. You signed the legal stuff. You can still say *no.*"

"But then you can't tell me anything."

"No."

James thought about it. He could call his supervisor in the Pentagon and explain the situation at the Debongos' reception Surely Vega and Blake had already pressed all the alarm buttons. But then what? Return to his job? After the suitcase fiasco, he would likely face a lawsuit if the Debongos haven't made sure the money disappeared and convinced Joana not to betray him. And she would certainly never talk to him again, no matter what he tried.

"All right, I'm in."

"You'll be paid twenty thousand dollars a month for at least two months. The length of the project can't be predicted yet, hence the long-term time frame," the major explained calmly so they wouldn't be heard over the roar of the engines, even by someone in the next rows of seats— even though they were unoccupied.

Norton pulled a single photograph from the inside pocket of his uniform jacket and held it out to James. It showed an oval object, pitch black, at least thirty meters long and perhaps five meters wide. It was being pulled out of the water by two cranes in the photographed scene.

James licked his suddenly dry lips. "What is it?"

"We don't know. But so far analysis by our scientists suggests it has been deep under Lake Maracaibo in Venezuela for about four hundred thousand years," Norton said, putting the photo back in his jacket pocket. "A European-Russian corporate conglomerate stumbled upon it while drilling for oil."

"Four hundred thousand years? But that means—"

"It's not man-made, yes. It is possibly alien technology that can generate an extremely strong magnetic field." The officer pulled a second photo from his jacket; it showed a shot of a crushed lump of metal that looked about to sink. Several ships surrounded it.

James gasped as the scale became clear to him. "What is it?"

"That's the *Deep Sea Explorer*—or what's left of her. She was a drillship from the company I mentioned, and what you're seeing there is the effect that an hour of violent lightning strikes had on the object. It just crushed the *Explorer* before dropping into a kind of inert state."

"You... you recovered it?"

"Yes."

"And this company, Russian, did you say?"

"European-Russian. We bought the wreckage from them and generously compensated the staff."

"They made it look like a military incident. Some failed test," James thought aloud. "The classic ruse."

"It's a little more complicated than that. It only worked because the EU Council and the Kremlin played along, but in return they wanted to be part of the research team studying the object after it was recovered." As James was about to ask several more questions when Norton raised a hand and continued in such a matter-of-fact tone that it made James want to shake him. "The photos are two months old. Since then, a total of eighteen researchers and two hundred soldiers have been working around the clock in a high-security underground facility that's part of Warren Air Base to extract its secrets."

"Did they find out anything about who might have built it?" James could hardly believe he was really asking that question. An alien artifact? The oval object had looked a bit alien, mostly due to the deep, contour-free blackness that seemed to soak up all light, but not as much as he would have expected in a science fiction movie. Was he seriously talking to another man about *aliens*?

"Just enough to know they were, or are, far superior to us. Inside, where the ellipsoid is thickest, there is a single room."

"A *room*?"

"Yes, and there are twelve chairs or seats in this room. Their shapes are somewhat odd, but definitely designed for humanoid bodies," Norton replied.

"A four hundred-thousand-year-old sitting circle that was deep underwater?" James asked, confused.

"No, it's a machine. Our engineers haven't been able to determine much else, so far, except this: Above and below the room with the seats are strong magnetic fields that absorb all the energy in their vicinity and store it in a hitherto unknown way. It seems there is a threshold at which these magnetic fields reverse and the stored energy is then discharged."

"Is that what happened in this Maraca Lake?"

"Lake Maracaibo," Norton corrected him. "Yes. That's what we're assuming. The seats are connected to the machine and charge along with it. There's something like an induction field in the armrests, but no theories yet on what they're for."

"Is there any sign of the builders of this object?"

"There's no instruction manual, if that's what you mean. No removable parts in the interior. It appears as if the entire object was made from one casting or piece, and it also shows no damage from erosion or tectonic action, which would be expected for something that old, even the hardest alloys."

"I don't understand."

"Believe me, we all feel that way."

"That's not what I mean." James looked up. "What you're telling me sounds so unbelievable that I can understand why you were assigned the project. If anyone else had told me about it, I would have laughed at them, but you're not kidding, are you?"

"Never."

"Thought so. So, you've assembled the best scientists you could find, and based on what you've already told me probably six American, six Russian, and six European."

Norton nodded and gestured for him to keep going.

"A group large enough to help each other and come up

with new ideas, but not so large that it splinters into small groups and gets in its own way because of Group Think and aggressive balancing acts. I understand that because it's easier to enforce confidentiality with a smaller group. Presumably, the participants will live on base for the duration of the project?"

Another nod.

"The only question that remains is why you want *me*, of all people, to be there. I am neither a scientist nor military. I have no political influence and I'm not suitable as a spokesperson since most people don't even know that the job of ransom negotiator exists."

Norton still said nothing, then reached into a small pocket on the seat before him and pulled out a file. He opened it then set a pair of reading glasses on his nose.

"James M. Hamilton, master's in cultural studies, bachelor's in contemporary drama." The major raised an eyebrow. "After graduation, hired as junior consultant at Benson & Schuster communications agency in New York. Promoted to senior consultant just two years later and reportedly initiated a merger with Bretoni & Partners, a competing Washington agency that was quite successful in political communications. After the merger was completed, you were elevated to partner, earned a prime contract for four years, and began a relationship with the senior partner's daughter, Joana Bretoni.

"Then you suddenly decide to push her father out of the company. Augustus Bretoni dies a week later in a car accident, and you quit three weeks before completing your fourth year as a partner, after which, according to the contract, you could have left with a golden parachute. Who does that? You lose not only your job but also your princess. Following the recommendation of a friend you step in as a ransom negotiator for an extortion case in Sudan. For the last three years you've had numerous assignments as just that: a ransom negotiator."

James's lips narrowed more with each word, but he forced himself to remain impassive and stuck his chin out.

"You seem to know quite a lot. Bravo," he said laconically. "But that doesn't answer my question."

"Your resume makes no sense, but it shows that you seem to have principles beyond money and that you can keep secrets. Your success rate in your new job is remarkable. It wasn't easy to get the records, but when I finally received approval, I was still amazed. In your second negotiation, you freed a family in Yemen with a fraction of the available ransom budget by revealing that they were really two families at odds with each other who had no ties to terrorists at all. A year later, you got two kidnapped arms dealers to work for the CIA after making the kidnappers believe that, for a lower price, they would henceforth have *two* double agents. How do you pull something like that off?" Norton pointed at the file and plucked out a few sheets, one by one. "This is full of examples like that. Supposedly, in your job interview, you sold Secretary of State Annelie Petterson, an avowed evangelical, a leather-bound copy of the *Necronomicon*."

"My ex-girlfriend would say I'm a manipulative asshole," James muttered indignantly.

"You can read people and get them to respond the way you need them to. Maybe you can manipulate for my sake. It's exactly what I need you for."

James mused.

"Your eggheads," he finally said, understanding. "They're not working together like they should."

"Mhm," said the major.

"Russians, Europeans, and Americans... genius scientists, so probably giant egos."

"Mmm."

"And in their midst, something that pushes them to the limits of what they previously thought they knew about themselves and the universe. Sounds like an explosive mix."

"Yes. Collaboration is far from smooth, and a critical point of the project is coming up."

"What critical point?" James asked.

"One of our scientists believes he has calculated the minimum energy threshold to activate the object. However, the previous power supply to the facility was not sufficient to test this, even though it's a nuclear weapons silo. Therefore, we are having a special line laid from the nuclear power plant in Washington. In exactly four days, we will be able to access the full power of the reactor for a total of one hour, which was not easy to accomplish considering the secrecy of the project. Only the president, the secretary of defense, and the secretary of state know about it. If we actually succeed in activating the object, I need a team that will pull together. A lot can go wrong, as you saw from the Lake Maracaibo picture, and a setback could mean an immediate halt to the project."

"You want to power it up? Do you even know what its function is?"

"Some of the team believe it's a transportation device, a teleporter of some sort, others think it's a sophisticated cinema, and a few think it's a Trojan horse that will drag our world to its doom," Norton said dryly, making James's hair stand on end.

"Then you can't just turn it on! You can't hit the red button just because it's there!"

"We will because it's the only way to find out what the

object's function is, and the civilian management of the project wants it that way." Norton closed the file, slid it into the folder, and closed it before stuffing both into his pocket. "I want *you*, Mr. Hamilton, to make sure that the team is unified and in line so the test can take place."

4

Wyoming, in the heart of the United States, was not particularly exciting. Beautiful landscapes, wide-open spaces, and few inhabitants, who cared more about their herds than about world politics.

The Francis E. Warren Air Force Base was a sharp contrast. Not only was it the oldest operating Air Force base in the United States, but it was also the headquarters of the 20th Air Force, the unit that controlled all of America's intercontinental ballistic missiles. Not that James knew anything about it without consulting his cell phone, which also told him that over three thousand soldiers lived and worked here permanently.

From the plane, the barracks looked like shoeboxes strung together among trees and vast meadows, forming their own small town just outside the state capital of Cheyenne, about five miles away. Knowing that nearly two hundred nuclear missiles, ready for immediate use, were stored here, capable of pouring fire and death around the world from their hidden silo, was a strange feeling.

There were only two runways, not particularly long,

touching in a sort of accidental T. They were surrounded by several Patriot air defense emplacements, mobile versions that, judging from the deep tire tracks around them, had probably been erected recently. They landed on the longer runway, which was apparently long enough for their jet, contrary to James's feeling on the matter. Norton and two civilian officers, who had introduced themselves during the flight as Jeena Pavar and Ralph Kowalski but had otherwise remained taciturn, led him to the main barracks, a two-story concrete structure with a green roof. Two soldiers standing outside the building saluted them as they approached. The entrance area was deserted and there were no other sounds to suggest any form of habitation. They walked to a nondescript elevator, which Norton activated with a key card. Next to it was a large plastic box, into which he placed his wristwatch and a cell phone.

"I'm going to have to ask you to put all electronic devices and metal objects in here."

James frowned but followed his instructions, as did the other civilians, who were less surprised.

"We need retina scanners," Pavar decided. The Indian-born woman with the stern look and attractive figure nodded to Kowalski, who set down his bag and made notes on a tablet.

"Key cards do the trick. Retina scanners are expensive and error prone. They're only for movies," the major replied.

"The president takes the security of this facility very seriously, Major, so you should too. Retinal scanner," she repeated, and Kowalski, who had paused briefly, continued his notes. James was surprised when the old officer nodded reluctantly.

"You're the new leader of this project?" James asked, and

almost flinched when Pavar looked at him like a lioness eyeing her prey.

"Yes, Mr. Hamilton. I'm also the reason you're here. You came highly recommended by Marcus Pollock to get our team down there on track."

And I hope you won't let me and Marcus down, her flashing eyes seemed to add.

"I, uh, will do my best, ma'am."

"Good, I assume that will be enough." She turned back to Norton. "Where are we with moving the test reactor?"

"It's more complicated than we thought."

"That wasn't my question."

"Three more weeks. At least."

The major looked like he'd bitten into a lemon, and James now had some idea of what was going on. The military had been in control for the first two months until a civilian leader had been agreed upon in Washington's inner circle, which was quick for the political mills.

"So, you're the new boss," he noted and caught her appraising look.

Political veteran, I'd wager, he thought. *Behind every statement, a motive, behind every glance, a complex maneuver, and behind every piece of writing, an intricate labyrinth of traps and lures.*

"I am the acting dean."

"Dean?" James nodded. "Fitting for a research project, I guess."

"Will you be my friend, Mr. Hamilton?"

"I'm here to make everyone friends, I've heard."

Pavar barely smiled, and James thought it looked good on her. It removed some of the severity from this austere woman in a pantsuit.

"Fine. Start by checking with me or Kowalski every step

of the way. Your job begins"—the elevator announced itself with a bright *ping!* and the doors opened—"right now."

"I've worked long enough in the tension between the CIA and the State Department to know the drill," he assured her. "Can I ask you a question?"

"In fact, you *should*. The more often, the better."

"How exactly how does Major Norton tie in?" James asked as they walked into the large, unadorned elevator emblazoned with the Air Force crest. The officer unlocked the control panel with his key card before pressing the bottommost of three buttons. Again, the dean eyed him, as if weighing and measuring him thoroughly. He could not tell from her gaze if she was considering how best to eat him or if she was remeasuring his value.

"Major Norton will be my primary advisor here on the ground, and on military matters, his word will carry a lot of weight. Now, what did my answer tell you about me, Mr. Hamilton?" Pavar asked, looking at him curiously. "That was the point, wasn't it?"

James did not try to deny it and smiled noncommittally.

"Several things: The politicians are trying to avoid unnecessary friction between civilian and military leadership. They realize they are new and need support from him and his soldiers. You want him close, that's smart, and it helps you in Washington because the Joint Chiefs of Staff are likely to be in the loop and are known to have a lot of influence with the president," James said. "So, you don't want to mess things up."

Pavar nodded slowly. "Not bad, but with a catch. The image of the career-focused politician has a few cracks. First, I was a candidate for the position of secretary of state and then in talks to be a UN ambassador starting next year. I gave up that opportunity for this. I am disappearing from the scene. My career in Washington is forfeited. Second, my severance package is so good that I never have to do anything again unless I want to. Under normal circumstances I would have congratulated you on your political insight, but things are different here. I want to know what we are up against while protecting our country, and I like difficult assignments. I'm not here to make the president happy, and I told him that."

"I understand. Thank you."

"Don't thank me. I said that mostly so Major Norton would hear." Pavar looked at the officer, who nodded slowly and seemed a little relieved. "So, thank you for your assessment, Mr. Hamilton. That's the last time you try to talk your way into my head, do you understand?"

"Yes, ma'am," he said, swallowing.

"Very good. Then we'll get along just fine."

The rest of the elevator ride took another minute. The doors opened into a plain hallway with rough concrete walls. A dark brown strip with "Sublevel 3" written inside led from left to right at about chest level. Two heavily armed soldiers snapped salutes as Norton led them to the right. Every ten meters, they passed below automatic fire bulkheads punctuated with alarm sirens. To the right were several doors made of some plain gray material. Each was marked with a huge number and was also only accessible with key cards.

"These are the living quarters," the major explained as they passed. "Since you requested to see the facility first, we can worry about moving you into your quarters later. I will get you key cards after the tour."

Pavar nodded.

There was a bend to the right at the end of the long hallway then the hallway changed. It was no longer angular but arched and much larger, with huge security doors at each end that led to enormous freight elevators. Emblazoned in each door was a prominent radiation warning sign. Thick cables and pipes ran along the ceiling, looking strangely soft. To the left, a steel door was emblazoned with "Maintenance and Safety."

"The engineers who maintain and monitor the nuclear weapons usually sit behind this door. This is the central silo, which was not built under the main building, but rather the other way around. The building merely serves as camouflage and is unused at all times, the walls are oriented so they lie between the individual silo doors. A total of eight Minuteman-III intercontinental ballistic missiles were stationed here. They have since been moved, along with all the other military equipment."

Can we finally see the object? James thought impatiently but restrained himself. Pavar seemed smart and direct, he could live with that, but she didn't seem like someone who had much patience with games or trickery. And he would need her if he was to succeed here, success he desperately needed.

What Norton had told him had become something of a bandage on his soul. For the first time in a long time, he wasn't thinking about Joana all the time, though every thought of her stung him, but instead about the photo of that black ellipsoid and what it meant.

"All ferromagnetic materials have been removed from this facility, and the rest of the barracks are currently being rebuilt to match. The blast doors are aluminum and plastic, and all wiring and piping has been replaced with complex polymer materials," the major continued. "Our scientists are working sixteen-hour shifts, four of them behind this door and the other fourteen in an identical room on the other side, where there is a similar corridor that was once used to deliver missile parts. At the end of this hallway"—he pointed at a freight elevator waiting about a hundred meters away—"there's a recreation room, a small mess hall, and two offices that are magnetically shielded."

"And in between, is *it*?" Pavar asked.

"Yes."

"We'd like to see it now."

"Of course."

As they walked along, James wondered how far underground they were. Most intercontinental ballistic missiles were extremely large, up to twenty meters long and two meters wide, and they needed correspondingly enormous launch shafts along with power and coolant supplies, a refueling system, ventilation, and exhaust pipes to carry away the resulting gases during a launch. Thus, each shaft was likely to be more than twice as deep as the rocket was tall.

The walls suddenly felt crushing.

They stopped in front of another door made of gray polymer. Two more soldiers saluted, which the major absently returned. He used his key card again and typed in an eight-digit code on an adjacent keypad before it slowly opened to the side like a tank riding on chains. Finally, they stood in front of a clear plastic sheet, which Norton flipped aside before leading the way into a fully lined room where a dozen hazmat suits hung from a pole.

"This is our airlock. For our safety and the protection of the object, we have to put these on. Beyond the next door is a germ-free environment."

To James's surprise, Pavar didn't hesitate to follow the major's example as he took off his uniform and, in his underwear, grabbed a suit off the rack and squeezed into it.

Eventually, they were all dressed in the pure white

plastic suits with large hoods over their heads and standing in front of another plastic tarp. They had packed their clothes in airtight boxes located under a long bench opposite the rack holding the hazmat suits.

James looked at the others through the large flexible visor then tightened the rubber cuffs between the suit and the gloves and rubber boots. He felt as if he had left the real world and was now in his very own microcosm, where the murmur of his breathing formed a background melody of urgency and every movement of his hands and fingers were clumsy and uncoordinated.

"Are you ready?" the major asked in a muffled voice. Small droplets of condensation formed on the inside of his visor, level with his mouth. Everyone nodded and he pressed a fist-sized button on the wall. White steam hissed down from several nozzles mounted above their heads, enveloping them in a dense fog that slowly dissipated. Only then did the aged officer open the plastic sheet in front of them and lead them to the next security bulkhead.

On the other side was a huge concrete hall the size of three tennis courts side by side and several stories high. Four massive pillars formed a square in the center of the space and four enormous white cranes were sealed into the floor, framing the ellipsoid. Its conical bottom disappeared into the ground, which had apparently been excavated to accommodate it, along with the ceiling. It was sitting in a former launch shaft, surrounded by five more shafts, identifiable by the round patches of recently poured concrete. Between them, the object looked like it was suspended, like an arrowhead rammed into the earth by a divine hand.

The shell of the object was so black that he couldn't make out a single contour, as if it consisted not of something solid but the total absence of any light. The edges seemed to flicker slightly, the same way heat shimmers on an asphalt road in the desert. But the claws of the plastic cranes were intact, so the impression of great heat was clearly an optical illusion. A long ramp on rollers led from between two of the pillars to the middle of the ellipsoid. It was crude and ugly compared to this thing of black perfection.

Speechless, James walked around the object at a distance, which wasn't difficult in the huge cavern. There was plenty of room, except for several wheeled tables covered with scientific instruments and tools spread every few meters around the ellipsoid. The front side was a bit wider, which he determined from the silhouette.

James's gaze fell on two large plastic containers marked with biohazard symbols. He could make out the fuzzy outline of a cow's head and a couple paws or hooves.

I wonder if animal testing was done on the object in the early days and weeks? But then the remains would have been removed. What had they done to them? And why were the specimens obviously dead? He wanted to say something, but the new facility manager beat him to it.

"It's very cold here," Pavar noted from some distance away.

She was standing with Norton and Kowalski at the foot of the ramp. James also noticed that his breath was forming thick clouds in front of his mouth.

"Yes. The object is very cold, two hundred degrees below freezing, to be exact. The scientists believe it must have superconducting structures inside. But that's just a theory, since we haven't been able to look through the shell with any imaging devices. It appears to be smooth down to the atomic level and cannot be damaged by any tool. How it keeps its temperature so low is also still a mystery."

"Any ideas what it's made of?" James wanted to know. He

joined the others between two of the large pillars, eyeing the object.

"No. Since the shell can't be damaged and it doesn't shed or lose even the tiniest particles, we're in the dark about that," Norton replied.

"But you were able to determine its age," Pavar said.

"Yes, but only from rock residue on the hull that we discovered during recovery."

"That means the object itself could be much older than four hundred thousand years."

"Yes."

"Does it respond to its environment in any way?"

"No, except that it gives off some of its cold to the environment, but not very much."

"Is there anything we *do* know?" James frowned and tried to ignore the goosebumps spreading over his arms and back, leaving an unpleasant tingling sensation.

The object was so powerful that even though he was standing at least ten meters away, he involuntarily felt small and insignificant. A menacing aura emanated from the thing, as if it were full of significance and danger, without him understanding why. The image of a powerful animal— or monster—manifested in his imagination, like a hibernating bear. James felt like an ant examining the sleeping bear, unable even to begin to comprehend what he was dealing with. He shuddered.

I wonder what will happen when it finally wakes?

"I've read the reports, the facts and figures, and I have to confess that I haven't slept very well in the eight days since," Pavar said from beside him. Her voice was almost a whisper. "But I don't think I'll be able to sleep at all from now on."

"I know what you mean," Norton said, nodding, never taking his eyes off the ellipsoid occupying the twenty meters between floor and ceiling like a giant splinter. "That's probably how everyone here feels, which is not particularly conducive to morale and cooperation, I must confess."

"Everyone's scared," James said. "I include myself."

"Fear will get us nowhere." Pavar stretched. "I read about the room inside. I don't see an opening."

"The ramp leads right up to it." The major pointed at a long pathway without railings resting on a complex web of struts. It was not for people afraid of heights. The dean raised an eyebrow and he added, "It opens as you approach."

"So, the object responds to us."

"Yes, but we don't know how. The team couldn't locate any sensors, and they can't detect any change in the object's temperature as it opens, which suggests it's either as perfectly shielded as we think it is, or it's using almost no energy."

"I want to see."

"Of course. It's quite safe. As far as we know." She gave Norton a quick sidelong glance at his last comment and barely hesitated when he motioned for her to go ahead.

"I'll go," James said taking a tentative step onto the ramp when no one objected.

The plastic material creaked slightly. It looked almost metallic, except for the white color, and the smell was more reminiscent of Tupperware fresh out of the packaging until he remembered he was smelling his suit. In good moments he felt protected, as if the thin layer of plastic crumpled around his skin was an effective barrier. It was probably wishful thinking. Nevertheless, he continued forward, checking each step to make sure he didn't slip, and the ramp wasn't tipping over. But it was more robust than it looked.

"Be careful," Pavar said behind him.

"I don't know how I'm going to do this," he muttered, but kept walking toward the growing ellipsoid in front of him, filling an ever-increasing portion of his field of view. "Keep it steady, big guy."

When he had crossed about half of the ramp, while avoiding looking down, he thought he felt a slight buzz in his ears. All the hairs on his body stood up. He stopped abruptly.

"You should feel the magnetic field about now. It is extremely strong and increases exponentially as the distance decreases," the major explained. He sounded as if he were very far away. Distant enough that James felt lost and incredibly lonely all at once, like a newborn baby in front of a wolf that had just bared its teeth. He kept walking, swallowing his fear and ignoring the lump in his throat that wanted to make him turn around and run away as fast as he could.

Although he never once took his eyes off the eerie featureless surface of the object, all at once, the opening at the end of the ramp was simply there: a rectangular cutout like a door, a little too high and narrow, but still recognizable as such. It consisted of a perfect white light and was such a sharp contrast to the shell that his eyes wanted to look away. However, he felt inexplicably drawn to it and had stepped forward before he thought about it. When he was one step from it, he stopped and reached out a hand. His rubber-gloved fingers slid through the light and he felt nothing at all. He was still cold, but otherwise there was nothing. He envisioned Pavar waiting behind him and gulped. He stepped forward into a hexagonal room.

It measured perhaps five paces across, and the floor and walls were a plain gray, forming a pattern of tiny hexagonal honeycombs that merged seamlessly, as if they had grown that way rather than placed by a hand. He saw no ceiling; it was lost in the impenetrable darkness above him. In front of each of the six sides of the room was a seat with a high back-rest, armrests, and footrests, tilted slightly back. Directly opposite each seat was another, so close that the footrests almost touched. The outward-facing chairs looked different, with eight small, jetlike openings in the backrest and a larger headrest. Compared to the eerie alien exterior of the object, they looked downright ordinary. Had it not been for their connection to the floor, which consisted of six shifting finger-thick tentacles that looked far too delicate to hold the weight of the twelve structures. In the center, where the backrests of the six inner seats almost touched, was a dark funnel.

He walked up to one of the seats and was about to touch it, but he withdrew his hand just before he did so. Some-thing about the piece of furniture in front of him that seemed so familiar also seemed *wrong,* although he couldn't put his finger on it. He also noticed the tingling on his skin and the subtle buzz in his ears had disappeared.

"It looks so *normal,*" Pavar said, echoing his thoughts, and he jumped, surprised, when he heard her voice beside him. He breathed heavily and tried to get his heartbeat to calm down.

"Um, yeah," he said, clearing his throat. "Strange, but also normal."

"Well, it's not." She ran the fingers of her right glove across the armrest in front of him. "Too long. And the seat's a little too narrow."

"Too narrow for *us.*"

"Yes." And the implications of her simple statement sent a shiver down his spine.

5

The team of scientists consisted of two groups, just as Norton had described. There were the leaders, one man and one woman from each group—US, EU, and Russia —with four colleagues under them, so they only had small teams to coordinate. He met with the team members first, but no one was overly interested in him once they learned he was merely a special advisor and would fulfill no scientific function. They just kept working after he shook their hands: standing in front of large posters with jumbled diagrams and notes, arguing over details, poring over aluminum tables covered with drawings and pages filled with columns of numbers. They were all focused, like students on the verge of handing in their theses.

After that, he turned his attention to the six team leaders on the other side of the chamber, which was accessible through a standard door, so he didn't have to go back through the heavily guarded corridors, which were even more claustrophobic than the compact concrete rooms where he was staying.

But the room was empty. They were probably in the

"cave," what they were calling the former maintenance area under the launch shafts where the object was housed. He considered joining them to introduce himself, but finally decided against it. Trying to manage introductions from inside a rubber suit probably wouldn't make the best impression, especially since he would be disturbing them, and he imagined the scientists wouldn't be particularly pleased.

So, he moved into his quarters instead, a small room off the main hallway near the elevator. There was a sink, a bed, a tiny desk and closet, and a single lamp that he could turn on and off with an old-fashioned pullcord. It was a strange contrast to what they were doing down here, though possibly an extremely fitting one. Toilets and showers were at one end of the corridor and were shared by everyone. James tried not to think too much about the lack of privacy.

He opened the files Norton had had the leadership team bring to his room. They contained an astonishing amount of detail about each person, including photos where they had not realized they were being photographed. It was a very heterogeneous group made up of a wide variety of person-alities.

Dr. Kathryn Chazelle was a forty-five-year-old particle physicist at Stanford University, originally from Utah. She was so thin that she looked like a skeleton covered with fresh skin. She seemed aloof and absent in the photos, as if she had several things going on in her head leaving her no time for worldly things. Divorced for ten years, never married again, and no children.

Dr. Vincent Meeks was fifty. A big man with a mighty belly and a thinning fringe of hair wrapped around a shiny bald head. He grinned like a clown in every other picture. He was a nuclear physicist and engineer with twenty years of professional experience in Boeing's research and development department. His wife had died in a car accident two years ago and his children, twins, were studying in Germany and Italy.

Dr. Mette Laudrup was Danish and the oldest at sixty-two. She was chubby with rosy cheeks and a shock of hair that would have been enough for three. She sweated visibly in the pictures and looked like a comfortable mom, but by no means a brilliant scientist much less the best in her field. But she had over thirty years under her belt as a civilian chemist in NATO's NBC units.

Dr. Justus Falkenhagen, also from the EU and a German citizen, was the exact opposite of Laudrup. At thirty-nine, he was the youngest in the group, well-trained, tanned and almost cartoonishly attractive with a radiant white smile and powerful muscles. He was also the only one who was married, albeit childless. James had to read the astrophysicist and quantum researcher's details twice to make sure it wasn't a mistake, and the photos hadn't been swapped with those of a stock photo model.

Dr. Mila Shaparova was from Novosibirsk, Russia. She was forty-one years old and an engineer and materials researcher at a well-known Moscow institute James could not pronounce. Unmarried with no children, she was pretty, with blond curls, an elfin face, almond-shaped eyes, and a melancholy expression.

Dr. Adrian was the second Russian and the last of the bunch. He was a colonel in the Russian Air Force and a former cosmonaut with two tours to the ISS in the early 2000s. Besides his many years in the cockpit, he had worked on and off after his astronaut career as a training consultant at Star City near Moscow while simultaneously working as a superconductor engineer for Gazprom.

Overall, James was dealing with a distinguished group, that much was certain. He imagined they were not always in agreement since the only similarities they had, with one exception, were that they were all divorced and unattached. Unfortunately, there was nothing in the files about what the team disagreed on. Sure, Norton had mentioned that some wanted to activate the object—or at least try—and others considered the danger too great, but it was hard to imagine that that was what this group was fighting over.

He got a preview of what the major might be talking about at dinner. He made sure he was the last to enter the small mess hall at the end of the underground complex. The scientists were spread out across the four tables, with the leadership team sitting at the largest one, right next to the food counter.

The room was plain with a small window with two warming cases, behind which stood a massive soldier in an apron. There were several tables, two trash cans, and a rolling cabinet for the used trays, and every surface was aluminum. There weren't even the obligatory Air Force posters adorning the gray concrete walls.

There was no sign of Pavar or Kowalski. Major Norton was sitting in a corner with a small group of researchers and nodded curtly at him when he entered. The rest either didn't notice him or only glanced at him. After a quick look around, he spotted his worry group, which he recognized from their files. He headed right for the food line.

"Good evening, Sergeant," he greeted the portly Black soldier behind the window.

The soldier eyed him with a raised brow and tapped his badge. "Private."

James raised his hands. "You look like a sergeant to me. You're Hawaiian, aren't you? My name is James."

"Ruby," the soldier replied, nodding. "Oahu."

"I love Hawaii; my mother-in-law was from Maui. Well, almost mother-in-law. Anyway, she passed her love for it on to her daughter, that's for sure."

Ruby broke into a grin. "That's what our women are like. They have fire."

"Oh yeah. I've been burned by that several times, thank you, but then again, it was my fault."

"It always is." The soldier seemed to thaw a bit. "What'll it be? Spaghetti Bolognese or ratatouille?"

James winked at the private as he pointed inconspicuously at the spaghetti. "The spaghetti, please." Ruby started loading his plate and he pretended his hands hurt. "Was always my fault."

"What?"

"Well, everything. Was that normal with your wives?"

"If you have something dangling between your legs, it's your fault. It's an easy life with us."

"Women are just better people," James sighed. "Ua Mau ke Ea o ka ʻĀina i ka Pono."

The soldier's face lit up. "The life of the country is preserved by righteousness. You know our state motto in Hawaiian?"

"Oh yes, I've used that to get myself out of harm's way many times." He turned to the scientists at the large table, then sighed. "Which I guess I'll have to get *into* now."

"You're the special advisor, right?"

"Mmm. Seems so."

"Good luck then. These people aren't actually that bad, just a little crazy."

"Great." James grimaced, then nodded to the chef one last time before heading toward the scientists with his tray and a fresh set of plastic cutlery.

"Good evening, ladies and gentlemen. May I sit down?"

He looked around the table of scientific directors, who stopped their conversation and scrutinized him for an uncomfortably long moment. Kathryn Chazelle merely widened her eyes a little while the two Russians looked at him with open suspicion. The German, Justus Falkenhagen, seemed irritated, and Mette Laudrup, the plump woman with the wild hair, gave him a broad smile and beckoned him over.

"Hello. You must be the special advisor Major Norton told us about." She stood and waddled to the nearest table where, after a brief inquiry, she took one of the chairs and set it down for him, between her and Vincent Meeks, the American nuclear physicist.

"Thank you." James set his tray down and noticed they had all finished eating and were looking at him as if he were about to perform some feat they didn't want to miss. He glanced at their faces before lowering his fork and nodding. "Special advisor, yes. I know that's what they told you, but you probably think I was hired as a babysitter to get you to act in the project's best interests."

No one answered, but they didn't need to. He understood what was going on behind their eyes. So, he delivered what they expected, just not the way they expected it.

"You're absolutely right about that. They want me to observe and make sure you activate the object."

That surprised everyone. Dr. Laudrup and Dr. Falkenhagen exchanged meaningful glances, Dr. Meeks snorted, and Dr. Smailow clicked his tongue.

"I have no idea about the object itself, except that the hairs on the back of my neck stand up just looking at it and know I probably won't be able to get a peaceful night's sleep since I know of its existence. Now that I'm so close to it, I'm more likely to get *none at all*." James nodded to himself and gave everyone a moment to absorb what he'd said by twirling some spaghetti onto his spoon with his fork and popping it into his mouth. He chewed, swallowed, then continued, "I'll have trouble getting used to the cutlery too. A prong from a plastic fork once broke off and got stuck in my throat. It wasn't my best day, I must admit."

"That's happened to me too!" Dr. Laudrup said, her face contorting. "Terrible feeling! But aluminum is a bad alternative if that's what you're thinking. It's toxic to the body if any of it rubs off."

Dr. Meeks gave her a stern look, but she didn't seem to notice.

"If aliens walk out of this thing, at least we have a line of defense. Let them eat with our cutlery and wait to see if they choke on the broken tines or die of plastic poisoning. Maybe they'll be allergic to it."

Laudrup laughed, her red cheeks bobbing up and down. The others, however, remained tense and clearly annoyed by the childish, carefree behavior of the eldest in their circle.

"All right, folks, let's make this simple: I'm here and I'm not leaving, not as long as the major and the dean want me here. I've never been in the military, and I distrust anyone who pulls out a gun and throws their life away for a piece of pretty cloth because old farts in fine suits think that makes sense. Pavar is one of them. I'm not a scientist like you, but I'm someone who believes in facts, not talk. So, you can have in me an ally who may not understand everything you explain to him, but who—and I promise you this—will listen to you. I'm supposed to make sure you all pull together, and I can only do that if I get to know *you*. Not to manipulate you—and I admit that's probably what I'm expected to do—but to help you reach a consensus. You don't have to be a social scientist to do that. Thank God."

"The dean you said?" Dr. Smailov asked in a rolling Russian accent. "Pavar?"

"Yes. She's a little implacable, but very direct and honest, from what I can tell." Then, to show them he was their ally and willing to talk openly, he quickly continued, "If you ask me, it's a good thing a civilian has taken over, then we don't have to worry about the military using this extraordinary find. At least for now. She's a careerist, for sure, but she obviously believes in this project because she gave up a UN ambassadorship and forfeited her political future to take this job. I think that's a good sign."

The Russian looked at the others and then nodded to James. Only then did the rest of the group relax.

So, he's the ringleader, James thought, making a mental note. That made sense since he was a scientist through and through, older than the others—except for Dr. Laudrup, who, as he'd expected, wasn't taken very seriously. On top of that, he'd been a cosmonaut, which was a superhero among academics. James turned toward him a little more, pulling his right arm back a bit.

"You've been in space. Surely you know how to handle difficult situations better than any of us here. Can I ask you something?"

Smailov nodded.

"When you first saw the object, what went through your mind? Your first impulse, I mean?"

"Impatience."

"Impatience? Are cosmonauts allowed to be impatient?"

"Yeah, they just can't show it."

"Why impatience?"

"Because we've been searching for traces of extraterrestrial life for decades, and now we've found one, here, under our noses for hundreds of thousands of years."

"Any concerns?" James asked.

"No. If it were dangerous, I think we would have noticed something by now. After all, it was there in Lake Maracaibo for four hundred thousand years getting bombarded with energy."

"But it destroyed the *Deep Sea Explorer*," Falkenhagen objected. The tanned German looked even less like a scientist in real life. He was wearing a simple shirt that looked like a muscle shirt on him, and his hair was short but perfectly styled, as if he'd just come from a photo shoot.

"That was because of the magnetic field," Meeks said. The tall American with the light fringe of hair and his prodigious belly pressing against the tabletop, leaned back in his chair and gestured at the entire room. "An accident. Now we know and have taken precautions; we should be safe."

"Unless something happens that we can't foresee beforehand; something we can only react to afterward," the German astrophysicist insisted. "What else could happen that we *aren't* prepared for, and how many can we survive? Fourteen people died on the *Deep Sea Explorer*!"

"We already know it's neutrino impermeable," Dr. Chazelle replied. The spindly American spoke at a normal volume, yet her voice seemed fragile. "It may even be absorbed. That should at least make us cautious."

"And why? Because we don't understand," Smailov snorted. "When we don't understand something, we instinctively, immediately turn away because we're scared. But where would we be today if great figures in history hadn't done exactly the opposite? What if Wilhelm Röntgen hadn't discovered radioactivity for fear of getting cancer?"

"We'd be without nuclear weapons and a hundred thousand dead Japanese," Falkenhagen suggested.

"To understand something, we have to research it, Justus. Thanks to research, at some point, we knew about the dangers of X-rays."

"Yes, and before that, the first devices were used for years as fairground attractions to make bones visible. I don't want to know how many people died of cancer until we learned better."

"I have a question," James said cautiously, surprised that conflict had heated up as quickly as Norton had implied. All eyes turned to him. "From what the major told me, you don't know anything about this object yet, do you?"

"Nothing at all?" Meeks looked as if he had been insulted, but then grinned abruptly. "Boy, we haven't slept the last few weeks! What's clear is that the seats were made for humanoids, which roughly approximate the human body. We know we can feed it any energy source just by holding cables up to the hull. The thing sucks up whatever energy it can from the environment, but only above a certain strength. It doesn't absorb body heat, for example, or the weak electromagnetic radiation from lamps."

"But neutrinos!" Chazelle said excitedly, raising a finger like a tiny branch. "I think it's sucking them up."

"How do you know all this?"

"The energy level increases," Meeks replied. "We can measure it with thermal imaging cameras. Heat is nothing more than atoms in motion, thus energy. This energy level can also be read from the seats."

"Do you have any theories about what happens when a certain energy level is reached?" James asked.

"It's a means of transportation!"

"A spaceship!"

"Impossible, it has no engine!"

"Impossible for *us*. Not for those who—"

"A kind of virtual library. An ark for knowledge! Why else, should—"

"A time capsule from the past, I say. We just need to find out—"

"Maybe nothing more than a work of art? Who knows?"

James interrupted the scientists, each trying to voice their particular theory. "Okay, okay. So, we don't know."

"Nah," Dr. Laudrup laughed, wiping fresh sweat from her brow. "But we'll figure it out. We just need more time, and this major is a very impatient man."

At last, everyone nodded agreement, though Smailov hesitated.

James leaned forward, and the others instinctively did the same.

"I'm going to tell you something, but please keep it to yourself; the major wants the object activated as soon as possible, and he'll put pressure on you until you do. Now me," he said quietly, "if you all agree that we need more time"—he put a slight emphasis on the "we"—"then I'll do my best to see that you get it."

"Good evening. Ladies, gentlemen." Major Norton stepped up to their table and looked around. Everyone leaned back and looked up at the officer. "I see you've all met our new special advisor. I have some good news: the line from Washington will be ready ahead of schedule."

"Early?" Falkenhagen asked, surprised.

"Yes. Tomorrow. I want everything set up by 1600."

"We're supposed to have another week!" Meeks protested.

"Things are going better than expected. Dr. Chazelle,

you've said that you believe the energy level could reach a critical point if we double the current one."

The American nodded slowly.

"Then tomorrow we should be able to find out what happens when the time comes. I suggest you get everything ready."

Norton left, and there was silence around the table.

6

"This is not right," Falkenhagen grumbled, shaking his head repeatedly as he held a small metal rod the size of a crochet hook against one of the seats inside the object. The rod was connected by a thick cable to a small box-shaped device on which a pointer bounced back and forth. "Absolutely out of order!"

The German astrophysicist, in his white, Type 2 chemical protection suit, looked like an alien speaking English. The five other scientists on the leadership team were also in the hexagonal room, with its twelve seats facing each other in pairs.

Meeks was setting up industrial infrared thermometers, each standing on thin tripods against one of the six walls. Chazelle was doing the same with the seats, clamping spiderlike clips with small sensor probes that looked like guns to the headboards, the muzzles pointed inward.

Mette Laudrup, the portly Danish woman, was kneeling in the tiny area between the backs of the outward-facing seats where they almost touched at head level. She was bent over a large case assembling something James couldn't see from his position. He wondered how she had managed to get the thing over the funnel and into place.

Smailov, the Russian superconductor engineer, was connecting six bulky battery cells to cables, presumably to be coupled over the next quarter of an hour to the equipment his colleagues were setting up.

"So, what does this look like to you?" Mila Shaparova asked, standing beside him and laying her arms across her chest. Being almost a head shorter than him, she almost looked wider than she was tall with the huge helmet hood of her protective suit.

"Oh." He acted surprised, though he had seen her out of the corner of his eye, irritated that everyone on the team seemed to be working except her. She was free enough to think he was a bit distracted, apparently. He was scared, yes, and the goosebumps covering his body made no effort to recede, but it helped him do his job. Remembering what he was good at kept him from running away, hammering frantically at the elevator's control panel, and running for the hills —something his mind had been demanding loudly of him all along.

"Don't be alarmed. It's just me, the superfluous one."

"Superfluous? Are you trying to take my job away?"

"Mila."

"Excuse me?"

"My name is Mila."

"James," he replied with a smile and was about to hold out his hand to her, but as he looked at his bulky rubber glove, he felt the gesture was ridiculous.

"We're all on a first-name basis down here."

"Does that mean you're not about to chase me away?" He smirked and turned to her so she could see it through his plastic visor. Even under the hairnet and hood, her face showed her elfin features with its curved Slavic features and almond-shaped eyes.

"For now, no. After all, we have a common opponent."

"Norton?"

"Time."

"I see. And they're both working together against us." James nodded and pointed at the others. "What exactly are they doing? And why would you be unnecessary?"

"I'm a materials researcher, and so far I've been able to find out next to nothing. I just haven't found a way to take any samples. Not even with a diamond drill." The Russian woman snorted and shook her head, her hood unmoving. "At least with these chairs I should have been able to sample something with a cylindrical pry bar. Those are normally used for sampling bulk materials. I also tried using a Nobbe sample pricker to pick up smaller pieces and—"

"Sorry? I'm afraid I haven't the faintest idea what that means. The surfaces are too hard to scrape anything off, aren't they?"

"Something like that. They're too compressed. I don't know how it works, but apparently it does *somehow*. Since I've been here, I've been taking notes and making guesses while the others measure."

"But even diamonds can be damaged."

"Yes, but here we are dealing with something different. Normal atoms are held together by electromagnetic forces which can be disturbed, for example, by gross physical action. My theory is that the atoms of these surfaces are held together by strong *nuclear* forces."

"Don't they control what happens *inside* individual atoms?" James asked.

"Yes. Equal electric charges usually repel each other, so it seems surprising that atomic nuclei are stable. After all, there are many positively charged protons there, and in a small space. But they do not fly apart. This is due to the *strong nuclear force*, a much stronger force than the electromagnetic one. Sometimes it is also called strong interaction. It acts among nucleons, not on electrons. Normally it has such a small range that only protons and neutrons attract each other and not the nuclei of neighboring atoms." Mila eyed him, then raised her hands. "Too much, I see. In short, by some unknown effect, there seems to be a strong nuclear force between the atomic nuclei of these surfaces, making it downright impossible for us to damage and sample them."

"But you can split atomic nuclei, can't you?" James thought about it, then shook his head. "Stupid idea, I guess."

"Yes, but our inability to do so explains as to why, after hundreds of thousands of years of exposure to Earth's tectonic forces, the object's shell does not show a single scratch. It might also explain the energy absorption, which appears to operate without any directly identifiable connections. But I'm not sure about that, nor am I the expert on it." Mila pointed upward. "In fifteen minutes, the Air Force will provide the energy output of an entire nuclear power plant to power this alien machine. Raw power that hasn't been run through a substation, mind you."

"Like the lightning that crashed into Lake Maracaibo?"

"Something like that. A simulation of that, only significantly stronger."

"You are against this attempt, am I right?" James looked directly at her and waited until she looked at him. To his surprise, she shook her head.

"This object is as far superior to anything we can understand and build as a space shuttle is to what a swarm of bees can create. We understand virtually nothing about it except these seats." She pointed to the normal-looking seats in front of them. "Their function seems pretty clear; you sit on them. But because of the utter strangeness of the whole package, we have no clue what their function might be beyond simple sitting. Justus—"

"The German Sunnyboy?"

"Yes. He doesn't think we should try to enable anything we don't understand in principle, and his argument makes sense."

"But you don't see it that way."

She shrugged. "I'm Russian."

"More practically oriented."

"Yes. Pragmatism never hurt anyone. When I cried as a child, my grandmother always waved it off and said, 'You go ahead and cry, kid, you don't have to piss what you cry.'"

James barked a laugh, earning irritated sidelong glances from the others, but they quickly continued with their work.

"Sorry," he said, grimacing before turning back to Mila. "That's *very* pragmatic."

"The way I see it, we are facing an endless enigma we cannot easily resolve. Justus and Mette have suggested that we should keep the object away from major energy sources and study it, for many generations and centuries, if necessary, until science and technology are advanced enough to better understand what we are dealing with. The argument is good, and I would support it if we lived in a scientific world, but we don't. We only ever think in terms of the span of a human life, and that is very short in cosmic terms. Until we have a larger scope of consideration—and we simply don't have the means or the social opportunity to do that right now—we're going to push every red button we can find. So, we might as well get it over with. We've always been better as a species at picking up the pieces and reassembling them than putting aside the hammer and *eyeballing* the glass."

"I understand what you're saying. Thank you."

"Thank you for what?" the materials researcher asked in surprise.

"I realize I'm not the most popular person in this room."

"Oh, I think you're reading too much into it. My colleagues are pretty good people and basically distrust any politician."

"But I'm not a politician!" James protested.

"You're not a scientist, are you?"

"No."

"So, you're a politician."

"How should I understand this?"

"Among us scientists, there is—at least at work—a deep-rooted suspicion of all non-scientists who are involved in our projects and have something to say about it. In the pharmaceutical industry, that can be business economists in project management who put monetary issues and process optimization ahead of methodology and gaining knowledge; in mechanical engineering, it can be bosses who cut away the best features of a product because they want a larger margin." Mila waved it off. "There are many such examples. All the people who don't do research and development have political motives. They want to get promoted, make money, look good—take your pick. Politicians, that's what they are. We have suffered with them since the beginning of science, when politicians were still called clergymen. Hence the caveat. But you did it cleverly in the mess."

"What did I do?"

Mila's curved mouth started to smile and seemed about to answer when a voice sounded in the earpiece of James's headset.

"How far along are you?"

It was Norton, and he wasn't about to be put off.

"Done," Meeks reported. The tall American stepped away from the last infrared meter, and the others also gradually stepped back from their equipment.

"Done," Falkenhagen also said.

"Ready," Smailov confirmed.

"If there are any gases leaking out of here now, we'll be able to catch them," Laudrup said, waddling away from the open case in the center of the room. Her rosy face beamed behind her visor as if it was all great fun.

"Just a second." It was Chazelle, the smallest of them, who was still fiddling with one of the seats. She was tinkering with one of the shiny metallic induction strips on an armrest.

"Clear the object now," Norton urged them, and his meaning was clear.

"All right. We're coming out now," Smailov said, raising a hand and making circular motions with an outstretched index finger. "All right, people, let's get out of here."

Like cosmonauts, they walked carefully around the seats, stepping over the cables like they were in microgravity. James waited for them to go first.

"We have a problem," Norton said, louder and more urgent.

"A problem?" James and some of the others asked at the same time.

"The energy level is rising," Meeks replied instead of the major. He had stopped at one of the infrared meters next to the door and was looked at the small display. "Holy shit. It's rising fast. We should get out of here!"

"What exactly is happening, Vincent?" Smailov stopped

at the door of pure light separating them from the "cave" and turned around.

"I don't know; maybe it's pulling the power out faster than we thought. I don't know. But we should get out of here," the American repeated.

"Get out!" Norton shouted over the radio. This time he could be heard clearly despite the scratching and cracking in the connection. "We haven't started the feed yet, but—"

The rest was lost in static.

"Out! Out! Out!" Meeks roared. Smailov turned on his heel and disappeared through the light barrier. Laudrup followed, waddling, then Falkenhagen.

"Kathryn!" Mila exclaimed, urgently beckoning to her petite colleague, who was still standing at the armrest fiddling with two cable ends she had attached to the induction strip with duct tape.

"Just a second," the particle physicist replied without turning around. The Russian was about to run toward her, but James held her back.

"No. Go! I'll grab her."

"This is—"

"I could use another piece on the chessboard, couldn't I?" James turned her around and gave her a gentle push. She passed into the light as if it had swallowed her.

"Ma'am?" He stopped at the opening and glanced at Dr. Chazelle standing not four feet away at the seat facing in his direction. She merely raised an arm and continued to fiddle with her cables.

"Dr. Chazelle, the others seem very upset; we really should get out of here!"

When she still didn't budge, he screwed up his face and ran to her, fast enough to give in to his growing fear but slow enough so he could still step over the cables lying on the floor and avoid tearing his protective suit on an edge from adrenaline-fueled carelessness.

He wondered why he was doing this, staying behind. He could have carried the Russian out like a clichéd would-be hero. He wasn't a hero, he was a master con man, as he'd had to admit to himself more than once. He could read and understand people because he knew their negative sides from personal experience, and he knew how to play those sides off against the positive ones to get them to do something. Conveniently, his job had brought him into contact exclusively with bad people over the past few years. James Hamilton was not one to put himself in danger for others, so why was he still in here now and not out there with a few feet of concrete between him and this creepy artifact?

The many voices on the radio startled him out of his thoughts before he could lose himself in them.

"Dr. Chazelle!" he shouted emphatically once he was standing next to her, and to his great relief, she turned and nodded.

"All clear. Ready. Let's go!"

"Finally!" James said relieved, and gestured for her to go ahead of him, though he would have preferred to run right away.

To his horror, the particle physicist stopped. "Wait! Do you see that?"

"What?" he asked impatiently, but she just extended a finger and pointed the white rubber material at a tiny glowing dot.

He froze. "What is it?"

"A light. It wasn't there before."

Fascinated and spellbound, he blinked a few times and leaned closer.

Sure enough, between the two parts of the headrest—or

what he instinctively thought of as a headrest—a red light was shining. It was tiny, perhaps the diameter of a needle, but definitely a red light. At first, his mind wanted to dismiss it as a visual disturbance, especially since it was hard to see when he looked directly at it. But from the corners of his eyes, where his vision was stronger, it remained clearly visible.

"This is new." Chazelle ran to the neighboring seat on the left before he could stop her.

"Doctor, we should—"

"It's glowing green here." She walked on to the next one. "Here, too."

"Doctor—"

James broke off when something struck him. It was silent. It was deathly quiet, although just a moment before the voices on the radio intense and made his right ear ache. He turned toward the glowing opening to the room and was horrified to see it had disappeared. Instead of a doorlike passageway of light, each of the six walls were just that, walls. They consisted of the same honeycomb pattern as before, except there was no way out—or in—and no sign that such a thing had ever existed.

"All the seats have tiny glowing green lights," Chazelle said, apparently not taking any notice of what was happening around her. Like a white dervish, she moved quickly between the seats and back toward the one she had prepared with the cables. Only now did he notice that her right hand was no longer gloved and were touching the fittings without protection.

"*Doctor!*" he roared, and at last she turned to look at him.

"What, don't you see that..."

"The passageway!" he interrupted her. "It's gone!"

Instead of answering, the scientist frowned and spun around.

"Oh," she finally said. "That's interesting."

"Interesting?" James snorted. "We're locked in!"

Cold sweat formed on his forehead. Small droplets pressed through the pores of his skin until they grew heavy and ran into his eyebrows and over his nose, leaving a barely noticeable burning sensation like a trail of fire.

"That's probably an automatic mechanism to prepare for activation. It's a good sign."

"What?"

"It's reacting to the energy feed," Chazelle explained slowly as if she were dealing with an obtuse child. Her rate of speech alone nearly drove him crazy. "That means the object is changing. Taking up its work, possibly. It's working."

"We can't get out!" He ran to the wall where the opening had been, but then he wasn't sure. They all looked identical, and it could have been one further to the left or right in the hexagon. There were no switches, no buttons, no levers, there weren't any joints in the smooth material, just the strange honeycomb patterns that blurred together as if they were optical illusions. "It's gone! Just gone!"

Stunned, he stretched out his hands in a desperate attempt to feel for an exit—in vain.

"The energy is building. I don't feel anything, but it's possible this room is shielded from the magnetic field," Chazelle said as if James's panic was none of her concern. "But I'm sure there's potential energy increasing here. A nuclear power plant generates about eleven billion kilowatt-hours of electricity a year. Across three hundred and sixty-five days, that makes thirty million one hundred and thirty-six thousand nine hundred and eighty-six point three kilowatt-hours per day. That makes one million two hundred and fifty-five thousand seven hundred and seven point... seven-six kilowatt-hours an hour. A day has... eighty-six thousand four hundred seconds. So, all told, just under fourteen and a half kilowatt-hours a second." Chazelle nodded, satisfied. "That's a lot of energy that has to go some-where. But for a machine like this one, it's probably just a trickle."

"Excuse me," James said indignantly. "Didn't you catch any of what just happened? We're locked in here!"

To his surprise, the particle physicist turned to him and held out her hands, palms up, startling him.

"Yes, I understand that, Mr. Hamilton. So? Does it help to get hysterical now? I don't think so. We're in here and can't get out. At least not at this moment. These are the facts: Given the size of the room there's enough oxygen here for half an hour or more. I don't see any acute danger to our lives. Instead, we have a great scientific mystery that we can observe from the inside as it becomes active. So, if you have nothing useful to contribute, I suggest that you at least be quiet. Okay?"

Taken aback, James nodded. For the first time in a long time, he didn't know what to say, and it wasn't from fear, which had a firm grip on him. He felt like an animal locked in a cage. But she was right, even if he didn't want to admit that to himself.

"Wonderful."

Chazelle looked satisfied and turned back to the seat.

James, meanwhile, thought of Joana, and memories of the money case in Mombasa; her face filled with deep disappointment as he was escorted to the helicopter by the soldiers. Images of their heated argument after her father's death, which had hit her so hard. If he died here, he would never see her again, would never be able to tell her all the things he desperately needed to tell her. Things which had kept him awake for hours every night—for years.

"Hey, what are you doing?" He interrupted his gloomy thoughts. His heart was in his throat as Chazelle sat in the seat with the tiny red light illuminated in the headrest.

"I'm testing a hypothesis."

"What?"

Instead of answering, the scientist fiddled with the fastening on the hood of her protective suit. Before he could say anything to stop her, she had pulled it off and laid it carelessly beside her, revealing her sweaty, bony face. She took a deep breath.

"Are you crazy? This is far too dangerous!" He protested. He went to her.

"Why?"

"I don't know, toxins in the air, foreign environment! There must be a reason why we we're wearing these things!"

"Yes. Caution. We don't need them now, and I need to check my hypothesis," Chazelle repeated, peeling her arms out of the suit, making crackling noises as she did so. When James tried to intervene, she gave him a warning look. "Leave it!"

"All right, so what's your hypothesis?" he grumbled, looking out of the corner of his eye for any changes around them.

"These induction panels here." She rested her forearms on the shiny surfaces on the armrests. "I think they provide some kind of electromagnetic interaction. The fact that the room is magnetically shielded could mean that there are electromagnetic processes that shouldn't be disturbed, and since humans have their own electromagnetic field, an exchange or alignment via these fields here would make sense."

"I didn't understand a word of that." James pointed to the headboard. "But this one is glowing red, so of all the seats, I don't think you should sit on this one."

"And why not?"

"Red?" he asked as if she was the one who was slow. "Red always represents *danger*. Evil, bad, no!"

"That's an extremely anthropological view," she replied, unimpressed. "Most living things on Earth don't have any such concept of the color red because it's only our brains that interpret reflections and their wavelengths as such. Whoever built this will have a very different system of symbolism."

"Oh, just like they build completely different seating than we do?"

"There is one more clue. We can assume that the energy supplied to the object is a drop in the bucket. So, like any machine, it's going to run on low power, like an emergency generator. There are twelve seats here and they all have the same color lights except for this one. So, it's much more likely that the one different light indicates functionality. And if it doesn't—what's going to happen? We can't expect to find answers by studying this thing for centuries without reaching for the possibilities that present themselves." Chazelle leaned her head against the headrest and placed her feet on the footrests before closing her eyes and exhaling.

James saw the hair on her thin arms stand on end and he recoiled. But the scientist looked very relaxed.

"Amazing," she breathed, then all at once she went limp.

A violent headache hit James at the exact same moment. He held his temples and screamed. It felt like thousands of glowing needles were being jammed into his scalp at once, and everything went black for a moment. Then, as suddenly as it began, it was over. His ears roared.

Chazelle still lay limp and unmoving even when he gently shook her arm. There was no body tension, so her hand slipped off the armrest and hung down at her side.

Startled, he stumbled back a stepand collided with something. He screamed and wheeled around and saw it was just the nearest seat, not a monster trying to eat him.

"Chazelle! Can you hear me? Oh, damn!"

He recklessly tore his hood from his head and removed his right glove. He stretched out two fingers and searched for her pulse as voices burst from the radio in his helmet on the ground.

7

The atmosphere in the management team workroom was like that of a funeral.

When James had stumbled out of the object, supported on either side by two soldiers as if he were a frail old man, he had hardly noticed what was happening around him. He had seen figures in the same protective white suits, except their faces were still behind their visors. There had been great excitement, and someone had spoken to him, but he hadn't understood a word.

Now he was sitting at a long worktable covered with drawings and spreadsheets, staring indignantly at his hands, which he had placed over the wrinkled sleeves of his protective suit. Around him, Meeks, Smailow, Falkenhagen, and Laudrup sat in their chairs, scowling or looking aghast at nothing. The emergency lamps provided light, bathing them in a red glow that only heightened the sense of disaster.

"James?" someone asked, and when he looked up, he was looking into the sweaty face of Mila Shaparova. He didn't know how long the engineer had been sitting on the table in front of him. "I know this is difficult right now, but can we ask you a few questions?"

They're curious. Shocked but curious, he thought and felt anger rise inside him. Anger that, even now, they were pursuing their scientific curiosity. He knew this anger was irrational and he was bothered by his reaction. Where did this deep-seated horror, that had spread through his guts, come from?

Dr. Kathryn Chazelle had been lying in the infirmary for over an hour, in a coma. From what little he had witnessed since sitting silently in the twilight, she was brain dead. Whatever had happened had simply drained her brain, erased it, wiped it out.

Watching the scientist simply die hadn't been a pretty sight, but then he had watched a warlord amputate a child's limb with a machete just to send a message. He'd seen mothers hanging from a tree in Chad, where a negotiation was to occur, and many more similarly traumatizing things. Although these experiences still haunted him and caused him to bolt upright from horrible nightmares several times a year, he had come to terms with them. It had also hardened him in some ways. So why was he so afraid, unable to get rid of the images of Chazelle helplessly slumped over?

He knew why , of course, if he was being honest with himself.

"She shouldn't have taken the red seat," he muttered, shaking his head.

"Excuse me?" asked Mila.

"The seats. Tiny lights came on in the headboards. All of them glowed green, except one was red. She was eager to find out the object's function and believed the induction strips on the armrests provided an electromagnetic balance between the body's field and some other. I didn't understand it." James paused and rubbed the his hands across his face. When he looked up, he noticed everyone was watching him. Meeks looked as if he hadn't slept in a month, Smailov had his arms folded in front of his chest and was chewing incessantly on his lower lip, and Falkenhagen was holding Laudrup, who was crying softly.

Mila nodded for him to continue.

"I told her that red always represents danger, but she thought that was too anthropological a view. She was convinced the object consumed a tremendous amount of energy and therefore could only power one of the seats." He shook his head. "But an anthropological view of this thing is the only logical thing so far. I know you're all smart scientists with PhDs and outstanding reputations, but maybe it would help to have someone with simple skills look at your problem.

"The seats in that chamber could be from any office complex. The passageway fits our height and there are green and red lights. In every culture, red indicates a warning of some sort, doesn't it? Among other things, many plants and berries use red as an indicator of poison to deter predators, warning symbols for vehicular traffic, alarm signals—they're all red. And green is the color of life. Why would we regularly observe anthropomorphic cues right under our noses but completely ignore or turn them upside down just because we expect extreme complexity or maximum strangeness? Even a complex rocket engine is made up of simple parts."

The others were silent for a long while, exchanging glances.

"Did she say anything else?" Meeks asked.

"Amazing."

"Excuse me?"

"She said 'amazing,' then she was dead."

"So, she saw something," the tall American said firmly. "Or felt it. Something!"

"We don't know that, Vincent," Falkenhagen said. "We know absolutely nothing, except that she is now brain dead."

"Don't you think I know that?" Meeks hissed, and the German squeezed Laudrup's shoulder as she sobbed loudly.

"Calm down, Mette," Smailov said calmly but with a slight rebuke in his tone. "That won't bring her back to us. We need to pull ourselves together so we can think clearly. The object is still active."

"What?" James asked, half dismayed, half surprised.

"There was hardly any energy consumed and the connection to the power plant is severed, but the object itself is still extremely warm and its surface is crackling with energy."

"Only the magnetic field has subsided. That's why the current flow has returned to normal. Now all we have to do is repair the damaged wiring. You wouldn't believe what happened when you were in there," Mila said.

"What about Pavar?"

"The politician? Haven't seen her again. But Norton is in crisis mode. Can't blame him. After all, the object absorbed the full power of a nuclear power plant for nearly ten minutes and, by all accounts, gave none of it back." The Russian looked at her colleagues. "We have to get back in while it's active!"

"Are you crazy?" Falkenhagen said, shaking his head vigorously. "We don't even know what happened to Chazelle!"

"Yes, we do," Smailov said. All eyes turned to him. "We know she's brain dead because she was sitting in one of the seats—with the red light active. According to Mr. Hamilton's testimony, she was experimenting with the induction fields on the armrests. Nothing happened to him. *Those* are the facts. Everything else is our fear and consternation."

It didn't escape James that he was still being called by his last name by everyone except Mila, even though everyone on the team was supposed to be on a first-name basis. It was a linguistic statement that wasn't needed.

Mila nodded agreement, and Laudrup seemed to calm down a bit, pulling a handkerchief out of her sleeve and blowing her nose audibly. Only Meeks kept scowling and turned away while Falkenhagen seemed to struggle with himself.

"*These* are the facts," the former cosmonaut repeated, and his Russian accent gave his voice a particularly emphatic tone. "That's what we're here for, *facts*.

"So far, there is no evidence that we are in danger if we return to the object—and we *need to* return to the object. We are here to study and investigate it, to find out its purpose and function. Each of us knew there was danger in the unknown, but as scientists it is our job to bring light to the darkness, to bring knowledge to the ignorant. Hiding and giving in to fear is not part of that. So, I suggest we move on."

"Now?" Meeks asked, shaking his head, bewildered. "She's *dead*, Adrian. *Dead!* And you're just going to keep going?"

"If you fall off a horse, you get right back on," the Russian insisted. "Otherwise, you never get on it again."

"Unfortunately, we're not dealing with a horseback ride here. Kathryn didn't fall off a horse. She died in a damn alien artifact because her brains were fried!" Meeks growled.

"That was an example, but it applies here, too."

"He's right." Laudrup had broken away from the young Falkenhagen and was wiping tears from her red eyes. "I'm terrified to go back there, but that doesn't mean you bury your head in the sand. Continuing is the right solution."

"On the contrary," Mila said, agreeing with her, James immediately recognized she was cleverly using momentum to reinforce it. He would have done it the same way. "We owe it to her to keep going. Kathryn was extremely brave, we all know that, and she may have paved a way for us to better understand the object with her courage! We shouldn't throw it away."

It appeared to work.

The former Boeing engineer wrestled with himself, running his hands over his bald head and saying nothing. He slid off his chair and paced restlessly up and down.

The mood was tipping.

"And what exactly did we find out?" Falkenhagen asked.

"The red light. It does seem to be a warning or an indicator of malfunction," Mila replied.

"A hypothesis."

"Yes, but one with circumstantial evidence."

"A clue you'd bet your life on?" the German asked.

"When in doubt, we have to ask ourselves how far we would go to discover this object's secrets," Mila said.

"How far? Best get prisoners and put them in there as expendable guinea pigs, maybe?"

Smailow intervened. "Hey, there's no need to throw things at each other. We're all upset about Kathryn, and that's fine, but we're not going after each other, all right? We're better than that. We've been working for six weeks on something that would be the envy of millions of our colleagues around the world. So, get your act together."

"I'm going," James said, straightening. He felt week and his limbs protested, but he forced himself to go. He knew everyone was on edge, and Smailov was right with every word. However, he couldn't stand sitting in that concrete tomb wracking his brains any longer. "I'm going back inside."

Everyone looked at him. Smailov nodded appreciatively. Mila's expression showed a mixture of sympathy and criticism, while Meeks and Falkenhagen looked incredulous. Laudrup looked as though she felt sorry for him because he was sacrificing himself.

The entire plant was bustling with activity that could not have been imagined from within the management team workroom. Everywhere, technicians were opening pipes and lines and making repairs. Welding equipment flashed in several locations and there was a bright confusion. James wondered how many of these people knew what was going on down here, or still assumed it was a missile silo. Mila explained in a whisper that the facility's EMP-safe electrical circuits had survived the object's extremely strong magnetic field, but that many wires had been burned out by the magnetically induced surge. Since there was no alternative, they were simply being replaced.

In the airlock, they dressed silently and mechanically. Mila helped James with the fasteners around his arms and legs, and he returned the favor. The others assisted each other after Smailow approached Meeks. There was a mournful but determined atmosphere, and somehow that helped him see the door into the "cave" with a little less fear. It was still threatening, seemed darker than it should be, and he felt like a prisoner on his way to death row, but an increasingly powerful voice inside convinced him he was reacting irrationally.

Major Norton was standing against the far left wall with two soldiers, also in hazmat suits, taking notes on clipboards and pointing at the object. Otherwise, the huge cavern was empty. Even the wheeled tables and containers with the researchers' work equipment had been taken out, so only the ramp remained where James had last seen it.

The ellipsoid was still stuck between the ceiling and the concrete floor as if nothing had happened. Its featureless black shell still shimmered at the edges, and James could *feel* cold that gripped him emanating from it.

"What are you going to do?" the major asked, leaving his soldiers and coming toward them.

Smailov answered for the group. "We're moving on."

"I don't think that's a good idea. We should wait to see if the dean gives the green light first. We're in a repair phase right now and can't afford another magnetic surge."

"I understand that. But Ms. Pavar is the leader, isn't she?"

Norton's mouth narrowed.

"Just ask her, and in the meantime, we'll get back to work." Smailov, well aware the phone lines hadn't been repaired, nodded to the officer and turned away. Norton left the cave and pulled his radio from his belt. "All right, let's get going."

They approached the ramp, the bright white of which stood out sharply against its pitch-black background. James swallowed hard, more from the fresh memory of his panic when they had been trapped than of Chazelle's death. Even though it felt heartless, he hadn't known her very well and she been very sympathetic to him. His feeling was more from the way it had happened. Abrupt and downright gentle, without a bang, blood, or any visible effect. She had closed her eyes and died, just like that.

Smailov did not stop at the foot of the ramp but boldly

took the first step and allowed the rest to fall in behind him, single file. James feared the opening might not appear this time, but before he finished the thought, it was there again from one moment to the next, an upright rectangle of glistening light. The cosmonaut stepped through without hesitation, followed by Mila and James.

Everything looked as he had left it. The seats were still there, facing each other, one row outside, one row inside. The open case with the chemical sensors, the battery packs with cables leading from them to the infrared meters and the many cameras. And there was the seat where Chazelle had died. The honeycomb patterns of the walls seemed to darken and close in, making everything tighter, more threatening, but James tensed and took a deep breath.

"Or not?"

James shook his head when he realized Laudrup was addressing him. The woman with the rosy cheeks and the mighty shock of hair smiled sympathetically at him and grabbed him by the arms. Her hands were soft and warm.

"Excuse me, doctor," he said, blinking a few times. "What did you say?"

"It's all right. Take all the time you need."

"It's okay."

The chemist squeezed his wrists one last time and released him go

"The open wires that Kathryn... that she connected to the induction strips. Do you remember exactly where that was?"

James looked over her shoulder, which wasn't difficult since she was so short. The blue and red cables Chazelle had taped down were lying on the floor to the right and left of the seat. He showed her what he remembered. Meeks and Falkenhagen watched him closely and discussed "equalizing voltages," "induction fields," and "frequency bands." He didn't understand a word. Then he watched as the others checked the instruments and studied the seats as if there was something new to discover, which there wasn't.

It's just a room, he reminded himself. *And Joana is not here. You had your chance and you blew it. Accept it already. You're down here and you can't contact her. Even if you could, what would you say to her? What could you ever say that would explain what happened? You can't even reveal why you were taken away by the soldiers! "I wasn't arrested," maybe? And why should she believe you? It's over, simple as that. You'd best to get used to the idea.*

Except that he would *never* be able to get used to it, and he knew it.

James looked up as an argument suddenly broke out between Meeks and Smailov. The tall American was standing in front of the cosmonaut, his arms crossed over his belly.

"What is this supposed to be? Russian roulette?"

"No. We simply connect Kathryn's wires to one of the seats with a green light and test the hypothesis that green stands for 'functional' or 'safe,'" the Russian replied, seemingly calm.

"Oh yes because we just have a guess. How are we supposed to die? Clockwise or counterclockwise?"

"Preferably neither."

"Oh, come on." Meeks shook his head and snorted. "I'll tell you what, in Siberia, you probably hit anything that doesn't work with a hammer, but here we use our brains."

Smailov raised his hands placatingly. "I know you're concerned about Kathryn, but that's no reason to lose your nerve. We have a clear lead, and if you don't want to volunteer, I can understand that."

"A lead in the form of a color? In what test series is that an indication?"

"We are talking about an experiment here. Without experiment, there is no gain in knowledge."

"He's right," Falkenhagen cut in, pointing at Meeks. "It's too dangerous, Adrian. We can't just send one of us into brain death. Think what that would do to our team? We shouldn't rush into anything."

"I agree with Adrian, to be sure," Mila said from across the room. Then she pointed with a crackling glove toward the opening of light. "But the object doesn't seem ready for another try at the moment."

"What if Kathryn's idea of equalizing voltage was right? The object undeniably reacts intelligently in some way, which we can see because the opening forms only when someone approaches from the outside. Remember the first attempts? It didn't work with animals. There is a breathable atmosphere in here, and we still can't find any toxins. This" —Smailov tugged at his bulky suit—"is purely a precaution against the unknown. Maybe the object detected that one of the seats was ready."

"Ready for *what*?" Meeks asked. Falkenhagen also looked promptly at the Russian, who shrugged his shoulders.

"I don't know."

"Of course not! We don't know anything! We are like ants who want to play with fire and therefore burn in their burrow!"

James saw Smailov glance at Mila, who nodded imperceptibly. Someone else probably wouldn't have noticed, but someone like him, who specialized in micro-gestures to succeed in his job, didn't miss it.

"Can I have a word with you two?" the cosmonaut finally

asked his two colleagues, and after a moment's hesitation Meeks and Falkenhagen nodded. "Outside. I think we need a little rest and distance from this place."

The three exited the ellipsoid through the opening, and suddenly James was alone with Mila and Laudrup. The Russian engineer, as if on cue, ran to the seat with the red light and picked up the wires from the floor before grabbing the large battery behind it.

"What are you doing?" James asked, irritated.

"Making the most of the time," she replied curtly, waving him over as she positioned the battery next to the neighboring seat and held out a roll of duct tape to him. "Take this and tell me exactly how and where she placed the ends of the wires."

James did, and she followed his gestures carefully, tearing off pieces of the tape again and again and attaching the cables to the end of the induction strips until it looked just as he remembered. Fortunately, it wasn't complicated.

"What are you going to do now?"

"What do you think? We're testing your hypothesis."

"We shouldn't do that," Laudrup said. "It's not right."

"Do you think they'll come to an agreement before Norton gets back and puts a stop to the whole thing, shoving it so far up our asses we won't be able to move for weeks?" Mila shot back without pausing.

"The object seems to see it differently." The Dane gestured to the opening. "Maybe it doesn't have enough energy left?"

James looked at the seats and the tiny green lights inside them.

"Why would it need or have used that much energy in the first place?" the Russian asked. "Kathryn died, but nothing happened that we would associate with high energy consumption."

Again, James surveyed his surroundings and looked toward the opening, trying to remember exactly when it had disappeared.

"Maybe it decides for itself when the time is right?"

"But then we shouldn't trust it if it interpreted Kathryn's attempt as the right time," Laudrup said.

"It may not be *that* intelligent. It could be intelligent sensors, not full AI, or maybe multiple AI systems that follow certain criteria. Condition A is met, so condition B is initiated," Mila explained. "Hey. What are you doing?"

James carelessly threw away the glove from his right hand and placed it on the armrest of the seat Mila was preparing. He looked over his shoulder and heard Laudrup gasp loudly. The opening had disappeared.

"I tried something."

"You—"

"Yes, me."

Mila looked him in the eye and pursed her mouth.

"Not you," he affirmed.

"I know that kind of look, James. It's the look of a broken man. You shouldn't be doing this."

"Why not?"

"Because you want it to not work."

"Part of me wishes that, yes," he admitted, embracing the sadness in his heart that he had been trying to suppress for years, because he hadn't given up hope of correcting his past mistakes after all. "But that isn't it. I harmed someone once, and I won't do it again. This project needs you more than me, believe me, and it's *my* theory. I should check it out and stand up for it if necessary."

Mila looked into his eyes for a long time. Then she took

his hand and squeezed it before nodding and helping him free his other arm and his head from the hood and helmet.

He took one last deep breath, turned around, and sat down. The skin touching the induction fields first felt cold; then it tingled but eventually subsided.

"Are you all right?" Laudrup asked anxiously.

James nodded.

Are you tired of life now? Or are you trying to buy your way out of this by doing something heroic? he thought to himself and didn't know the answer. The only thing he knew with complete certainty was that his decision not to watch Mila take the risk was the right one. It felt good not to think about himself or what others were asking of him, but to just stand up for his idea and do something selfless. Why? Because it was so easy. There was nothing difficult about this decision. He simply had to protect others from danger. What could be easier?

"The battery shows moderate voltage. Is anything happening?" the Russian asked. She looked at James with a mixture of criticism, compassion, and respect.

"No. I don't know," he answered hoarsely. He looked for signs of excitement inside him, a lump in his throat, a heaviness in his stomach, or a vibrating restlessness in his bones, but there was nothing. He was merely sitting in a chair, but he had a lot going on in his head: Thoughts of the aliens who had built this strange object, of a machine that, in its complexity, made everything ever created by humans look like wedge tools and came across as sophisticated. That was his current reality, and it was so surreal that his mind tried to avoid dwelling on it.

"You didn't strike me as the cavalier one at all," Mila said, smiling at him as she checked the connections of the cables to the induction panels. She sounded casual—she had probably misinterpreted his calm expression as fear or at least tension.

"I'm not. I was once, I think."

"Well, now it's you again."

James looked at the seat in front of him, which was close enough that the footrests—or what they had interpreted as such—almost touched. He closed his eyes, relaxed his body, and leaned against the headrest.

8

J ames opened his eyes and immediately felt the cold on his skin. He shivered as his gaze fell on the seat opposite him. But something was different. Mila was no longer there, and there was no trace of Dr. Laudrup either. He looked down at his arms and frowned when he saw he was naked, no protective suit, not even underwear. He raised his hands in front of his face and examined the fine grain of the many folds that were so familiar to him, turned them a few times and wiggled his fingers. He looked between them again at the opposite seat and noticed the perspective was different.

He was sitting in the inner circle!

"What..." he mumbled and swallowed. Carefully, he grabbed the armrests and stood.

There were no cables leading to the induction strips, no battery behind his seat, no chair across from him with its back facing the honeycomb wall. Startled, he turned around a few times and found absolutely nothing: No infrared meters, nor those little guns on tripods, no battery pack above the funnel in the middle where the backs of the six inner seats almost touched, no cables, no cameras. The room was empty. Empty except for himself.

There was no sign anyone had ever been here. But also nothing proving it was *not* the strange room he had just closed his eyes in. Everything was exactly as it was before: The honeycomb pattern on the walls of the hexagon he was in the center of, the seats with their immaculate cushions of strange material, the floor that looked like a mixture of hardened metal and plastic, the ceiling above him that wasn't one at all because it was simply lost in a contourless black that appeared to be both solid and empty darkness at the same time.

But the opening was there. That perfect rectangle of light from which photons seemed to lick over the edges like glistening plasma. Bright, yet not so it hurt the eyes.

"Where is everyone?" he asked aloud, turning around again a few times.

No answer.

"This isn't not funny!"

What did they do? Undress and move me? Why didn't I notice anything? He touched the skin on his stomach and hips. Everything felt normal. He was not tired. On the contrary, he felt more vital than before, as if he'd had a great night's sleep. The first in many years. *Do they want me to come out naked? Or had there been an accident?*

James froze. What if he had also fallen into a coma like Chazelle and was now in a permanent delirium, a mental dream world that wouldn't let him go? That would mean his brain was trying to process this last experience in a continual loop. It even made sense since he had internalized the space well but hadn't understood any of the scientists' equipment. Cables conducted electricity, he knew that much, but that's was the extent of it. So, had his comatose mind just blanked out all that and given him what he subconsciously wished for? The exit? But then where were the others? He liked Mila, and Laudrup with her motherly appearance he somehow found reassuring. He realized that now that they were gone.

Brain dead, he thought and swallowed hard. *Is that possible? Am I lying in the Air Force base infirmary right now just like Dr. Chazelle, while the others are below me in the depths of the missile silo making long faces at each other and trying to determine who's to blame for all this?*

The idea made him shiver and reminded him how cold he was. Should a man in a coma be cold like that? What would happen if he walked through the light now? Would the dream be over and start all over again with him waking up in the wrong seat?

Following an impulse, he went to the chair diagonal and to the right of his and looked for the little light. He found it. It glowed green. One by one, he ran to the other chairs and found that each light was green.

No red!

James went to the center and stood between the six headrests that came together like a cocoon surrounding him. There was not a single deviation, no threatening red flicker or flash. What if he wasn't in a coma at all, but something had happened to the object? Maybe an even stronger magnetic pulse that had destroyed it, or a burst of radiation that had merely spared the chamber inside?

But then where were Mila and Laudrup? If they had been evacuated they would have taken him with them, wouldn't they? Again, a chill came over him, and he shivered. He had to warm up somehow, and that was impossible in here. So, he went to the rectangle light in the honeycomb wall. Without the scientists' equipment to guide him, it was impossible to know in which wall the opening had appeared since everything looked exactly the same and symmetrical. Though in the Air Force facility, it had always appeared in the same place. He wondered if it would have been the same if they had put the ramp on the other side of the object? While the chamber was symmetrical, the object itself was ellipsoid. Not for the first time, he wondered why its builders had chosen such a shape. For aesthetic reasons? Or functional ones? If the latter, wouldn't a sphere have made more sense?

He stopped in front of the light and carefully pushed his hand into it, first with the fingertips, then a little more, until it disappeared to the wrist. It felt warm. Very warm, in fact.

He took a deep breath and passed through... and cried out as he fell into the void. With a *smack*, he landed in a viscous mass and groaned. Dazed, his shoulder aching, he scrambled to his feet. He found himself in a muddy morass of stinking slush made of old leaves and soil. The ellipsoid rose from a drab, earth-colored tundra, black and feature-less, a mighty monolith in the midst of desolate nature. Nothing could be seen of the opening, but it must have been several meters above the ground.

The entire area was covered in the dark morass, punctu-ated by clusters of tangled, waist-high bushes that looked as if they had been through a fire a few days or maybe weeks ago. Dark browns faded into even darker browns, creating the depressing image of a lifeless environment looking out for a sun that didn't exist. Mountains of dense gray clouds covered the sky like a stained shroud and a stench of rotten eggs lingered in the air.

"Where the hell am I?"

James straightened and held his shoulder, ignoring the stinking mud that oozed down his body like tough chewing gum in no particular hurry. Contrary to his fears, wading back to the object was not strenuous, although the mud tugged at his feet whenever they came slurping out of it. In front of the black shell, it grew cold again, and as he almost pressed his nose against it because it was hard to tell where the object began. He noticed drops of water beading off it as if they could find no purchase. The black object was smooth and dry, and it took a quick eye to see the drops at all. Overcome by sudden thirst, he opened his mouth and pressed his cheek against it, catching as much of it as he could, and drank greedily.

It was a little bitter but quickly quenched his thirst. As soon as he moved away from the object, he warmed and instantly broke into a sweat.

"Where am I?" he breathed, suddenly feeling lonely.

The environment in which he found himself was so desolate that it seemed to suck all the life out of his veins. Visibility was limited to about a hundred meters because of a hazy veil of fog around the area. But there was nothing to see anyway, except the same colorless bushes in the mirk.

"Is there anyone there?" he called out, feeling stupid. It was obvious he was as alone as one could be.

After a few endless minutes, he started waking south. He had no way to determine cardinal points but decided to define the black ellipsoid as his personal north. The object stood out clearly against the hazy surroundings of the stinking swamp, a sharp outline against the cloudy horizon, always closer than he would have liked.

James put one foot in front of the other, looking back every few steps so he could be sure the object was still there and in sight. There was no sound, except for a slight rustle carried on the warm wind to his ears, probably from the bushes that always to move slightly.

No birds, he thought. *No insects. Nothing.*

He walked to a bush and squatted in front of it. He wiped the sweat from his forehead with the back of his clean hand, then touched a branch. He rubbed it lightly with his fingers and raised his eyebrows as damp ash came off the wood, which was very dry underneath. Tiny buds appeared, barely larger than a few millimeters in diameter. There was a hint of green in them, but they were mostly rust-colored spots that looked like disease and decay.

When he squeezed a harder to expose more buds, the branch snapped with an eerie *crack* that seemed loud and made James wince. He jumped up and looked around like a startled deer scenting predators in the shadows. Every tremor of a branch, every rustle, sent goosebumps tingling across his heated body. He searched for the object, having trouble at first as he spun in circles. He breathed a sigh of relief when he recognized the ellipsoid on the horizon, black and steady. It interrupted the monotony of the dismal atmosphere with its simple shape, and stood out from it like a minimalist work of art.

James kept walking, looking for someone or something, tracing concentric circles, with the object as the center. He found small, gnarled trees with yellowed leaves, many broken branches, and gray stones overgrown with dark moss saturated with moisture. He smelled it but pursed his mouth in disgust and quickly threw it away. The stench threatened to eat into his brain and overwrite his childhood memories of the earthy scent of the moss that grew under the terrace of his childhood home.

He didn't know how long he walked around trying to figure out where he was and if it was even real, but eventually he settled in the mire against the object, crouched onto his buttocks, enjoying the chill that contact with the shell sent through his body. His shoulder still ached, but he found no injury, so it was probably just bruised. It didn't bother him much, and it gave him the feeling that this was real, that he wasn't in a dream.

Then where was he? And why did everything around him seem to be dying? Besides the object, of course.

James rubbed his hands over his face. At some point he buried it in them, blocking out the ugliness of the dead landscape, the ominous mountains of clouds, and the stench, trying to fathom what had happened.

"I sat in one of the outer seats; there is one per wall," he said, his voice forming a strange echo in his hands. "I closed my eyes and... something must have happened. Chazelle died when she closed her eyes. She said 'amazing' before she was dead. Is that it? Does closing the eyes initiate some kind of transition? But then why was I sitting in one of the inner seats facing outward when I opened my eyes? Was it the seat opposite mine? But even if it was, how did I get there? And why?"

A rustle made him freeze. It stood out clearly against the constant breeze. It was brief and then it was cut off. The chill in James's back abruptly spread throughout his body and he slowly pulled his hands away from his face.

In front of him was a figure.

They stood about five meters away, , a person a little smaller than him perhaps, wrapped in dark scraps of cloth, several layers on top of each other. Around their waist was a sturdy cloth belt, into which a crude hatchet, a knife, and a jute sack were stuck. Their face was covered by a bandana so only the eyes and part of the nose were visible. It was undoubtedly human, from the rather slender silhouette possibly a woman, although it was impossible to tell.

Since she had drawn none of her weapons, he swallowed his initial fear and raised both hands, palms facing forward.

"Uh, hello!" he said hoarsely, then cleared his throat.

At the sound of his voice, the figure startled and took two steps back.

"No, no!" He raised and lowered his hands placatingly. "I-I need some answers: What happened? Where am I?"

Instead of answering, his visitor tilted her head and scrutinized him. James licked his lips and stood, increasing the distance between them.

"I'm unarmed and injured," he said, smiling kindly. "Not a very great danger. On the contrary, I should probably be more afraid of you."

The figure stepped closer, cautious as a cat on the prowl, eyes always on him and shifting restlessly back and forth.

"Really, no." He followed an impulse and turned his back to her, placing his hands on the object's hull like someone under arrest. "You can see for yourself, I'm a naked, mud-covered guy who doesn't know where he is and has a real pain in his shoulder."

Why doesn't she speak?

"Mahru tek qasadu?" said a voice behind him. It was soft and yet slightly strained. And it was closer than he had expected.

"What? I don't understand. Do you speak English, by any chance?" James asked, then snorted at his own words. He turned to look at her and just barely kept from flinching. She was standing right behind him, and stepped back when he turned around. Suddenly, he remembered he was naked and he tried to cover his shame with his hands. "Um... my name is James."

"James?" She awkwardly mimicked him. She had a very strange accent that reminded him of none that he knew. But maybe that wasn't even possible because he was... not on Earth?

"Nasaku!"

"Nasaku. That's your name?" James pointed at her without taking his other hand off his genitals. "Nasaku?"

In response, she raised a gloved hand toward him and turned the palm upward.

"What does that mean? Do you want me to give you something? I'm afraid I have nothing." Before he finished, she lowered her hand and silently eyed him. "Nasaku, I need to know where I am! A coma room doesn't seem to be it; that much is certain, but where am I? Has there been an accident? Was the facility destroyed?"

Again, there was no reaction.

"You don't understand me," he muttered, half-turning to the object he was still touching with one hand. "You know this one, don't you?"

Nasaku followed his gesture and again extended her hand with the palm up. It was a quick, casual movement. It had to mean something. Perhaps a nod in their culture? Many examples of gestures had evolved differently depending on the culture, such as the nod of the Europeans, which meant approval, but among the Indians, it meant disapproval, while a shake of the head meant approval. He had not yet seen a hand gesture, but he was not an anthropologist.

"ASAR!" the woman shouted—by now, he was sure it had to be a woman. Her voice was a bit distorted but definitely feminine.

"Asar?"

Again, she raised her palms.

"Asar..." he muttered. "What does that mean?"

"ASAR!" Nasaku repeated, holding a finger under her

right eye. James believed it was green. He pointed to his own.

"Eye?"

She frowned. A form of facial expression he understood. To clarify, he blinked a few times, and she raised her palm again. He imitated the gesture and smiled carefully. As he did so, he noticed open sores had formed on his hands that itched and burned terribly, now that he saw them. The edges were dark, almost black, and deep red on the outside. In the center was a viscous fluid that looked like pus. Startled, he frowned and examined his fingers. He immediately found several places where similar oozing abscesses were forming.

Nasaku came at him so fast he flinched. She grabbed his right wrist, pulled it toward her, and inspected the injury. She smelled like a mixture of mire and cinnamon, and her clothes were even dirtier than he had thought. The fabric of her glove was scratchy, like matted wool.

"Timbak anu!" she said, emitting a long-drawn-out growl before backing away and gesturing for him to follow her. Without checking to make sure he was following, she ran off, each of her steps producing ugly smacking sounds.

"What is it?" he asked anxiously, running after her. "Wait!"

9

Nasaku ran through the mud as if she were dancing with it. He felt like a trampling animal. Each of his steps produced an ugly *smack* that sounded like an acoustic outrage in the silence of this place. Still, he couldn't get rid of the vague feeling that he was being watched, that the many shadows had eyes. The strange woman was proof enough that his hunch had been confirmed. What if there were more observers? What if all this was not as deserted as it seemed?

But how could people survive here? There is nothing to eat, only dying vegetation and stinking air, he thought, panting as he tried to keep up with Nasaku. She deftly dodged the bushes, which seemed to tug at her ragged clothing like claws snapping back and forth in the wind. She led him further and further away from the object, and this made him nervous. The ellipsoid became paler and paler the longer the strenuous march lasted.

"Wait!" he gasped as they threatened to run out of sight of the object.

When she didn't respond, he stopped. He looked back

and forth, torn between her receding back and the towering shadow far behind him. Two impulses warred within him: Cling to the only person he had encountered or to the only thing he knew that gave this place some constancy. He should have been afraid, of the stranger, her weapons, her motives, but instead there was merely the desire to cling to the company, to no longer be alone in this bleak mustiness. The object, too, should have sent a shiver down his spine, as it had done before, and yet he saw it as a hand that had beaten him, but which was a hand he could hold onto.

"Manatu?"

James looked up and saw Nasaku had stopped and was looking in his direction. She was too far away to see her eyes, but he imagined that she was looking at him questioningly.

"I..." He sighed, then let go of everything going through his head, as if he could get rid of it. "I don't know you; I don't know all this." He gestured with his arms, moving them back and forth to include the entire place and sat in the warm mud at his feet. "I'm sitting here *naked* who knows where and I don't even understand what happened. My colleagues are gone. You speak a language I don't understand, and I'm scared. Yes, me." A snort escaped through his nose. It was depressing. "A great ransom negotiator I am. *Nerves of steel,* I've been told in reports. I've negotiated with warlords, leaders of militias full of child soldiers who have brutally slaughtered more people in their lives than could fit in a Rambo movie. That was a thrill for me, a break from my thoughts of a time and things I can't change. But this... this scares me so much it makes my throat close up."

Nasaku tilted her head and came closer.

"You don't understand me, either, I know. But you know what? This might be a good thing. At least I can say what I really think for the first time in a very, very long time. That object back there, it did something to me. I don't know what, but I seem to be trapped in some kind of dream. What does that make you? A dream walker? A figment of my subconscious?" He shook his head and looked down at his filthy hands.

"James."

Startled, he looked up at his name—said with a somewhat strange intonation, but clearly understandable. Nasaku squatted in front of him and untied the panels of cloth sewn onto the brown scarf from her face. It revealed an oval face with a curved nose, slanted green eyes, and a narrow mouth with wrinkles at the corners. She did not look as soft as her voice suggested, but still friendly.

"Iwok Dab," she declared.

"I... I don't understand you. Iwock dap? What does that mean?"

Nasaku pursed her lips in frustration, then grabbed his right hand so quickly that he didn't have time to be startled. She pulled it toward her and turned it so he could see the wound, which by now had grown alarmingly large. What had looked like an ugly abscess before was now oozing and had developed a fiery red wreath around a powerful pus blister.

"Iwok Dab," she repeated, pointing upward, then at the bushes around her. "Noctum Dab."

"I don't know what it is. But it doesn't look good."

Impatiently, she bobbed her head up and down, which looked like a rather strange nod, but probably meant something completely different. After a frustrated hiss, she folded her hands above her head and then made movements with two fingers as if two legs were walking.

"We have to leave?" he asked.

"Gone," she repeated, seeming to taste the words on her tongue, then turned her palms upward. Before he could say anything, an eerie roar pierced the gathering darkness. It reminded him of the rutting cry of a moose, only much deeper and more terrifying.

"What was that?"

"Gone." Nasaku was visibly tense now and looked around grinding her jaws before jumping up and running off without looking back at him.

James blinked in dismay as the roar sounded again, only much louder this time.

"Wait!" He scrambled to his feet and, heart pounding, followed her as fast as he could. *But not so alone,* he thought, panicked.

Nasaku ran so nimbly that he had to ignore the burning in his legs to avoid falling behind. The resistance of caused by the sticky mire caused his strength to fail him quickly. The eerie sound that followed them, however, did not allow him to catch his breath. In his mind, he imagined the worst horror, a many-headed monster with huge claws right on their heels that would eat them at any moment.

After a while, the environment changed, became rougher, and the ubiquitous mud was replaced by rocky ground covered with black moss. It looked like mold that had formed a soft, dense turf. Judging by the smell, it seemed quite likely. Large monolithic stones protruded from the ground, like teeth that had been abraded and gradually knocked over by wind forever blowing from the same direction. They looked bizarre and became more numerous with each passing minute.

The screams of the monster increased, too—or were they echoing through the monoliths, towering up to ten meters high? Nasaku stopped occasionally and changed direction, seeming to orient herself with things James could not recognize. Again and again, he turned briefly, for fear of losing his connection. He peered into the haze to find the object, but it was too far away.

It was getting dark when Nasaku finally stopped, and he almost collided with her because he heard the roar again and wheeled around.

"What is it?" he asked, panting.

"Dak."

"Dak?"

"Dak." She narrowed her eyes, then seemed to listen to the wind before gesturing for him to follow her.

They slowly crept around a mighty monolith with a rough top and were suddenly standing before a large structure of shiny material. It was elongated, twenty or thirty meters long, with a triangular spur projecting toward them like a roof. The front was small and squat with pale windows, and the back looked like a series of disintegrated funnels.

"Is that... a *spaceship*?" he muttered in disbelief.

"ASARU," Nasaku replied, walking toward a dark space beneath the mold-strewn wing. James followed her, gazing in wonder the solid metal from which the craft was constructed. It looked alien, yet familiar enough that it looked like a cross between a space shuttle and a fighter jet, albeit slightly larger and beefier. Clearly, it had crashed. There were deep scars in the flanks where whole chunks were missing as if a giant predatory cat had slammed its claws into it.

The dark place was an opening, a large hole which they stooped through. Nasaku pushed aside a curtain before sticking her head halfway inside and making snuffling noises. Then she waited and finally went in, holding the fabric so he could follow her.

Inside was absolute chaos. There were no real walls, just metal plates wedged in and over each other from which cables and thin strands hung. Piles of fabric and numerous objects, from cans to debris to crude axes and knives, were knotted together with battered, rounded boxes by pieces of rope. There was a lot of space, about as much as half a badminton court, and yet everything looked squat and cramped because of all the trash—there was no other way he could describe what he saw.

There was also a rather large area of sand spread in a semicircle in front of the entrance, which Nasaku was blocking by clamping prepared loops in the fabric to curved hooks around the hole in the fuselage. The blanket—if it had ever been one—flapped at the edges in the stronger wind gusts but seemed sturdy enough to withstand it, creating something like a sense of protection and security.

"Is this your... home?" he asked as he slowly turned around and looked closely at everything. His eyes fell on a charcoal drawing on a piece of sheet metal, but Nasaku jumped in front of it and turned it over so quickly that he backed away, startled. He thought he had seen a little boy or girl.

"What was that? Your child? A sibling?"

"MOKADAB!" she hissed and looked at him sharply.

He raised his hands defensively. "None of my business, I understand."

She calmed down and went to one of the boxes before beckoning him to join her. Obediently, he followed her and sat on a thick stone polished smooth on the top.

She opened the box, he blinked in wonder. It was full of strange implements: small rectangles with buttons that glowed from within, improvised cylinders made of rubber tubing, a plastic bag barely marked by the expected decay, and lots of blister packets with pills inside.

Nasaku grabbed a finger-thick cone that looked made of plastic and had a smooth surface with tiny holes on one side and a red button that looked like a thimble on the other. She pressed the flat end against his neck and he flinched.

"Hey!" he protested. "What are you doing?"

Exasperated, she rolled her eyes, held it just below her own ear, and pretended to press the button.

"You're not going to inject me with that, are you? What is it? A medication? A drug?" James asked, swallowing. All at once, he felt threatened, recalling that he had no idea how to get back to the object from here, let alone with whom he had escaped. He was locked in the wreckage of a machine that must have been exposed to wind and weather for decades, or centuries, and now this strange woman wanted to shove something down his throat?

"No!"

"TIIT!" she hissed, glaring angrily at him. Again and again, she tapped the little thing in her hand. "TIIT!"

"I. Know. Don't. What. That. Means!" he growled, infected by her anger, frustrated that they couldn't communicate. *A great ransom negotiator I am.*

"I can't understand you, but this stuff... *wait!*" James stood so abruptly that Nasaku jumped, scrambled back a bit, and let a hand wander to the axe in her belt. He didn't even register it, nor did he think about the fact that he was still stark naked and covered only by a thick layer of mud.

"What did you just say?" He focused his gaze on her like a hawk on a mouse. Fear and anxiety fell from him like old leaves from a tree. "That word!"

The stranger looked at him as if he had lost his mind.

"TITT? TI-IT?"

"TIIT?" she repeated, blinking, irritated.

"TIIT, yes! I've heard that before!" He clapped his hands and she flinched as if he had slapped her. "My former fiancé, she said a phrase to me, in Sumerian or something, the last time we saw each other. What was it...?"

He paced restlessly between the box and the sand in front of the door, stubbing his toe painfully against the stone he had been sitting on a moment ago, but ignored it as he tried to concentrate.

"Some wisdom she'd found on a dig," he muttered, tapping his chin incessantly with his index finger. *I should have been more interested in this old crap!* "Life takes place before the future, or first life, then the future. *TIIT* was the first word, I think. I memorized it because I thought it sounded funny. That would mean *IIT* must logically be *life.*"

"TIIT." Nasaku turned her palms upward.

"Life." James pointed to himself and repeated it, "TIIT." Then he pointed at her. "TIIT." Next, he tapped the stone and wiggled his index finger in denial. "No TIIT."

She tilted her head.

"Ul Tiit."

"Ul, no."

"No." Nasaku opened her palms, and he nodded eagerly before imitating her gesture.

She calmed and let go of her axe. Then she lifted what he thought was a modern injector, out of keeping with the post-apocalyptic setting. He paid no attention to it.

"You speak *Sumerian.* How is that possible? Have I traveled back in time?" The idea ran through him, making him shiver. "A time machine... that's a time machine!"

When she pressed the injector against his neck, the area briefly warmed. He wasn't even startled and didn't fight her off. Helplessly, he plopped down onto the stone behind him, only to realize he hadn't been in front of it and had landed on something else. That did not interest him either.

"You speak a dead, ancient language. The Sumerians spoke it. The first people with their own writing and recorded language. Do you know what that means?" He looked up, saw her puzzled expression, and sighed. "No, you probably don't."

"TIIT," she replied, wiggling the injector in front of his face, then tossing it carelessly to the floor. Outside, the wind howled hard enough that it whistled above them through the many small holes and cracks. Eerie sounds filled the hideout.

"Yes, *Tiit.* But when? That is the question. Is this what the world looked like ten thousand years ago? Did the Sumerians even live at that time? I really should have been more interested in Joana's work." James paused and frowned. "But that can't be right. The Sumerians lived in Mesopotamia, and the name they gave themselves was *saggigo* or *saggiga,* which means 'blackheads.' That's what I remember. You don't look dark-skinned, though."

He looked down at the empty injector at his feet.

"And they certainly didn't have medical equipment, let alone airplanes."

Nasaku waited out his soliloquies and then knelt next to the large, silted area in front of the twitching and whipping fabric covering the hole. She beckoned him over. Slowly he came closer, knelt, and watched as she drew with her index finger. The first shape was clear: an ellipsoid.

"That's the object," he said, nodding. She gave him a long sideways glance and then imitated his nod.

"Ob-Objeck." Nasaku drew five more ellipsoids in the

sand and connected them one by one with direct lines until they were all connected to and among each other.

"They're connected. There are six of them? Is that what you're telling me?" Thinking, he rubbed his chin. "But there are twelve seats."

When she looked at him without understanding, he traced a poor image of the seating circles in the object. One row outside, the chairs farther apart, and a closer row inside facing outward, toward their counterparts. Underneath, he drew a twelve.

"Ah," she said, pushing his hand away and drawing a line next to the number, only to write a six behind it.

"We share the same math. There are only six. But why?" Again, he thought, looking at the ellipsoid she had drawn first. He pointed to it and then to himself. Again, she nodded, as if getting used to the gesture.

Nasaku drew an arrow from the lowest object in the circle to the one where she found him, then one in the other direction, but she crossed it out and set a small broken twig next to the empty space.

"Damaged. The connection only works in one direction because the other is broken?" he thought aloud. "What you're saying there looks like it's a connection I came through."

Excitedly, he tapped his chest and tapped the lowest ellipsoid, said "TIIT" and then tapped the one at the top. "TIIT."

She raised her palms.

"Yes. You think that's how I got here. Traveled from one object to another. Like in a teleporter?"

She seemed to understand him. She pointed to his origin teleporter and said, "James TIIT." Then to the arrow. "Ul."

"Wait, *Ul* means no."

"James TIIT. James Ul." A tap on the local teleporter. "James TIIT."

"You mean to say that I live on both sides, but not on the path? If what you say is true, then I'm on both sides? That's why I woke up on the seat opposite... But how is it possible that my body exists twice?"

He looked up and into Nasaku's eyes.

"You're not from around here, are you? There's nothing here."

James pointed to her local teleporter and wiggled his index finger. She didn't seem to know what he was trying to say at first, but finally she opened her mouth and raised her palm. She tapped the right ellipsoid with a piece of the small twig she had broken, and her expression turned somber as she cut all the connecting arrows leading to or away from it with a furrow in the sand.

"It doesn't work anymore? Broken? Kaput?"

"Kaput." She seemed to taste this word, so foreign to her, on her tongue, then sadly lowered her eyes. "Anak Tab. Ina Pani Aksu."

"You can't go back to your home country. I'm... sorry to hear that." A loud roll of thunder came from outside as if to underscore the depressing realization of that sentence. "How did you get here?"

Nasaku looked at him for a long time. She drew a woman and two smaller people—children?—in the sand before pointing to her teleporter, which was no longer functional. Under the woman, she drew a one, then a two under one child and a three under the other. She grabbed her chest.

"Situ Bas." Now she pointed again to her local ellipsoid, drew herself and her two children below it in the sand and pointed to the destroyed connection before crossing out the two little stick figures. The corners of her eyes filled with tears.

"You were stranded and they died. Oh, damn. But why did you come here? This place—this... *world*? It's horrible." James plopped onto his buttocks and rubbed his temples. "Unless whatever happened here happened after you got here. But what could that be? Do you know what destroyed this world? A natural disaster?"

He looked at the wreckage around him and swallowed.

"Or something else?"

"Aksu," she replied, tense. "Rabum Aksu."

"Rabum Aksu?"

Nasaku drew a jagged sphere in the sand.

"What is it? An explosion? Danger?" He pantomimed wrapped his arms around himself and looked around demonstratively like a skittish animal.

"Rabum Aksu!" She raised her palms.

"Danger. Great danger. This is taking too long. You obviously know a lot about these machines, but I don't speak your language. With us"—he pressed an index finger to the local teleporter—"there are people who speak your language. I can take you with me. But you have to show me how, okay?"

Nasaku frowned, then pointed at him and himself and the teleporter.

"Yes. We have medicine, food, water." He nodded eagerly. "You know how to use it. You can help us understand; then maybe we can help *you*."

James's gaze fell on his hand and he noticed that the weeping abscess had visibly receded.

"This medicine, is it yours? Or did you find it here?"

Nasaku looked at him questioningly, and he nodded in frustration.

"Yes, I know. We don't understand each other and these drawings have their limits." More thunder, this time so loud his bones shook. Rain began to fall, pelting the hull of the wrecked ship from a quiet patter one moment to a deafening roar.

"Damiq," she said and made a reassuring gesture.

"Thunderstorm?"

Nasaku drew a plus sign in the sand. "Damiq."

"Plus? Positive? Could also mean good. You don't want me to worry, do you?"

She didn't say anything, but drew some lightning bolts across her teleporter, striking into its tip.

"Damiq."

James nodded knowingly. "The lightning is charging the teleporter. Like Lake Maracaibo."

"Sittu," she said. "ASAR damiq."

"ASAR is the teleporter; you said that before. The teleporter is charging, it's good. I understand. Sittu."

Nasaku folded her hands and rested her head on them.

"Sleep, rest."

He was veryexhausted but not tired. He probably wouldn't be able to sleep a wink, certainly not with all the crazy thoughts going through his head trying to make sense of what he had learned. He watched her curl up in a corner of the wreckage, where several blankets lay on top of each other, and close her eyes. He saw something glittering in them, probably reflections from the glowing mushrooms sprawling across the ceiling like a spongy lawn. He hadn't noticed them before, although they had been their only source of light.

"Luminescent plants," he murmured, fascinated.

Nasaku watched him with doubt, but he couldn't blame her. It was amazing she had been so trusting and helpful in the first place. After all, he was a dirty, naked man from an alien planet—a thought he still couldn't fathom. Six teleporters on six planets, all connected. If true, the potential consequences and sheer unlikelihood were so great that just trying to foresee them all made him dizzy.

So, he sat on a piece of cloth and listened to the violent thunderstorm, wincing a few times in a sort of half-sleep as exhaustion spread through his limbs and settled over him like a heavy blanket.

He didn't realize he had fallen asleep until someone shook him. He looked up into Nasaku's face, his eyes gummy. It was quiet and the air was cooler than before.

"SITU," she said softly.

"Go? To the teleporter? Um, ASAR?"

Her palms turned upward.

"It's fine." Groaning, he stood, trying to drive the fatigue from his bones. He pointed to the blanket he had been lying on, and when she nodded, he wrapped it around his body.

"Arhis! Arhis!" she urged him. A little surprised, he followed her through the hole in the ship, from which she had pulled the curtain. To his surprise, she did not re-hook it and instead ran.

It was still dark, but not so dark that you couldn't see your hand in front of your eyes. There was no wind, not even a gentle breeze. The silence was almost eerie. James rubbed the last of the sleep out of his eyes and looked around he knew why.

Above them, in a huge circular area, the sky was clear. The black firmament seemed filled with dozens of lamps, they were not lamps but gigantic chunks of debris. The local moon had shattered in the middle and the fragments trailed behind it like an irregular string of pearls.

"AKSU!" Nasaku shouted from the ahead, hastily waving him over. James turned his gaze away from the glowing pieces of debris and looked at the pitch-black clouds surrounding them in all directions. They towered thousands of feet high and looked as if someone had sliced them open with a scalpel. Flashes of lightning twitched silently back and forth, branching into glistening fractals. They were in the eye of an enormous storm the likes of which he had never seen before, not even in a feature film with computer effects. He couldn't imagine what it would be like once the eye had moved on.

"AKSU!" the she repeated emphatically. He shook his head and turned away from the spectacle of nature to follow her. The soles of his feet ached from the rocky ground after only a few meters. Yesterday he had hardly noticed it because of excitement. Now he ignored it and ran between the large fangs that made up the bizarre field of gray rock formations around them. In the absolute silence, he heard every single sound of his footsteps, every crunch of gravel, every breath so loud that it was disturbing.

They reached the edge of the rocky area, which was slightly higher than the muddy swampland stretching before them, when the eerie roar of the previous evening sounded again, followed by a bloodcurdling scream.

"Nasaku!" he shouted and looked over his shoulders for a monster in the shadows.

But the shadows were so numerous and long that each seemed to give birth to monsters. Adrenaline surged through his veins, spurring him on to even more haste.

Unlike the day before, the walk back felt much shorter, and he breathed a sigh of relief when he saw the dark silhouette of the teleporter in the distance, appearing out of the twilight of the moonlit night.

The roaring and screeching behind them swelled and became so loud that he kept expecting something to jump at them. He couldn't stop to think about , so instead he focused on running for his life and praying incessantly in his mind they would make it in time. The mire, which again enveloped his feet, made every single step much more strenuous and only aggravated his feeling of being defenseless prey.

They were finally standing in the mud in front of the ellipsoid and the environment was already getting cooler. Nasaku dug in the mud to the left of the narrow side.

"What are you doing?" he asked, spinning around several times, his eyes narrowed, his knees slightly bent. He examined the many shrubs, tangled and jagged against the ground, motionless in the stillness air, while around them the giant storm described frantic circles around the calm center. The cloud wall was getting closer and would arrive in the next few minutes; that much was certain. The only question was whether the howling monster would reach them first.

"Nasaku!"

"DAMIQ!" She shouted triumphantly, and he wheeled around. She pulled a crude ladder made of branches tied together from the mud and held it up like a trophy, dripping and dripping, before running to him and placing it against the teleporter. She tried to make him go first, but he shook his head and shooed her up. He held the lower rungs so she wouldn't fall, looking over his shoulder the whole time.

A shadow moved! Big as a minibus, with a spine like jagged swords.

"Nasaku," he muttered and swallowed. Then louder, *"Nasaku!"*

The woman had almost reached the last rung and did not turn around. Then the passage of light appeared and she disappeared into it. Quickly, he climbed after her, but jerked violently at a mighty roar that was so close the volume made him tremble. Whipped up by panic and adrenaline, he scrambled through the light and knocked the ladder over with his foot so nothing could follow him.

Relieved, he rolled onto his back and breathed heavily as the glowing opening became a familiar wall of small honeycombs. The whole world seemed to have been locked out with it, and James felt a sense of security fill him, although the teleporter still made the hairs on the back of his neck stand up.

He got to his feet and gratefully took Nasaku's hand when she held it out to him. She walked to the seats, looked around, and pointed to one on the right, which had its back to the outer wall and was aligned with its counterpart in the inner circle.

"This is the connection to Earth?" he asked, coming closer.

Although she could not understand him, she raised her palms.

"You follow after me, okay?" James pointed to himself and then the seat, then to her and the seat.

Again, she raised her palms and beckoned him to hurry.

"All right. I hope it works." He thought about how his body was still sitting on the other side, comatose. What if they had thought he was as dead as Chazelle? What if she had actually traveled to one of the other planets? Or maybe she had sat in the seat that led to Nasaku's home, which was no longer accessible? Maybe that's why the dot glowed red ?

His forearms touched the induction strips. He laid his head back and looked at Nasaku one last time.

"We'll help you, Nasaku."

"Damiq."

She nodded, and for the first time something like a smile played around her mouth, though her eyes still expressed pain and sadness. He thought about the two children she had painted and crossed out and closed his eyes.

10

James opened his eyes and inhaled like a drowning man breaking the surface of the water on the last of his oxygen. His heart raced as he looked anxiously to his right and left. All around him were lights, so many lights, and colors that mingled wildly but remained out of focus. His pupils protested the onslaught on his retinas and his eyes ached, like he could feel them penetrating into his skull. There was so much noise, frantic and disturbing, and so loud that his ears were ringing. Only gradually did he realize they were voices, including some familiar to him.

"James? James!"

A bright surface appeared above him. A face?

"James, can you hear me?"

"Ow!" Something pricked the crook of his left arm.

"James, it's me!"

"What?" he murmured, confused, and blinked several times. He recognized the face of Mila Shaparova, her big eyes, the blonde hair that framed her oval face like liquid gold, and her curved mouth. The worry and strain in her looked seemed to like a travesty marring her countenance.

"So beautiful..."

"What, James? What happened?"

Slowly, his confusion subsided like a patient waking from anesthesia. He also saw Laudrup standing next to Mila from the seat he had just been sitting in—only in a different teleporter with Nasaku standing next to him.

What if she tries to come over and the seat is taken?" he thought, his panic rising before his gaze fell past Mila to the seat in front of him and he calmed down a bit. *The outer seats are for departures, the inner ones for arrivals. It has to be that way.*

"What happened?" he asked, smacking his lips to drive the metallic taste from his tongue.

"I just asked you that," the Russian woman said. "You were in a coma for several hours."

"Several hours?"

"Yes."

"But I'm still here?" He looked around and saw the walls' honeycomb pattern, the black infinity above him, and the other seats. There were the cameras and infrared sensors, the many cables and battery packs. Two women in white lab coats were busy managing the many needles in the crooks of his arms and unhooking an IV hanging on a plastic stand beside him.

"Yes. I was able to convince Ms. Pavar to have you examined and treated here after the staff physician certified you were not brain dead as..." Mila cleared her throat. "Like Kathryn. You just went into a coma with normal vitals, at least those of a sleeping person."

"So, you left me in here?"

"Yes. It wasn't easy to convince Norton, but Pavar seems a little more open to some risk." Mila's still looked worried, which in turn began to worry him.

"What is it? Is something wrong?" He wiggled his fingers and his feet and exhaled in relief when he could feel and move them.

"I made that decision," the Russian said. "I was worried, but I was convinced there was a difference here. We have to wait and see."

"You feel bad about stopping the major from moving me into the infirmary?"

"Yes."

James snorted. "You probably saved my life with that one."

"I wish we had succeeded," Laudrup said, sounding sad. However, when he looked at her, her rosy face was relaxed, and she gently squeezed his shoulder.

"Yeah, me too," Mila agreed with her. "But at least we tried."

"Wait a minute, what are you talking about? It worked!" he protested. "I was... on the other side."

Mila and Laudrup exchanged a look and frowned.

"Believe me, someone is about to come through here. Her name is Nasaku and she speaks Sumerian!"

The wrinkles on their foreheads deepened.

"You don't believe me," he breathed in frustration and was about to jump up, but the two nurses and two scientists gently, but firmly, pushed him back into the seat.

"Easy. You'll have to sit tight for a bit until they give the green light and the staff doctor has seen you. I'm sure the others are on their way by now, too."

James looked the Russian woman straight in the eye.

"I'm serious. I woke up in another teleporter..."

"Teleporter?" she asked.

"Yes. This machine, it's a teleporter—or at least that's its function. I woke up in another one, identical to this one.

The only difference was that I woke up in the seat across from it. I was naked, but it was my body as far as I can tell."

Again, the two exchanged a glance, which caused a creeping anger to rise within him.

"Hey, look at me! I'm not talking nonsense, and I wasn't in a coma."

"All right," Mila said in a neutral voice. "What exactly happened?"

"I went through the opening made of light and fell; there was no ramp there. The teleporter was in the middle of a swamp, a stinking morass. There were bushes, dried up and covered with ash, and thick mountains of clouds. The air smelled of sulfur and ozone. Then I met someone, or rather *she* found *me*. Her name is Nasaku and she's from another world. It's also connected by a teleporter, but she can't go back. Her two children were there with her but died—"

"Wait a minute," Laudrup interrupted him gently. "Another world? A third?"

"Yes, there are a total of six teleporters on six different worlds. They form a network with each other, so you can use any teleporter to reach any other. Except for the one that doesn't work anymore. There's no way there or back."

"That's what this *Nasuku* told you?"

"Nasaku," he corrected her. "The wasteland is a terrible place, there's no life except shrubs and bushes and mold, and everything seems affected by a creeping decay. It even made me sick, but Nasaku gave me something from an injector, which made the abscesses recede. There were also several monsters there, or maybe just one. I only saw its shadow, I think."

James paused as he realized how crazy it all sounded.

"Ah, the patient is awake." A new voice said and a lean man in a white coat came into the object, a plastic clipboard under his arm. "I'm Captain Miller. It's good to have you back with us, Mr. Hamilton."

"You're the doc?"

"Yes." The doctor came closer, pulled out a small penlight, and shone it in each eye before speaking a few short sentences to the two nurses which James barely understood.

"He says he traveled to another teleporter," Mila said, and James wanted to scold her for talking to the captain and not him. How was a doctor supposed to understand something like that?

"Ah, quite normal. There are many studies about coma patients who have woken up. Some wake up after hours, like Mr. Hamilton here, others after days or weeks or years, and others not at all. Since we know nothing about the induction of the coma state, no reason can be identified. However, dreams during a coma are quite normal and commonplace, so I wouldn't worry about that." Captain Miller smiled encouragingly at him and made notes on his clipboard.

"Wait a minute, I wasn't fantasizing!" James protested. "I was really on the other side. I was hurt and in real pain. I was scared and didn't know where I was. It was all real!"

"The brain processes in dreams what it experiences in waking life. It sort of sorts out its neurons, if you will," Miller explained without looking up. That he didn't even seem to consider whether there was a possibility that James was right was disheartening. He nonchalantly dismissed it as the ravings of a coma patient.

"That wasn't a dream!"

"No? You were afraid of this strange machine, just mourning the loss of a colleague, and maybe even blaming yourself for being in here with her. Then you slip into a coma and wake up in a different seat than the one you were so afraid of; you must have been nervous. You are naked, which subconsciously indicates that you felt defenseless. The vegetation outside that you described was desolate and a reflection of death and decline—what you experienced before. But then you meet a savior figure—a woman who speaks Sumerian, of all things. Your former fiancé speaks fluent Sumerian, am I right?"

Now Mila and Laudrup were looking at him with a mixture of irritation and understanding. The latter was the hardest to bear.

"Yes, she does, but..." James swallowed. Could he say anything to convince the doctor it hadn't been a dream? Could he even be completely sure? "It wasn't a dream; I don't believe that. It was too real. I wasn't flying or anything. Time was linear. Sensations were not abstract but immediate. I know what dreams feel like!"

"Have you ever been in a coma, Mr. Hamilton?" the doctor asked, making a final note before passing the clipboard to one of his nurses.

"No," he admitted.

"Then you don't know what it's like to have a coma either." Miller squeezed his arm and gave him an encouraging wink. "It's good to have you back with us. You should take it easy and get some rest. You'll be fine! I'd like to do another MRI scan when you're ready, but we'll have to do that upstairs in the clinic. Ladies?"

The captain nodded to them and left through the light passage. Shortly thereafter, Meeks, Falkenhagen, and Smailov appeared. While the latter looked rather subdued, the American and the German seemed relieved when they saw him and smiled.

"You're back!" Meeks rejoiced, nudging his shoulder as if they were longtime friends. "We were really worried!"

"I'm glad you're well again," Falkenhagen said, nodding at him. Now, surrounded by a bunch of people, the center of attention, James suddenly felt even more uncomfortable. Although they all looked at him kindly, he couldn't shake the feeling they pitied him and thought him insane.

"Thank you," he said, pointing to the cameras. "I know you've been listening to me. I know you don't believe me."

"James, it's not like that, it's just that..." Mila rose to protest, but he silenced her with a raised hand.

"No, it's okay. I do understand. I probably wouldn't believe me either because it sounds so unbelievable. But I want to ask you to think outside the box for once. This arti-fact here, the teleporter, is a miracle. A technical miracle of extraterrestrials who are or were vastly superior to us. You said so yourself. Why shouldn't it be possible that what I say is true?"

"Because you've been here the whole time," Meeks replied gently. "You went into a coma. Your green lights theory seems to have turned out to be an anthropological trap, I'm sorry to say."

"You need proof." James nodded in understanding. "You'll get it when Nasaku shows up in the seat across from me."

They all looked at the empty seat across from him, and silence fell as everyone looked expectantly at the dark seat made of the unfamiliar material. Nothing happened.

Come on, Nasaku! he thought, chewing on his lower lip. *Where are you? You were right behind me!*

He thought of the roar of the monster and shuddered. Could it have gotten her? But that was impossible. It would never fit through the passageway, and besides, the opening was high enough that no one could get in without a ladder.

Or?

They looked at him again, and the pity in their gazes hit him like a slap in the face.

"You don't believe me," he breathed and sighed, disappointed. A spark ignited in his mind; it was a spark of doubt. Was it possible they were right? They were, after all, pretty smart people.

No! I know what I saw, I did not make something like that up. The Sumerian vocabulary, I've never heard it before!

"It doesn't really matter if we believe you," Falkenhagen said, looking as if he had bitten into a raw onion. "Ms. Pavar is extremely angry about you going it alone."

"And so are you."

The German pursed his lips. But Meeks answered clearly uncomfortable. "You were in a coma; I don't want to argue with you."

James gestured carelessly. "It's okay."

"Smailov lured us out; we got that already!" The American fretted, as if a dam was breaking inside him. "Going it alone like that"—he looked out of the corner of his eye at Mila, who defiantly thrust her chin forward—"is neither informative nor wise! We're here as a leadership team, do you understand? We can't just resolve our disputes by some of us doing what we think is right."

"This is *dangerous*!" Falkenhagen said, agreeing with his colleague. "We can't afford to just go for it. We need consensus and smart decisions supported by all of us. Otherwise, how will we ever trust each? We come from three different cultures and groups with different beliefs, and we need to work together for the good of everyone and science. You have undermined that trust."

Mila looked like she wanted to protest, but James beat her to it. Enough damage had already been done.

"I understand that, and I'm sorry," he said. "*I* take respon-sibility for that. I'm not part of your team. But I'm telling you, at least listen to me. Let me tell you everything from front to back and document it. If you change your mind, at least you'll have the knowledge that only I can give you."

Meeks and Smailov exchanged a quick glance, then the American nodded.

"If it's up to us, we'll do it for sure," he said.

"But it's not up to you, I guess?" James wondered where Major Norton was.

"No, Pavar was beside herself with rage, and she prob-ably still is. I expect she's on her way here now."

"That's her," a firm, deep voice interjected into their conversation. It was Major Norton, coming through the light opening, his uniform freshly pressed, his face hard as gran-ite. "I'm glad to see you're out of the coma, Mr. Hamilton, but it's the end of the line for you."

"What?" he asked, horrified.

"You are out. This solo effort was the first and the last. You are out of the project. But don't worry, you'll get your first month's pay."

"But Major, I have—"

"Save it. Ms. Pavar has already prepared the appropriate paperwork. She had to make a decision and I understand it."

"But you don't agree!" James said hopefully.

"That's irrelevant. She doesn't trust you anymore, and you don't seem to understand how delicate this project is with all the parties involved. It wasn't easy to get the EU and Russia to sit down with us and agree to do the project on our soil. If someone like you comes in and jeopardizes all this because he doesn't consult with us before doing what he wants, then no genius in the world can make this project a success."

"Major, we have—" Mila said, but the officer cut her off.

"No, you be quiet, understand? Don't talk yourself into any foolishness. This management team must remain in place. Or do you want to explain to the Kremlin that the project has failed?"

Mila fell silent and gave James a pained look.

"Shouldn't we at least hear him out?" she asked defiantly.

"Pavar wants him out because he's unpredictable."

"But what if it's true?" Falkenhagen, of all people, said. The German poster boy shrugged as Norton glared at him. "It may sound unlikely, but on a project like this, can we afford to not consider all possibilities? This is still an incredible alien artifact; what did we expect? That we'd understand it right away?"

"No, and that's why we can't assume that we can assess whether the effects we see are real or not. We have to set completely new standards," Laudrup agreed, squeezing James's shoulder. Only now did he realize that her hand had been there the whole time, and the touch made him feel good.

The others nodded emphatically, except for Smailov, who folded arms and looked thoughtful. James couldn't believe that despite their doubts, they were standing up for him, though Meeks and Falkenhagen had reason enough to be angry with him—and obviously were.

He was touched by their support.

"So, you're going to believe him and go up against Pavar for this?" the major asked, raising an eyebrow. "You should think twice about that."

"There's nothing to think about," Mila grumbled. "It's

not that we want to *go up against anyone*, it's that we don't want to discredit someone because their story sounds unbelievable. We should at least listen—he's only been awake for ten minutes!"

"I'll save you the time because you know absolutely nothing about Mr. Hamilton. But I do."

James scowled at the officer.

No!

"Mr. Hamilton initiated a corporate merger several years ago between the PR agency where he worked as a senior consultant and that owned by the father of his then-fiancé. The reward was a seat at the table as a partner. He made a lot of money from that deal. After some time, he then made sure her father and his patron were pushed off the board. Her father later took his own life by driving into a tree."

"It wasn't a suicide! The road was slippery that night!" James growled.

"So, you're not saying that your action made him depressed?"

When he didn't answer, Norton nodded.

The major continued. "But that's not all. For the last four years, he's worked as a ransom negotiator for the State Department. They always used him where Americans were being ransomed by terrorist, with groundbreaking success."

"That's classified!"

"Everything down here is classified, and everyone here has signed NDAs that don't even allow you to pee behind the nearest bush and tell yourself about it!" All eyes were on Norton. "His track record is quite impressive, except that he's also made deals with the blackmailers to line his own pockets."

James froze. Liquid fire suddenly seemed to flow in his veins.

"Yes, Mr. Hamilton. They knew about your machinations. They just ignored it because the results were good, and you never got *too* greedy. You're not stupid, after all." Now the horrified looks turned to him. "He is a professional swindler and fraud who has made crooked deals with the worst terrorists on this planet to enrich himself. His whole life is a construct of lies, which makes him a perfect manipulator, but not someone you'd believe with a story to get him off the hook."

"What?" James said indignantly, but he felt the stares on him as if they were boiling him with laser beams. "I didn't tell a story to save my neck, I—"

"Oh, no?" Norton snorted. "Come on, man! You wake up and tell some confused fantasy story about a woman who rescued you on another planet and pretend to have vital information about a supposed teleport network, knowing full well that you'll be held accountable. What does that look like to you? You just want to make yourself irreplaceable. You can sell your crap to these people here, but not to me. And not to Pavar, either, for that matter."

James swallowed hard as he saw the somber looks of the scientific leadership team surrounding him. "It's not like that."

Laudrup seemed sad, Mila confused, and Meeks and Smailow openly hostile, while Falkenhagen looked as if he were trying to assemble a difficult puzzle in his mind.

"And what about this?" Norton pulled out his tablet, tapped on it, and turned it so everyone could see the photo.

It showed James amid a whirlwind of paper currency being maneuvered toward the camera by two soldiers. Joana's disappointed face was just visible in the background, though indistinct, distorted in the still image like a ghostly apparition.

James knew he had lost the fight. He saw it in the looks that pressed on him like the weight of whole worlds. He opened his mouth and closed it again, unable to say anything. Instead, he stared at the empty seat across from him.

Where are you, Nasaku?" he thought, discouraged. *Did you ever exist?*

11

James paced in his room, incessantly messing up his short hair. It was cramped and stuffy and he felt like he was running out of breathable air. Several times he held his hand in front of the ventilation grill, just to make sure there was still a slight breeze and that he would not suffocate.

Norton and two of his men had escorted him to his quarters, and James felt as if he were walking through a dreamlike drug trip. The team's looks, some horrified, some disappointed, haunted him like arrows stabbing him in the back, and made it hard for him to breathe. They reminded him of Joana's last look, and that hurt. But what could he say? Deny everything? Invalidate the last several years of his life and some of his most important decisions? No, he couldn't, and he wasn't allowed to. Pavar wanted to get rid of him. He could even understand it from her viewpoint, if he cared to put his frustration aside for once. But what did that mean for him? Nothing. It had no meaning because it would change nothing.

When the major had put him up against the wall in

front of the others and paraded him around, something almost escaped his lips. That had never happened to him before. And it was because of Nasaku. He just couldn't—or wouldn't—believe that he had imagined it all. It was real because it *had* to be real. He knew what a dream felt like when awakening from it, sometimes even while he was in the dream itself. But if it had been real, where was Nasaku? Why didn't she come through?

There was a knock at his door and he jumped. The major had given him two hours to pack his things—much more than he needed for the small backpack, of course. Were they here to pick him up already?

"Come in," he said hoarsely and swallowed, preparing to face Pavar, or two soldiers who would escort him to the elevator and make sure he didn't cause any trouble.

Mila poked her head through the crack in the door and then slipped inside. He was surprised to see her but waved for her to enter.

"Uh, hello," he greeted the Russian woman, shame welling up inside him.

"I know we don't have much time, but I need to talk to you again."

James took a deep breath, then nodded. He pointed to his bed, and they sat next to each other but left some space.

"What the major said, is it true?" she asked bluntly.

"Yes," he admitted after a pause, forcing himself to look determined. Self-pity had never helped anyone, and he was in danger of drowning in it. It was over, so the least he could do was walk with his head held high before he inevitably collapsed. A person could take only so much, and his limit had been reached four years ago. He had just managed to keep going like a robot, even though he was eating himself up inside.

Mila's expression stiffened, but she did not leave, instead she folded her hands on her crossed legs and looked at him.

"You probably don't want this, but before you go I want to hear the whole story. You're a fraud, I understand that. We shouldn't believe a word you say, I understand that too," she said, each word hitting him like a physical blow. "Still, you are right about at least one thing, we can't afford to ignore your story out of hand. Even if it's simply a transcript, we may still be able to get something out of it, even if it's just inspiration."

"Mila," he said quickly and slid toward her, but she immediately moved away from him. He stopped. Sadly, he went on, "I swear to you that I didn't imagine it. Am I a liar? Yes. And liars aren't believed, I know that. But I traveled to another teleporter, I'm sure of it. Either that or I'm a madman."

"Tell me," she said without apology.

James nodded and told her. About first closing his eyes and waking up in the opposite seat, meeting Nasaku, his fear and her shelter, the monster's eerie roar, the storm, the broken moon and his abscess, the injector and their escape in the eye of the superstorm. He told her about the monolithic rocks and how they had looked like teeth, the obviously advanced technology in the wreckage, and the ladder he had knocked over behind him after returning to the teleporter with Nasaku.

He realized he wasn't telling his story in the correct order and kept jumping around, Mila admonished him to take a deep breath. He did so and tried to tell it again chronologically, leaving out feelings and thoughts and focusing on the facts. The Russian materials researcher nodded every now and then and asked him to explain if something wasn't precise enough for her, but otherwise let him finish, didn't criticize or question, and made notes on a small pad she had pulled out of her pants pocket.

After he finished, he felt exhausted—mentally, but also physically, as if all his strength had drained out of him along with his memory. Or maybe it was just the stress that his experiences might have been for nothing. After all, Nasaku was still trapped on that terrible planet.

"Let's assume all of that is true, and we should as long as we're talking about this subject because, otherwise it doesn't make sense," Mila said, tapping the end of her pen against her chin. "You woke up in the opposite seat and you were naked. On our side, you didn't disappear but continued to sit or lie in the seat where you had your eyes closed. With your clothes on."

James smiled at her joke, only to quickly wipe it away when he saw no sign of amusement in her expression.

"So, *if* it really is a teleporter," she continued, "it clearly doesn't teleport the body."

"Only consciousness." James nodded and got up to pace, as he liked to do when he needed to think. "But then where does the body come from?"

"A clone."

"A clone?" He was surprised by her immediate answer to his question. He stopped and looked at her, frowning.

"Yes. That's obvious. If the teleporter doesn't teleport bodies—which would be virtually impossible physically anyway—then perhaps it merely does it with information. A DNA sequence would probably suffice." Mila nodded, deep in thought. "That would require much less energy and could be done through the induction fields or some other pathway —perhaps even the air you breathe. On the other hand, your body could then be built in the form of a clone and your consciousness, which, after all, doesn't seem to be made of matter, would simply be loaded into it. A perfect copy."

"So that wasn't me at all?"

"That's a good question." She waved it off. "The correct question is 'where did the material for the clone come from?' He was biological, you said, not a machine. Otherwise, you wouldn't have suffered from the formation of an abscess."

"A human body is just a bag of flesh and blood held upright by bones, isn't it?"

"Yes. It's very simple in its basic structure. It's only the emergence that makes it something complex, the interplay of very many *stupid* individual parts that, when added together, form a complex, intelligent being," she explained. "Sixty percent is water, with about sixteen percent proteins, ten percent lipids, one point two percent carbohydrates, and another five percent minerals and one percent nucleic acids, such as DNA, among others. At the elemental level you are fifty-six percent oxygen, twenty-eight carbon, nine hydrogen, two nitrogen, one point five calcium, one percent chlorine, one percent phosphorus, some magnesium and sulfur, and a few more electrolytes like potassium and sodium. That's it. Every complex living thing is made up of these substances in slightly different compositions."

"But where does the teleporter get all that?"

"It has to have a source of biomass that it somehow extracts."

"Or that needs to be fed to it," he suggested.

She nodded and stood. "Or that, yes. I have to think about it."

"Wait!" The word escaped before he knew it. He didn't want her to leave. He liked Mila and seeing the coldness in her eyes pained him.

"For what?"

"I..." James bit his tongue and grimaced.

"Do you want to tell me something?"

He thought of the moment in the teleporter when Norton had confronted him and revealed him, that one moment when he almost said something—said *everything*—but he wasn't allowed to.

"I know that look in your eyes," Mila said. "From my father. He fought in the Afghan war and experienced things no one should have to experience. He never talked about it. He said he didn't want to burden us with it. He finally died of cancer, and I'm sure it was the wall inside him that he had to build between himself and those he loved. At least that's what he believed he had to do. To protect us. I would rather have had my father than the decision he made for me and the whole family without us having a say."

James swallowed but said nothing. Mila nodded.

"You are supposed to be a liar, a cheat. You are, I see it in your eyes, but I see the same thing I saw in my father. Lying has become a habit with you, this inner wall that you won't break down. It will kill you, eventually. It does that to all good men."

"Good men?" he asked.

"Yes. You could have ratted me out in the teleporter. I had a plan to try the seat without asking the others. That was *my* responsibility, and you went instead to protect me. What criminal does that?"

James remained silent. Mila sighed headed for the door before turning back once more.

"I don't know if you will hang yourself or spend the rest of your life in your self-created prison, but I do know one thing, before you die, you will be like my father and you will regret that you made all the decisions for others and never told the truth. The truth can take care of itself and doesn't need your hubris thinking it knows what's good for others. Just ask yourself if your past behavior has made the world better or worse." With that, she turned and opened the door.

"Wait!" He stopped her at the last moment. She stepped back but didn't turn around. "Close the door, please."

She did. He took a deep breath before dropping onto the bed and burying his face in his hands.

"It started with the agency merger. It's true; I was a senior consultant at Benson & Schuster when I met Joana. Her father was kind of the toast of the New York public relations scene. Everyone who was anyone wanted to shake his hand at one time or another. He was a true veteran of the industry. Many people accused me of throwing myself at his daughter to get to her father because I was, admittedly, very career-focused at the time. I had nothing else in my life that gave me meaning and purpose. I wanted money and success and to be on top. Maybe I did have certain ulterior motives when I first approached her at a reception for her father's agency, Bretoni & Partners. But if I did, it quickly changed.

"She was stunning. Intelligent, funny, and above all, so full of life. She wanted nothing to do with the money-grubbing of the New York upper class, the endless small talk, and the scrutinizing looks to see if you were wearing the latest fashions or were already on the decline. She wanted to change the world, to see it, feel it, make it better. And her father, Augustus, supported her in everything. He never pushed her in any specific direction, and she loved him. She loved him so much that she didn't talk about anything but 'her daddy.' I think part of it had to do with her mother dying of cancer when she was twelve. That left deep scars and ultimately, I think, led her to dedicate her life to helping children."

James let out a long, slow sigh. It felt strange to be talking about a past he had only reconciled within himself. There was something cathartic about every word that left his mouth, as if a layer of concrete was peeling away from him.

"He was a good man, you know," James continued. "He was strong-willed about things but soft on details. He always knew what he wanted but wasn't willing to hurt others along the way. His employees loved him, and the customers too. But he also had his shadows. And that included—"

"You've never talked about this, have you?" asked Mila.

"No, but it's past time. If not in an underground bunker, then where?" He smiled sadly and swallowed the lump in his throat. "That included an affair with Joana's former nanny, Dorina, while her mom was still alive. While she had cancer, he was completely overwhelmed and took refuge in the arms of another woman. Joana would have been destroyed by that knowledge, and he knew it. He was desperate to make amends and saw only one solution. He followed his own advice that he often gave to others: Steal two pieces of candy from someone, and you have to give them back three.

"So, he was faced with a dilemma. He had wronged his wife, and his daughter by withholding the truth from her. At the same time, he was not willing to lose her or destroy her life in the name of truth, so he sacrificed his agency. He made me a partner and signed over most of his shares to me. Joana would never have believed that he would give up his life's work just like that, so he also gave me some incriminating documents about inconsistencies in the accounting. I was to send them anonymously to the other partners. His though was that he would spend more time with Joana once he no longer had the agency. But the whole thing blew up, and eventually it became known that I had leaked the documents.

"Joana never forgave me and I couldn't tell her the truth. I had promised Augustus, and I saw how much she enjoyed spending time with him. They vacationed together, went skiing, moved closer to each other. She broke up with me. I considered, at my lowest emotional point, putting the truth on the table to get her back, but how selfish would that have been? Who was I, who had come into her life long after her father, to decide that she had to hate him to love me?"

Mila sat next to him, her expression calm, but he saw compassion in her eyes.

"At first things went well, but Joana started her own non-profit and considered moving to Africa. Her dad wanted to go, but it became increasingly clear that he missed his work. He'd been the center of attention all his life, part of New York's high society and on a first-name basis with senators and the governor. You don't just give up something like that from one day to the next. One day he visited me at the agency and asked about doing some pro bono consulting work for us, and of course I agreed. He also wanted to finally clear my name, which he never succeeded in doing, although he always assured Joana that he was not angry with me. On his way home, he ran into some black ice and hit a tree on 6th Street. He died in the ambulance. After that, Joana never wanted to talk to me again. She believed it was a suicide, although the police report didn't confirm that. But it was unclear enough to leave her opinion unchanged."

"She blamed you," Mila opined. "Oh, no."

"Yes. She told me to never come near her again."

"Is that why you started that new job? As a ransom negotiator?"

"I think so. I sold my agency shares, I didn't want

anything more to do with it, and anonymously donated all the proceeds, sixteen million dollars in all, to her newly formed charity. It sounds like I was trying to wipe my slate clean, but that's not what I was doing. Despite my grief at being on the outs with the woman I loved, I felt immensely sorry for her. I just wanted to do whatever I could to alleviate her suffering and help her start a new life with her charity, which was extremely close to her heart. So, it seemed like a good way to go.

"In my new job, I enjoyed the adrenaline, the fear of death, of my extinction, which seemed like a promising redemption. I know that sounds cowardly, but I probably wasn't brave enough to just throw myself off a bridge. Many times, I would have liked to do it to escape my self-pity, but I found another reason to live: I saw an opportunity and made crooked deals with the extortionists. I secured my own cut for passing on information that helped them do more business in the future. That secured me good results with lower ransoms, often up to half a million in commissions and good contacts."

"You donated those proceeds to Joana's organization, too, I assume?"

"Yes. I had a somewhat romanticized notion that I was taking money away from bad people and investing it in something good. At least that way, I thought, I could make up for something, even if she never knew. I actually felt better for a while."

"Do you know what your biggest mistake was? The biggest injury you caused her?" Mila wanted to know.

He did not answer but looked up and returned her gaze through watery eyes.

"That you didn't think she was strong enough to know the truth. Look what you have endured all this time. You must think very little of her if you don't think her capable. You have no right to pre-chew and sort the truth for her. Everyone has to find their own way with fate, and even if you had to break a promise, at least you could have done it after he died. The lesser of two evils."

"She won't believe me now," he was sure. "Not anymore."

"Again, you think for her!" Mila scolded him, punching his left shoulder so hard that, for a moment, he thought the injury was back from his tumble out of the teleporter.

"Ow!" He rubbed the sore spot and blinked at Mila in surprise. "I guess I deserved that."

"Yes." She stood. "You have to tell the truth."

"What? Norton and Pavar? The—"

"No, *slaboumnyy!*" Mila rolled her eyes. "It's none of their damn business. Besides they don't want you out because you lied to your former fiancé or cheated the state out of money, they knew that before they hired you for the job here. They misjudged you and think you're a loose cannon. My guess is that they thought you were flawed and egotistical. They thought they had sized you up and could manage you so well. See how good you were at keeping that promise to your almost father-in-law?"

"Yes..."

"When you're out of here, you're going to fly to her and tell her the truth, understand?"

"Aye, aye, ma'am," he promised with a sad smile. The very idea made him shiver.

There was a knock at the door, hard and short.

"One last tip," Mila said. "Talk to Pavar. Don't just leave without a fight. Try to convince her of your story. It may not help you now, but it will help us. Take the time to tell her everything you told me, then you can leave with your head held high."

She hugged him tightly, surprising him.

"Thank you."

Before he could react, she was already opening the door. On the other side stood Major Norton wearing a grim expression, with two soldiers behind him.

12

J ames got two surprises. One was that he really did ask Norton to talk to Pavar, to share his important information with her one last time. The facility manager really couldn't resist and agreed.

The other was that he experienced no anxiety about the conversation because he felt downright liberated.

His involvement in the project was over. There was no doubt about that but sharing the truth he'd been carrying around for so long with Mila had been liberating. He might be able to tell Joana the truth without perishing just thinking about it.

Norton didn't want to inquire with Pavar at first, but James convinced him he would cause less trouble for him and would leave willingly afterward. When the dean agreed, it was impossible to miss that the major had not expected it, nor was he particularly happy with the outcome.

Pavar's office, to his surprise, was on the first floor, well above the cave with its mysterious teleporter. A former storage room had been cleared out and furnished with two large desks—one for her and one for Kowalski—plus filing cabinets and televisions. She obviously needed her laptops and computers to work and judging by her assistant working madly on a keyboard, he needed them even more.

"Mr. Hamilton." Pavar did not rise as he entered but shooed out the two soldiers who accompanied him.

Major Norton had them close the door from the inside. She was still signing documents and did not raise her eyes. James felt like a schoolchild being summoned before the principal, but he could find no annoyance in himself about it. He was still too busy imagining what it would be like to call Joana. Would she even pick up the phone? Or had she blocked his number long ago? Maybe he'd have to go through her relief organization.

"I figured you wouldn't just pack up and leave," Pavar said, finally gesturing for him to take a seat in the only chair in front of their table. It was made of aluminum, and its arm and back rests were unpadded and cold. Just the way she wanted it, he guessed. "Under current labor laws, you're entitled to a four-way conversation, and, unlike certain people, I abide by regulations."

"Thank you," he said, not responding to her rebuke. "I understand your decision, and I'm not here to give you a long speech to change it."

"Good." She looked surprised but knew how to hide it well—even from someone like him. "So, what can I do for you then?"

"I'm sure you think I've gone off the deep end or made something up so you won't throw me off the project. I'm not, but I also realize you won't buy it either way."

Pavar untangled her fingers and intertwined in front of her in a gesture that seemed to indicate he had caught her.

"Nevertheless, I think you are a rational woman and make decisions according to their logical consequences. If you throw me out now without my information you may miss a piece of the puzzle that will cause you great conster- nation in the future," he said.

"I rate the chance as very low."

"Very low doesn't mean nonexistent."

"All right, Mr. Hamilton." Pavar deliberately pushed the stack of papers in front away and leaned back in her chair. "Kowalski? Protocol, please."

"Of course, ma'am!"

James cleared his throat and proceeded her every detail of his experience on the alien planet, chronologically and calmly, just as he had done with Mila on the second try. Now, the third time, it was much easier for him to bring order to the chaos. Being detailed also helped him to be acutely aware of everything. The dean did not interrupt him once. Only the incessant impact of Kowalski's fingers on the keyboard accompanied his words.

When he finished, Pavar nodded.

"Thank you for your report. My assistant will have you to sign it, then you can go."

James blinked in surprise. He had expected everything, protest, amusement, even a brusque rebuff, but he had been wrong. The dean remained as cool as an autumn wind. She leaned forward again and clasped her hands in front of her on the tabletop.

"That will be all, Mr. Hamilton."

"One more question," he said.

Pavar raised an eyebrow but gave a placating wave, presumably to Major Norton at his back.

"How do you think you're going to make this project a success if you don't tolerate risk-taking? I imagine that the political implications of forcing the Europeans and Russians to participate will involve daily wrangling, which is what worries you most. This project will have to deliver results before there can be any real differences between the parties. And you're not going to get results with a rule book that's too narrow." James leaned forward. "The teleporter is, perhaps, humanity's greatest opportunity, a gateway to other worlds. What you're accomplishing by throwing me out is intimidating the leadership team and warning them against going it alone."

Her emotionless expression was confirmation enough of his assumption.

"But consider carefully," he continued, "about whether this is the right way to go. If you put the researchers on too short a leash, you won't find out anything. To know what black powder is, the Chinese had to light it first, and there were many accidents before it could be used safely and effectively. Look how far we've come with it now—despite all the negative effects."

"Thank you for your input," Pavar said and waved him away with one hand. "You may leave now. Remember the confidentiality agreements you signed."

"Don't worry. I assume the NSA will keep a good enough eye on me to make sure that the words 'object' and 'Wyoming' don't appear in my vocabulary anymore."

"Goodbye." Pavar pulled her files back toward her and flipped open the top one.

"Come on," Norton urged James, grabbing him by the elbow. James stood and offered no resistance. He let the major lead him outside. On the other side of the fake reception area, two soldiers were waiting by the elevators started toward them but the Norton stopped them with an outstretched hand and stood in front of James.

"For whatever that's worth, I think you're right about this. We have to take risks, to do something, to step boldly into the darkness because that's the only way we can bring light into it," Norton stated earnestly. "And, for the sake of my continued work here, I'm glad you gave the dean that speech."

"You—you agree with me?" asked James, confused.

"Yes. I know I threw you under the bus in front of the others, and I'm not proud of that, but it had to be done."

"To bond the team together and not turn them against each other."

"That's right. This project is more important than me, and also more important than *you*. I stand by that. You should not have gone it alone. This thing is far too danger-ous! What you have done here and now, you should have done before. Pavar is cold as steel, but she is also smart, level-headed, and open to smart arguments. However, bypassing her and causing trouble without involving her was a mistake that has cost you your involvement. Perhaps you will remember that if you get another chance in the future."

"I don't think there's any going back to my old job, is there?" asked James.

Norton shook his head.

"No. They obviously turned a blind eye in Washington and Philadelphia because your results were good, but with your knowledge of a project that even their employers in the agencies don't know about, they won't let you near criminals again. At least, that's my assumption."

"I understand. It's probably better that way."

"You should be well provided for with your racketeering anyway," the major said, and the biting criticism could not be ignored. James sensed that the older soldier was torn between a strange sympathy and a moral objection toward him. He could well understand that since he felt the same way.

"No."

"No?"

"You wouldn't understand. But thanks for asking. I'll get by."

James took one last look at the elevator doors and sighed inwardly. He hoped Nasaku was okay and that nothing had happened to her. Although he had been terrified, he would have loved to travel to her planet again, just to make sure it existed. During his involuntary stay there, he had wanted nothing more than to get home, away from that eerie place with its stench, the depressing desolation, and the horrible noises. Now he wanted to go back. It was crazy. But the realization he would never go there again and would have to spend the next weeks and months—maybe even years— wracking his brain about what was happening, whether the other teleporters had been found and what else the team was finding out, saddened him.

"The two privates will drive you to the Cheyenne airport." Norton interrupted his musings as the soldiers pointed him toward the door.

So that's it, he admitted to himself. He merely nodded, unable to say anything. He felt like a stranger in his own body as he slowly shuffled toward the exit, flanked by the soldiers. His limbs felt as heavy as lead and his head strangely empty. Until now, he had been running on adrenaline, or at least under the excitement of what had happened: His return, the relief, followed by the shock of Norton's accusations in front of the team and their collective disappointment. Then the conversation with Mila, which had left him rattled. Now he was like a passenger in his own head, watching one foot being put in front of the other and realizing for the first time it was actually over.

What was he supposed to do now? Where was he supposed to go? To his apartment in New York? He was now unemployed with a decent amount of money in his bank account, but nothing to do. He hadn't had many friends in the last few years. His school friends were scattered across the country and he had neglected them after he met Joana. His job as a ransom negotiator had been something like the final nail in the coffin for his social life. He never knew when he would have to leave or for how long. Sometimes a week, sometimes two, and always spontaneously. But now he had no Joana, no job, and no friends, and the prospect of sitting alone in his Manhattan apartment, where he was never truly comfortable, terrified him. He would have far too much time to think about every-thing that had happened here. He had been part of something big, a swing of fate out of his morass of self-pity and into the greatest adventure in human history. What a gift that had been, despite the circumstances of his extraction from Mombasa.

How did I not see that? He stopped and looked back at the elevators, and it hit him like a blow. He wanted to rush off, take the two soldiers by surprise, and pound on the control panel, anything to get back. It just couldn't be over yet.

"Keep moving!" said the one on the right, a burly private with a cool look.

James swallowed and followed his instruction. His shoulders drooped The light shining through the milky glass of the front door hurt his eyes. To him, it seemed like an airlock into another life, the final proof that this would merely be a dream once he stepped through.

Suddenly, an alarm sounded. A high-pitched squeal went through his spine and made the windows in the door rattle. He flinched and wheeled around. The two soldiers were startled for a moment and looked around.

James took advantage of the moment of carelessness and stormed past them toward Pavar's office door.

"*Hey!*" one of them yelled, but by then he was already several steps ahead of them.

The sirens reverberated unpleasantly in his ears, and he would have preferred to cover them, but there was no time for that as he rushed toward the office. Adrenaline made his skin tingle, and the anticipation of being chased and suddenly grabbed from behind electrified him in an unpleasant way. He was relieved when he pushed down on the handle and heard suppressed curses behind him.

Before he could stop himself, he turned around and saw the soldiers were using both hands to hold their pistols in their holsters. His tongue tingled.

"The magnetic field!" he shouted, and stormed into the dean's office as his overseers regrouped and continued the chase. One of them almost grabbed him, but James dodged the hand and slipped through the opening in the door. One crashed into the door so loudly that it could be heard over the alarm. Fortunately for him, the impact pushed the door back into the lock.

Pavar and Norton were standing in front of one of the large televisions and had turned toward him, their faces contorted in a mixture of surprise and reproach.

"Has it been activated?" James said breathlessly. "The teleporter?"

"Possibly. There was another surge in the magnetic field, but I don't see how that's any of your business anymore. You should have—"

"Sorry, ma'am!" The voice belonged to one of his overseers and James's courage sank.

He was grabbed roughly by the arms and now the tingle on his tongue was gone. The dean and major seemed to notice, too, and she waved impatiently to Kowalski, who was closest to the television, who turned on the display and took two steps back. The picture showed the inside of the tele-porter far below them. Two figures in white protective suits stood with their backs to one of the honeycomb walls between two infrared cameras. They were staring at one of the inner seats where something was happening.

"My goodness!" Pavar breathed.

James noticed the grip on his arms had loosened and broke away to stand next to her and the major, they didn't seem to notice he was there, they were spellbound by what was happening on the monitor.

One seat—he believed it was the one opposite where he had been sitting—seemed to have started moving, although it was probably an optical illusion due to something moving *on* the seat. As if tiny beads of sweat were being squeezed out of invisible pores, a milky layer formed on the seat and flowed into each other like mercury, forming compounds that boiled with great surface tension. Gradually, the liquid grew as if filled with air in time-lapse. Two long outgrowths formed and crawled downward.

"What is it, Major?" Pavar asked in a thin voice, staring spellbound at what was happening in the teleporter.

Norton did not answer, apparently unable to concentrate on anything other than what he was watching.

"A clone," James muttered.

"What?"

"A clone!" he repeated hoarsely after clearing his throat. By now, the shape of a humanoid body was discernible, milky white and viscous, but the colors were already chang-ing, becoming reddish and yellow in some places before a creamy sheen settled over it. "The teleporter, it creates clones into which the consciousness of its travelers is loaded. Mila was right!"

"Doctor Shaparova?" Pavar grabbed him by the wrist. "What do you know about it, man?"

"If the travelers do not leave the home teleporter, then it must be a machine that transports only consciousness. But to use a consciousness, it needs a body. It needs *the* body because it's unlikely it would work in another. At the very least, one would have to expect negative psychological consequences. But how did it solve the problem of the biomass?"

By now, it was clear that a human body was forming on the seat in the middle of the camera image, which faltered occasionally and was interrupted with white noise. Hair sprouted from fresh skin, pushing through the scalp above the forehead. Toenails and fingernails emerged from the white mass, eyes took on color, then were hidden under lids with long eyelashes growing from them.

"Nasaku!" he shouted triumphantly as he recognized her bony face, slanted eyes, and mouth surrounded by wrinkles. She looked like a hawk, unmistakable. She was naked, of course, and he was amazed at how delicately built she was. Sinewy, with tight muscles, yet more delicate than the tough survivor he remembered her to be with all those layers of smelly fabric.

"This is the woman you saw?" Pavar asked incredulously.

"Yes! That's her! She's alive! And she made it here after all. Mila, you fucking genius!"

Pavar and Norton exchanged a glance. On the television, Nasaku blinked for the first time and looked at her hands, her brow furrowed. The two figures in the protective suits were still frozen against the wall, their hands pressed against the honeycombs behind them as if they were trying to disappear into the surfaces.

"She's scared," James said, reaching a hand toward the picture.

"Major, get Mr. Hamilton down there. Now!"

"Are you—"

"Yes. Now get on with it! This is a first contact scenario until we know for sure what we're dealing with. So, let's stick to protocol."

"You mean that I—" James said, but Pavar gestured for him to remain silent.

"Maybe you were right," the dean admitted. "As long as we have to assume that, I won't let you go."

"I wouldn't go for any money in the world. I need to talk to her. When she sees my face, it will calm her down, I'm sure."

"Then don't waste any more time."

"Thank you, ma'am!"

Pavar had already turned back to the television and was watching with a pale face as Nasaku cautiously stood and stared at the two scientists.

13

J ames stood in the airlock and bounced impatiently on the balls of his feet. The rubber of his boot soles made squeaking noises on the plastic. When the hiss of gas finally sounded and unlocked the blast door to the cave, he rushed forward.

The large cavern was noticeably more crowded than usual.

Ten figures in hazmat suits were standing in a wide semicircle around the teleporter and had assault rifles pointed at the passageway, which was lit up like a celestial portal at the end of the ramp. Three unarmed men stood close together nearby, obviously engaged in a heated discussion.

"Hey! Put down your weapons! She's not a threat!" shouted James, but they paid no attention to him, as if he wasn't even there. So, he ran to the scientists. Meeks, Falkenhagen, and Smailov stepped away from each other as he ran toward them.

"Mr. Hamilton!" the former cosmonaut said, blinking in amazement.

"Pavar changed her mind."

"You were obviously right," Falkenhagen said, nodding appreciatively.

But there was an unmistakable doubt in his gaze—just like in the other two. They were probably still trying to sort out Norton's statements about James for themselves. But that didn't concern him now.

"What's with the guns?" he asked, pointing at the soldiers. "Have they gone crazy?"

"There's some kind of golem that's formed in the object. What else are they supposed to do? Roll out the red carpet?" Smailov, snorted. "It's not just a sensation, it's a potential danger."

"Bullshit! I know Nasaku."

James tried to break away from them and run to the ramp, but a strong hand grabbed his shoulder and held him back. He turned around and looked into Meeks's face. Beads of sweat were running down the former Boeing engineer face as if he had just completed a heavy workout.

"Boy, even if you're right, you don't even know this woman. You've known her for how long? A few hours? Half a day? Even if all that is true, then she could be anyone. We don't know anything about her or her species."

"She's human."

"That should make us even more suspicious. As far as we know, humans exist only on Earth and—"

"As far as we know," James agreed with him. "Exactly. Maybe, thanks to her, we've learned that there are other things than what we know. Other answers. And this woman has them. Aside from the fact that she acted like a *good* person when I was completely scared and alone in her world, the least we can do is be on our best behavior."

With that, he broke free. The rubber of Meeks's gloves

slipped off his plastic suit like soap off a sink. He walked between two of the burly soldiers into their overlapping field of fire. But he didn't even want think about what might happen if Nasaku marched through the entrance to the teleporter now, and one of them did something stupid with a nervous finger.

It wasn't a dream, he rejoiced inwardly and gave free rein to his excitement and relief. *No imagination! She's here, and the teleporters are just that: Teleporters!*

He hurried up the ramp with long strides, causing it to sway a little, but he did not look to the right or left as if magically attracted by the glowing light in front of him. He slipped through, and, as always, it was as if he had stepped through a mystical portal from one world to another. The world behind him was ominous, filled with the roar of wires and heat sinks, the crackle of hazmat suits, a place of high ceilings and massive columns. Where he found himself now was cramped, alien and yet familiar with a feeling of security, from the compact construction to the prevailing silence.

Nasaku was standing in front of her seat, and in front of her—judging by the extremely different outlines—were Laudrup and Mila. The two scientists gestured cautiously toward the stranger, who spoke loudly in Sumerian but kept eyeing the many instruments they had set up.

"Nasaku."

His heart leapt when she turned to him. It felt strange, as if he had found a long-lost friend, despite not knowing her at all. Whether it had been the fear and the special circumstances of his experience on her planet, his need to see her again to prove that he had not lost his mind, or the relief he was not on his way to New York, excluded from this project, he didn't know, and he didn't care. Here and now, he could contribute, for her and the project. And for himself.

She looked at him in irritation. He tore his helmet off his head. Why hadn't he done that right away instead of scaring her like that?

"It's me. James. I'm sorry for the outfit; I don't want you to feel like a lab mouse."

Nasaku's features relaxed when she saw his face without protection and visor.

"James," she said, tilting her head slightly.

"ASAR," he said, gesturing around him before grabbing his chest. "Our ASAR. Our teleporter."

"Damiq." Nasaku looked thoughtful and covered her shame.

"Oh, sorry!" He peeled out of his rubber layer until he was standing there in just a formfitting bodysuit and handed it to her. "It's not Armani, but it should do for now."

She accepted it and got dressed. The suit was much too big for her, making her look like a child in her parents' clothes, except *these* clothes looked like packaging.

"Mila, Dr. Laudrup?" he asked the two scientists. "Are you all right?"

"Call me Mette if you like," whispered the Dane without taking her eyes off Nasaku. She had buried her short fingers in the back of one of the inward-facing seats as if she were trying to hide behind it. Her white suit was splattered with red paint.

"It's all right," Mila said, also taking off her helmet and placing it on one of the seats.

"This is Mila," he said to Nasaku, pointing to the Russian, who gave her a friendly smile. The visitor acknowledged it with her palms raised upward. "That's kind of like a nod."

"Ah. Nice to meet you."

"How did you... how did you do it?" he asked the scientist.

"The deceased lab animals," she replied. "I was thinking about our theory with the clones and the biomass, and then I thought about the funnel in the middle of the room."

James looked at where Mette's open case with the batteries had been the last time. It was no longer there, only the black funnel with the small hole at the bottom.

"If the theory was correct, there had to be a delivery method for biomass, to feed the teleporter with raw materials for the cloning process," Mila continued. "I think I found it."

James looked again at Mette and the red liquid staining the front of her suit and he felt sick.

"That's why you wanted me to go back to Pavar," he said. "You were trying to buy time to prove that I was right."

"A last attempt, so to speak. Though I must confess I had limited faith in it myself. But I had to try, and no one objected to Mette sawing up the animal carcasses and me throwing the pieces into the hopper."

"However, we have a communication problem now," the Danish woman said, staring cautiously at Nasaku as if she were a predator.

"We need someone who speaks Sumerian."

"I think they're already working on an appropriate solution," Mila said.

"I hope so." James turned to their visitor, who was looking toward the opening. "We should wait a little longer."

"Why?" the Russian woman asked. "We should let her out of here, give her something to eat and drink, and put her in proper clothes."

"Yes, but there are a dozen soldiers out there, and they're

all aiming guns at the door. Tell them to leave first. There's no second chance for a first impression, as they say." He looked into a camera and gestured with his right hand as if someone were talking. "Wait here." He looked at Nasaku and raised his hands, signaling her not to follow him as she started to do just that. Then he walked through the rectangle of light and stopped at the top of the ramp. If she ran after him anyway, at least this way she would bump into him and not into the muzzles of several guns.

"Lower your weapons, boys!" he shouted to the soldiers. Their faces were blurry behind the visors of their helmets, like washed-out drawings. Of course, they didn't move until the airlock opened and a new figure entered the cave. Judging by the gait, it could only be Major Norton.

"Do what he says!" the officer barked.

Immediately, the men lowered their weapons, secured them, and casually held them in front of their bodies. Norton walked up to them and gave instructions that James couldn't hear from his position. The men split into three groups and spread out around the room. It looked as if they were behaving casually, but he was sure they had instructions not to let the visitor from another planet out of their sight.

"Thank you," he said as the major walked up to the ramp.

"You took off your helmet."

"Yes. I was already in the teleporter without it anyway."

"What if she carries a disease that our immune system is not used to?"

"I don't think that's likely, because it's not from another planet; it was assembled by the teleporter—"

"Yes, a foreign biome is not to be expected," a third voice said, Falkenhagen. The German came around one of the concrete pillars with Meeks and Smailow and gestured to James. "But we don't know what exactly the clone looks like, whether it's adapted to the prevailing microbial conditions due to the extreme age of this machine."

"I think that a civilization that can create something like this," Smailov said, reaching out to the ellipsoid, "will also have thought of details like that."

"We don't even know fundamentally how they thought!"

"Yes, we know they—" Meeks started to say when Norton intervened.

"There's no time for that now. Hamilton, get our *visitor* out of there. That's an order."

"Where do you want her?" he asked back.

"Into the airlock, they'll examine her there and then assign her one of the free quarters if everything looks good. We have to test her for certain diseases and pathogens and that sort of thing. I want Captain Miller to tell me there is no immediate danger to this facility and its people. She's going to stay under guard but treated well until our interpreter finally gets here." Norton noticed the concern in James's face, and although his expression grew impatient, he continued calmly, "We'll show her videos of what we're doing and why, hopefully she'll understand."

James nodded and turned around. Back inside the teleporter, Mila and Nasaku were exchanging some vocabulary, pointing at things like the cameras, the seats, the floor, the walls, and then repeating the corresponding words in their languages. Mette and Mila had both taken off their helmets and looked like strange cartoon characters with the white band of the neck seal.

"Nasaku." When she looked at him he performed a little pantomime, pointing at her, pretending to hold an imaginary injector to his neck as she had done to him, and then pressing two fists over each other, hoping she recognized the gesture as a sign of safety. In any case, she opened both palms.

They exited the teleporter together and he worried that Nasaku would get scared. Instead, she seemed surprised and curious, looking around the cavern with wide eyes and would have fallen off the ramp if he hadn't caught her.

"Good afternoon. My name is Major Norton, United States Air Force. Welcome... welcome to Earth." Norton greeted their extraterrestrial guest, extending a hand. Nasaku didn't seem to understand the gesture and eyed the gloved fingers as if they were going to show her something. James tapped her on the shoulder, pointed to his own hand and then to Norton's. She understood and awkwardly squeezed the hand offered to her.

"Ubla Nasaku."

"Follow me, please." The officer pointed to the airlock to the right, which was open and had a cot and two people wrapped in white waiting inside, presumably Captain Miller and a nurse. Nasaku faltered at first and looked questioningly at James, who nodded at her after a moment's hesitation. Meeks, Falkenhagen, and Smailow watched everything from one side, their mouths open and eyes wide in amazement.

A quarter of an hour later, he was sitting with the scientific leaders around the round workroom table. The documents were scattered across it and many were on the floor. They were all sweaty, and it smelled like a predator enclosure, but no one seemed to care.

"We really don't know anything," Falkenhagen said. Unlike the rest of them, he did not look like a plucked chicken, but like a shiny Adonis who had covered himself with oil. "So, we should be careful."

"What don't we know about? About Nasaku?" Mila asked. "That's right, that's why we should not only be careful, but above all, friendly and helpful."

"Well, even if we assume that the teleporter built a clone from the remains of some of the larger test animals, there's still a chance that the machine responsible for it has bugs."

"A mistake?" Mila raised a questioning eyebrow.

"Diseases, ancient pathogens that have been waiting underground with it for hundreds of thousands of years to see the light of day again. Just think of all the stuff preserved in the permafrost in Siberia."

"I'm sure a civilization that can build a damn teleporter would also remember that the clones have to come to the world clean," Meeks said.

"But there is a mistake in that thinking," Falkenhagen said, and the American's expression darkened at this unintentional rebuke. "A clone cannot come into the world *cleanly*. If it comes into being in such a short time, it must have a functioning immune system, which means it must also have an intact microbiome. So, it's not clean, otherwise, the immune system would not have any training. So, it's very possible that certain pathogens—"

"Ah-ah"—Mila waggled a finger at him—"we have to assume that the clone was assembled from the material we fed into it. So, a goat and a cow. Everything that was in and on those animals was also likely used in some form to create Nasaku. So, we know pretty much what it is made from and what pathogens and microbes it's loaded with. There shouldn't be anything our immune systems don't know about."

"Sounds logical to me," Smailov said, agreeing with her. He was the only one not sitting, instead leaning against one of the cool concrete walls behind the table with his arms folded.

Falkenhagen was undeterred. "We don't even know the remotest thing about the builders of these teleporters—or whether they really are teleporters. It could be that this machine merely creates dreams or visions and then materializes parts of them."

"You mean James's journey only took place in some kind of virtual reality within the object?" Mette asked, rubbing her rosy, sweaty cheeks. "What for?"

"What for indeed."

"Every machine follows a purpose. It has a job to do, classically to make life easier for us humans. Why would someone build something so advanced just to create a VR world? It should be easier to do that than build something like this."

"There are machines that merely serve to pass the time. Game consoles, for example."

Mila snorted. "You don't think that's a game console, do you? We've only found one relic like it so far. Just one thing that has stood the test of time. I'm sure they're not game consoles built to last forever."

Some of the others chuckled in agreement. Still, the German didn't seem convinced.

"What I'm saying is that we look at everything from an anthropological perspective. How *we* would do it. What makes sense or nonsense to *us*. An alien culture could, and probably would, think and act very differently than we do."

"And what clue do we have to that?" Meeks asked thoughtfully. "I'm just saying, there are seats in the machine, obviously sophisticated and of a material we haven't figured out yet, but ultimately mundane seats like we use. The opening into the teleporter is the equivalent of the size of a human, or at least humanoids of our dimensions. Even hexagons have an established place in our cultural history. They are Euclidean polygons, perfectly symmetrical from all sides. If you connect its opposite corners, you divide it into six equilateral triangles. If you connect the non-opposite ones, a hexagram of two equilateral triangles adjoining each other, which in turn have only five vertices and thus fall out of symmetry. Honeycombs are rectangular, but so is basalt, which cools slowly in the magma phase. Even the north pole of Saturn has a hexagon."

"What does this machine care about the north pole of Saturn?" Falkenhagen grumbled.

"I'm just saying that we've seen a lot of signs that the builders of this thing must have been more like us—"

"Or still are," James interjected.

"Yes; or are *still* more similar than we think. You traveled to the other side, if there is one, and met what? Another human being! That can't be a coincidence either. Perhaps we should henceforth look at the ellipsoid *only* from human eyes and consciousness."

James said, "Two questions come to mind for starters: Why haven't we found anything from these builders except this teleporter? We don't even have a screw otherwise. And why is there no instruction manual?"

All eyes turned to James and he raised his hands defensively.

"I'm just saying that I don't think the teleporter is a relic that was deliberately buried for future civilizations like us. If it had been, I'm sure they would have taken care to explain its use and its dangers. But we've found nothing like that. That's why I think we won't meet the builders anymore. Either they didn't have time to leave us a letter, or they built the teleporters before they went under."

"Built for what? Why would you build it right before your demise?" Smailov wanted to know.

"I don't know, but we should consider it."

"We should be talking to this woman first and fore-most..." Meeks suggested.

"Nasaku," James corrected him.

"Nasaku. We need to talk to her."

"About what, exactly?" Mila's voice left no doubt that she was worried about what her colleague might be thinking.

"There's an elephant in the room here, but nobody wants to see it" It's either an alien or a possessed clone. I don't know which I like less. What I definitely don't like, though, is that we know absolutely nothing about her."

14

"She refused to be shoved into the MRI!" Pavar said. The politician tightened her pantsuit, and her cinnamon-colored skin seemed to turn a shade darker.

"That's no reason to lock her up!" Mila protested loudly. The light above the table in the work area flickered and all eyes briefly turned upward before it sank the room back into gloom.

"Oh, no?" Pavar glowered at the Russian woman belligerently. "Why do *you* think she refuses?"

"I know people who panic when they think about being squeezed into that narrow tube. There are more people who suffer from claustrophobia than you think!"

"We should also not ignore the fact that she comes from an archaic planet," Mette interjected. The Dane was devouring a chocolate bar and seemed to calm down more with each bite. "She's probably just afraid of an alien device that also makes very unusual noises."

"But Mr. Hamilton said she came from another planet and was merely stranded there," Major Norton pointed out. "So, we can assume that she didn't come from a primitive world, but from one that managed to use the teleporter and travel to another, from one that found out there were six of these machines."

"She could have found out in other ways," Mila objected.

"How so? A cave painting? Please."

"Her home planet must not be very developed. The teleporter I got out of was in the middle of nowhere. Like here on Earth in Venezuela, it was obviously charged by atmospheric energy. By lightning. Why wouldn't it work somewhere else?"

"She knew—according to your report—exactly which injection to give you. She understood the principles of the operation of the teleporter, which seats worked and which didn't. You also said there was more technology in that wreck of a spaceship—again, *your* words." Pavar paused briefly to make sure the others were paying attention. "All of this makes me doubt that she's just a droll savage, an Alice in Wonderland that we need to protect from ourselves."

"This is the typical distrustful talk I was afraid of," James grumbled. "Everything she says or does is understood and interpreted against the light of suspicion. So, after all, she doesn't even have a chance to make a good impression and work with us on a friendly basis."

"He's right," Mila agreed with him. "You only get a single first impression."

"Look," James said, looking in Pavar's direction and including Norton in his gaze. "We are in danger of losing everything through misunderstanding. In ancient times, the words for tool and weapon were often the same. An axe was a tool *and* a weapon, just like a knife, machete, and hammer. When Nasaku says tool, we may hear weapon, to give just one example. Tiny details can lead to a wrong reaction."

"But if she says gun, and we hear tool—or want to hear

tool—that's a mistake with a potentially large impact. That's where, as the leader of this project, I have to—"

"This *facility*," Smailov corrected her, unwaveringly parrying her sharp look.

"That's when I have to ask myself what risks I can allow. After all, we're talking about potential consequences for the entire planet."

"You say *potentially* very often," James observed and continued before she could get angry. "I recognize that we are dealing with a chain of doubt that cannot be resolved immediately. We don't know if we can trust her, and she doesn't know if she can trust us. There are also no direct ways to change that. So, we have the option to trust or distrust her."

"You choose to trust, am I right?"

James was surprised by her calm question, her expression curious.

"Yes," he said carefully, and Mila and Mette also nodded.

"Is that the opinion of the scientific leadership team?"

Meeks and Falkenhagen exchanged glances. Smailov had his strong arms folded in front of his chest and looked thoughtful.

We need unity, James thought, looking pleadingly at each of the three male colleagues. If they didn't stand up to Pavar now, showed them divided and at odds, she would add that as evidence that this was a situation where ambiguity meant her assessment had to remain in effect. Another notch in the wood of her argument. She needed that, after all. Every decision she made was being eyed by three power blocs. James could imagine it had been very difficult to convince the EU, especially the Russians, to install an American dean for the project. He didn't want to be in her shoes.

Smailov moved first, and James could see in his face he

would take his side, if only because the astronaut kept a reserved expression. But Pavar beat him to it like a snake waiting for the right moment to strike.

"Before you say anything, I have something for you here." The dean gestured to Kowalski, who had been standing behind her like a trained dog this whole time, and he pulled a piece of paper out of his pocket, which he passed to her over her shoulder. She took it without looking and laid it on the table. All heads—James's included—bent forward, as if attracted by a magnet, over the picture on the piece of paper.

"Is that an X-ray?" Falkenhagen asked, contorting his head so much that James's neck ached just from watching him. He eyed the surreal outline of a body that seemed to consist only of shadows and white, ghostly streaks, just as he remembered from his own X-rays. As a child, he had broken his hand and all his fingers playing inline field hockey. After the traumatic hospital visit, he had asked his mother if he was a ghost because he had not believed that his hand was being shown to him on bluish plastic.

Pavar nodded. "Yes. Go ahead and take a closer look."

The scientists' heads were practically butting against each other, and James could smell the mixture of sour breath and sweaty, unwashed hair they—presumably like himself—exuded. Long periods without eating or drinking, and without showering, were not favorable to the odor of the human body after wearing the -impermeable protective suits. He ignored their whispers so as not to confuse himself. Which wasn't hard to do once he saw the bright white outlines in both the neck, head, and along the spine. Bright spots meant that something was reflecting the X-rays or was opaque to them, if he remembered correctly.

"What is it?" he asked as the scientists discussed it in whispers.

"We don't know for sure," Pavar replied. "But Captain Miller believes they're implants. He's sent the images to a radiologist to examine them more closely. Apparently, pacemakers and cochlear implants look very similar on X-ray."

"How did you even get these?"

"This base has its own hospital and treats soldiers from all over Wyoming. It's just a kilometer away on the other side of the runway," Norton replied. "Not only is the MRI far enough away there to be unaffected by the teleporter's magnetic field, but some equipment from the sixties and seventies remains. Among other things, an X-ray wall that was used to X-ray five soldiers at a time."

"When you thought radiation was funny," Meeks snorted, shaking his head.

"She'll live," Pavar said. "I think we can put your nice story of friendly Pocahontas on file with this." She gave James a sharp look, which he returned with a sour expression. "This woman has implants, which raises several questions: Are they active? What are their function?"

"And how can it be that the teleporter co-created it? So, the theory that it creates a clone from biomass is only partially true," Falkenhagen countered. "That's a dangerous insight."

"Everything is always dangerous for you," Mila said, rolling her eyes.

"May I remind you that we are dealing with an alien clone from another planet!"

"They said Nasaku was being checked out at the hospital, but now she's locked up. Where?" James tried to stifle the emerging discussion, which was currently irrelevant, in his opinion.

"Down here in her quarters. She has food and drink, before you ask," Major Norton replied.

"I assume you took the X-rays with this *wall* without her consent? Presumably without her knowledge at all?"

"Yes. It's not like there are or ever have been rules for this investigation."

James wanted to protest again but he didn't need to look at the scientists' faces to know he had lost. Pavar's arguments could not be dismissed out of hand, and certainly not with counterarguments along the lines of "we have to take a leap of faith" or "I have a good feeling about Nasaku." The dean was not amenable to such things. That had been clear to him since the first moment he had met her. It was probably exactly why she had been put in charge here.

"So, her body could have implants whose function is unknown to us," James summarized, nodding. "I understand that might be troubling, but we don't even know if they're her own, or if the teleporter built them in by default, if you can put it that way. We just don't have any data on that, especially since—"

"That's right, we don't have any data," Pavar agreed, and she pursed her mouth. "That's why we're going to proceed very cautiously and not jump to conclusions that cause us to look at our guest through rose-colored glasses."

"So, what's supposed to happen now?" Meeks asked, his fingers crossed in front of him, their knuckles showing white.

"A translator is on the way so we can communicate with her."

When James heard "translator" an image of Joana involuntarily flashed through his mind, and he shuddered. The very idea that she, of all people, might have been called upon to use her skills at Sumerian stabbed him right in the heart. But even with the very small number of experts in Sumerian, the chances were slim that it was his ex-fiancé they were talking about.

"But that won't change your mind either," Mette said sharply. Her colleagues were so surprised by her tone that everyone looked at her and no one said anything, not even Pavar. The Dane continued, her cheeks red. "You have the task of making balanced decisions to the best of your knowledge and belief, but I see that you have strategically approached this conversation with your X-ray up your sleeve for your own agenda, your own narrative on the situation that you were determined to drag us into. That shows me that you already have an opinion and you're more focused on pushing it than looking for real facts."

Pavar blinked several times, as if she couldn't believe she'd been addressed. But the usually friendly chemist with the corpulent physique didn't let that upset her and placed the remains of her chocolate package on the table in front of her.

"What it takes is a cool, *neutral* head. No agenda, no preconceived ideas, nothing that puts all Nasaku's actions and statements in a corresponding light. Especially with a stranger—possibly alien—misinterpretation, which could be fatal. The danger is too great that we will drape our interpretive patterns over her like a shroud."

Mila was the first to nod in agreement, but Meeks and Smailow weren't far behind. They gave their colleague surprised looks until Falkenhagen also signaled his agreement. All eyes turned to Pavar.

"I understand your arguments," she assured them. "The interview will take place in half an hour, room four. For transparency, I suggest that one or more of you attend to ensure that we don't fall into the trap of any preconceived ideas. I would say, though, that it really should be just one person so our *guest* doesn't feel like a lab rat facing an entire panel of researchers."

Oh, now she's suddenly concerned about Nasaku's sensitivities? thought a very cynical part of himself, but James nodded instead. The others didn't appear to object either.

"I suggest that Mr. Hamilton be the one who joins the conversation from your group," Pavar suggested, to his surprise. This evoked a lively mixture of protest, disbelief, and agreement. Smailov shook his head and snorted, Falkenhagen said something about "not a scientist," and Meeks blinked furiously as if he had something in his eye. Only Mila nodded sympathetically, while Mette showed no reaction at all, as if she were the leading actress in a movie that had abruptly frozen.

"I know Mr. Hamilton is not from the science leadership team, but your actions so far have shown me that you trust each other," Pavar explained. James was under no illusions that any of them could misunderstand her statement as barely concealed criticism in the guise of good coaxing. "Also, we'll transmit everything here so you can watch, and we'll be recording, of course. So, unless the teleporter spontaneously decides to become active and intensifies its magnetic field, it should be like you're there live."

No one responded, but her words had not missed their mark. Pavar, with the deftness of a devious politician, had accomplished what she had intended: She had driven a wedge between the members of the scientific leadership team, which already had countless breaking points due to culturally diverse backgrounds, and the one who supposed to be holding them together—even if he increasingly doubted this was the case. The result she hoped for was, of course, greater ability to control those she must have felt were uncontrollable after everything that had happened. And if there was one thing politicians hated, it was a loss of control, whether imagined or real.

It infuriated James that he was again the odd man out, bringing a disturbance to the group simply by his presence and special treatment. Undoubtedly, every scientist at the table wanted to be present when the first alien who had ever set foot on Earth was questioned. He couldn't blame them since he passionately wanted to be there too and was secretly relieved that he didn't have to fight for it. He understood Pavar because, as devious and cool as she came across, she was also under pressure. He didn't envy her position as head of a dangerous secret project, perhaps the most important in human history, while relying on such a small, tenuous support structure. All located deep underground with a manageable number of employees but an incalculable number of risks and dangers that no one could foresee because no one had experience with an alien teleporter. It had to feel like she was riding a wild bull that kept kicking out in unpredictable ways, with no reins, saddle, or stirrups. What she was doing here was damage control, trying to build her reins and saddle before she crashed to the dirt and was crushed.

I would have done the same in her place, he admitted to himself.

"I won't go if you don't agree, and one of you can take my place," he said, addressing the scientists, knowing full well he would accomplish nothing by doing so because, on the one hand, they would not disagree with Pavar, and on the other hand, he or she would come across as selfish. But he saw no other way to possibly limit the damage.

"No, it's right that you go," Mette said. She offered him a warm smile, which obviously didn't come easily to her, so it meant more. "She knows you, and you have a past together, albeit a very short one. It will be good for her to have a familiar, sympathetic face sitting across the table."

Mila nodded as well. "She's right. The situation will be unpleasant enough for our guest. Besides, interpersonal skills are needed here, and you have the most out of all of us." The Russian looked pointedly at Pavar, who pretended not to notice. "We are scientists, not negotiators, and the latter is more in demand here, I think."

"Thanks," he muttered and took a deep breath.

"Good. Let's go." Pavar motioned to Kowalski, who gathered his things and hurried to the door to hold it open for her, much like the lapdog he was.

The "interview," as the politician repeatedly pointed out, took place a the room next to Nasaku's cell, which Norton euphemistically called "quarters." Four soldiers in heavy combat gear stood in front of it, posturing as they approach. The situation felt like a dream to James. The thought that Nasaku was here with him, on *his* side and not somewhere on a stinking, dying planet, was surreal. It was as though a character from a show he'd just seen on TV had suddenly stepped through the screen and become real. So, he kept looking at the wall of a room that looked exactly like his own. He imagined he could see Nasaku nervously pacing around it.

A table and two chairs were prepared, one on each side. Behind one, two more were positioned diagonally. More soldiers were busy setting up cameras on large tripods and orienting them toward the chair where Nasaku would be sitting; along the cold, unadorned concrete wall, lenses pointed at her like rifles. James could only imagine how she would feel looking into the strange faces, hearing their strange language, and seeing all the equipment pointed at her. He imagined what it would feel like if their roles were reversed and shuddered.

Once everything was ready, Pavar sat in the front chair and Norton in one behind her. Two soldiers stood in either corner behind the empty chair, their hands clasped.

"Would you bring them in, please?" the politician ordered.

"Sure," James grumbled and headed for the door.

Nasaku was already standing on the other side, flanked by two burly Airmen. She was a head shorter than him with a stocky, powerful body that was recognizable even under the Air Force's rather baggy gray leisure wear. Her birdlike face was strained but brightened some when she saw him.

"James," she said awkwardly. She sounded like she was trying to speak with her mouth full.

He gave her an encouraging smile, then waved her in. "Hello, Nasaku. The dean would like to ask you some questions."

Even though he knew she didn't understand him, it still mattered to him to suggest normalcy through his tone, to radiate calm and not give the appearance of proceedings out of the ordinary, even though that was exactly what was to occur.

Pavar and Norton stood when she entered and stopped in front of James. This kind of shyness just didn't fit the woman he had met on the other planet—decisive, pragmatic, no-frills. But he couldn't blame her for feeling like a cornered animal. She was alone among strangers, also human, but a stranger from another planet who looked somewhat different and spoke a different language, though they looked similar to her.

This must have been how European explorers felt when they first encountered the natives in Central America. A

different world but at the same time with just enough similarities to keep it from being completely alien. In many
ways, he had probably had it easier than she, stumbling
around naked and filthy on that dying planet. He would
have preferred that loneliness and danger to a scenario like
this any day.

"Welcome," Pavar said, pointing to the vacant chair on
the other side of the table. Nasaku looked at James, and he
nodded. Only then did she sit. He was about to pull the door
shut, but he encountered resistance and looked up in
surprise. A woman with dark hair and a dark complexion
appeared in the opening. She was juggling a massive stack
of papers and files and a coffee mug. For a moment—long
enough to sting him—he thought he saw Joana.

"Uh, hello."

"Hello. I'm Anosha Eikes." When he didn't respond, she
added, "Linguist."

"Ah, the translator!" James waved her in impatiently.
"Nice to meet you!"

"Thank you, you too, Mr...."

"May I introduce Ms. Pavar and Major Norton."

"We already know each other from the video call."

"Sit down, Ms. Eikes." Pavar pointed to a chair one of the
soldiers had added on the left side of the empty table that
separated her from Nasaku.

"Thank you, ma'am."

The translator looked out of place with her fashionable
civilian clothes and coffee, as if she had just come from a
meeting and now just had to quickly check off the next one.
Did she even know what this was about?

"Kowalski has already reported to me that you signed
the entire package of non-disclosure agreements. What you

see and hear here does not leave this facility," Pavar explained.

"Of course." Eikes's grin revealed that she had no idea the implications of what she had signed. She probably thought this was just a quick trip to a government site that once again didn't know what it was doing. "Just one question."

The dean raised an eyebrow as the translator waved a key card.

"It didn't work. I have to get back out via the elevator, don't I?"

"Just enter the code 1-6-0-4 on the control panel. This is reserved for you and is valid until tomorrow evening. If we need your services longer, we'll issue you a new card. Let's not waste time with this."

Norton cleared his throat and Pavar looked at him. He glanced toward Nasaku and she shrugged.

"She doesn't understand us anyway. All right, Ms. Eikes, I'd like to go straight *in medias res*, if you don't mind."

"Of course!" Anosha Eikes still seemed a little amused at the politician's serious tone, another sign she didn't have a clue what this was all about. She sat down, put the stack of files and books in front of her, and nodded to Nasaku. "This woman actually speaks Sumerian?"

"Yes."

"I see. Is she...?" Eikes winked as if they shared a secret.

"She's not crazy. Why?"

"Well, Sumerian is a dead language. Nobody *speaks* Sumerian. People study it, look for ancient slates and stone tablets to decipher the cuneiform even better. Some in my field who have studied both archaeology and ancient linguistics sometimes throw around single phrases among themselves, but that's about it."

"Nasaku—that's her name—speaks Sumerian. At least it appears so," Pavar said seriously, and when her expression didn't change, even when the translator chuckled, Eikes tightened her features and nodded hastily.

"All right. Let's get started then. How do you want this to go? You, uh, ask your questions? Is this like an interview?"

"Something like that, yes," Norton grumbled, impatient.

"Ask about her full name, age, and profession. We need to warm up a bit first," the dean ordered.

"I must warn you that this isn't going to be very precise. The Sumerians had a rather limited vocabulary centered mostly around their bureaucracy and mysticism. Don't forget that the Mesopotamian civilization, while amazingly sophisticated for its time, was still an agrarian society with a strong priesthood and without technology or modern social forms."

"What are you trying to say?"

"Their vocabulary—at least as we know it—was much smaller than ours."

"I understand."

"Good."

Eikes cleared her throat, looked at Nasaku, and a string of strange words left her mouth. She paused occasionally and finally fell silent. Nasaku eyed the translator with a mixture of surprise and amazement, then she replied in the same alien language he had identified as Sumerian, or at least similar to Sumerian.

"She says that her full name is Nasaku. She is seventy-eight years old and her profession is Mammi."

"Mommy?" Norton and James asked at the same time.

"Yeah, um, it's complicated. The Sumerian word Mammi means something like 'mother of the gods.' But as I said, Sumerian is hard to translate into our current usage. It could mean 'priestess,' but it could also mean something else entirely."

Nasaku began speaking again before Pavar could ask her next question. This time, after almost a minute, Eikes had to raise a hand to stop her.

"What is she saying?" Norton wanted to know.

"She came from humanity and wanted to bring the light to a new place, but this place was dangerous and she was not welcome. The wall imprisoned her before she could complete the union," Eikes translated.

"Excuse me?" Pavar blinked and looked over her glasses, which had slid to the tip of her nose.

"As I said, a vocabulary that is over five thousand years old—"

"Yeah, yeah, I got that!" The dean waved a hand impatiently. "But what does it *mean*? What kind of light? And what kind of humanity?"

"The word for man is complicated. Just as with us, *homo* means equal, actually from the ancient Greek 'like me,' so 'equal' means the same to the Sumerians. But they still had differentiated dialects between peoples whose land had been conquered, *nise matati kisitti qatiya*, various people groups—all known to them at that time—*salmat qaqqadi*, and the Sumerians 'civilized' them, *namlugallu.*"

"And which one did she use?"

"The latter. 'Those who are like me' seems like a strange term for those from whom it comes, but it's the same one we use for humanity, at least from a linguistic perspective."

James leaned back in his chair and mussed his hair. He didn't know what he had expected—that they would have a whimsical chat and after an hour, have clarity about who Nasaku was, where she came from, and what the secrets of her culture were? What the planet he was stranded on was all about?What happened over the next four hours, however, was quite different and tedious.

Just the back and forth, consisting of translation in one direction, Anosha Eikes's many notes, and then translating in the other direction, was nerve-wracking. The translator tried hard, but it became increasingly clear that she had been right to warn them about limitations. Many things remained unclear or vague, open to different interpretations and meanings, and it became increasingly apparent that direct communication was wishful thinking.

In the end, all they discovered was that she was from another planet—which seemed to amuse Eikes—her children had died on an alien planet—the dying one, apparently—and there was a barrier there that had something to do with her not being able to return home. She was seventy-eight years old and had occupied a high position in her society. There were others like her, but they thought she was dead.

But that was all they had learned with relative clarity. Along with a long list of things that were unclear and open to interpretation because there was no good translation: She was either a researcher, or 'tool woman,' which might be something like craftswoman or technician. Her fellows either flew to the stars or to the fish in the sea; there had been a war, or else a great gathering. Of the teleporters, there were six or twelve; they were all connected, or only half were. Nasaku was eager to make contact with her fellow humans or go to the other world. James guessed the former was likely in this case.

At the end of the lengthy and frustratingly slow process, Pavar was visibly tired. Norton showed signs of exhaustion and disappointment.

James had hoped that they would finally be able talk to Nasaku, only to find his naive hopes dashed.

"We'll repeat this tomorrow and prepare a list of simpler questions," the dean decided as Nasaku was led out. "I want you to set up a polygraph for me, Major."

"What, you—" James started to protest.

"Calm yourself. A polygraph is not an invasive procedure and doesn't even violate human rights."

"But it goes against—"

"Civil rights?"

Realizing that he didn't have a good argument on his side, he sighed.

"So. A polygraph and shorter, simpler, more concise questions. That wasn't very productive today, but at least now we know what we're dealing with and how to make it work."

"She just wants to make contact with her world. We can certainly help her with that, can't we?"

"How? Show her a star map and just have her send a message? Even if she could do that, I don't think it would be very smart," Pavar countered.

"She's good, you know?"

"No, I don't. And you don't either."

James wanted to offer a whole barrage of assurances, but one look at the dean's frigid expression was enough to sap his courage and convince him it would do no good. And she was right, too. They really didn't know much, factually, and he was just relying on his gut—something he wouldn't have advised anyone else to do.

"Let's at least supplement this process with research."

"Research?"

"Let me go back to the planet. We now know how the

biomass funnel in the center of the teleporter works. I can go back and look for more clues about it and the planet, so we have a clearer overall picture." He saw a protest building and quickly added, "You can send someone along to check it all out. A witness. Maybe a soldier, or Kowalski, someone you trust."

James wanted to slap himself for not thinking of it sooner. Since Nasaku was here, he had only thought to learn more from her, but while she was proof that the teleporter worked both ways, so far, it was still his word against everyone else's that what he had reported was true.

And I don't know myself because it seems like a dream by now.

"I don't think—"

"I'll go with him," Norton said, and James blinked in surprise. The major looked at Pavar. "You trust *me*, don't you?"

15

"Don't worry about the missing suits," James said as he settled into the teleporter seat he had used last time. Norton stood in front of him, his face as hard as chiseled granite. They were alone with the cameras and infrared sensors, surrounded by a tangle of cables that now seemed like a reassuring anchor, demonstrating that he was home and not somewhere among the stars.

Or in a dream? he added to himself. *I'll probably find out soon.*

"I won't. I thought I should go first," replied the major.

"Believe me, when you get to the other side, you'll be happy to see a familiar face."

"We don't even know if it's possible to send two people."

"We haven't tried it yet, but it should work as long as there's enough biomass on the other side to feed the hopper," James said.

"If there's not enough, I'll be stuck in the buffer, I guess."

"Do you still want to go ahead?"

Norton snorted and gestured for him to continue,

whereupon James pushed up the sleeves of his bodysuit so his forearms could rest on the induction pads.

After Pavar's surprising acquiescence and a short briefing, in which she spelled out the goals of their little expedition—check Nasaku's history, search the spacecraft wreckage for useful information or technology, and take no chances—she had directed the science leadership team to get everything ready for an efficient debrief. Since she had allotted a maximum of twelve hours, which corresponded with dawn of the next day, James and Norton had barely spoken to Mila, Mette, or the others, instead going straight to the teleporter room without donning their protective suits. It was obvious the major was tense, but not nearly as tense as James had been when he first crossed over. Probably because this time he was acting with the consent of the dean and had the possibility of company on the other side.

When the officer made no more effort to speak, James slowly exhaled a long-breath and let his head sink back against the headrest before closing his eyes.

Like before, the transition was unreal, as if nothing had happened at all. He merely opened his eyes and found himself across from the seat where he had just closed them. He looked at the empty seat and down at his naked body. The first thing he did was move his left shoulder experimentally and exhaled with relief when he felt no injury. Only then did he stand up and look around the teleporter room. He was alone with the cold light that seemed to have no source. All the seats were empty and the passageway as bright as ever.

He heard a barely audible hiss and he looked at the seat into which he had just come. The white mercurylike liquid was flowing from tiny openings that took a lot of imagination to make out. It squeezed out the material like sweat from skin pores, coalescing into a viscous mass that swelled as if greedily sucking up more of itself. The color changed to a dull gray and gradually protuberances formed, transforming into bizarre arm and leg shapes. Flesh formed in long strands, as if being assembled by an invisible machine according to a clear but invisible plan. Then came the head, a shapeless egg of expanding mass that soon revealed more detailed shapes until more and more of Norton's face became recognizable. As the outer skin changed to a brownish pink, James cleared his throat and looked up.

The major's eyes opened as if in slow motion, blinked a few times, then raised his newly created hands in front of his face and scrutinized them. He looked at James, gave a small not, and looked around.

"I'll be damned," whispered the aging soldier. "I'll be damned. You were right."

"Sometimes that's the way it is."

"It smells a little different here."

"Higher ozone levels, I think. It's probably all the equipment we managed to fit into our teleporter that's causing the weird smell on our end." James shrugged and held out his hand to the major, who accepted it with another nod and allowed himself to be pulled upright.

"I never thought about it because we always had the hazmat suits on, and those just smell like plastic."

"Now you know it's steak."

"Excuse me?"

"It smells kind of like steak in our teleporter, don't you think?"

Norton snorted. "After being burned, maybe."

James pointed to the passageway of light.

"We have to be careful when we go out. It's about two

meters to the ground. The last time I went out, I fell and had to deal with a bad injury."

"Is there anywhere we can get some clothes?" Norton asked, determinedly *not* looking at James's bare privates.

"There are blankets in Nasaku's shelter. I forgot how prudish we Americans are."

The major raised an eyebrow.

"I lived in Europe for two years," he explained. "They handle nudity differently. But that's not what we're here for. We should make the most of the time we have."

"Yes. Even though we have no way to measure it."

"I do wish watches could be taken. Or at least something," James grumbled. "Surely whoever created this could have found a way to synthesize items too."

"It's hard to say what it would take to do that when we don't even understand the basic principles on which the technology is based," Norton mused. It was clear he was trying to distract himself from something by saying so much, which was unusual for him.

Whether it was a general uneasiness proving his previous assumption right or if it was due to the alien planet that he could not yet see, was hard to say. What was certain was that the officer was obviously operating outside his comfort zone and his composure was crumbling, or at least it seemed so to James.

"Mhm," James said and walked toward the opening.

Norton hesitated then followed .

"Maybe there is a function for teleporting items. After all, Mila just discovered the function of the funnel yesterday."

"It's possible, but we can address that after we've delivered something to Pavar that will help her sleep more soundly regarding Nasaku."

"We are not here to exonerate anyone. We're here to find out more about our guest *and* this place. That only works if we observe with an open mind and don't follow an agenda through a lens where we perceive everything in a distorted way. If you're looking for clues that she's a well-meaning refugee stranded on a terrible planet, you're just going to misinterpret everything against that premise."

"You don't believe her, do you?" James turned around. The doorway felt like it was warming his back, even though he thought it was a figment of his imagination. "Why is it so difficult?"

"Our teleporter has been buried beneath the earth's crust for hundreds of thousands of years, and when we dig it out and use it, the very first time we use it, there's a person on the other side who was just waiting for that exact rescue. How likely does that sound?" Norton pointed to some of the seats that recognizably had red lights glowing. "She's no more than forty years old. Either we have damn good timing or she does."

"She's hardly likely to be an alien in a human costume who was merely waiting for an opportunity to become a Trojan horse."

"No, but she is conveniently a woman, helpful and potent, but not so much that she wouldn't arouse a protective instinct. She speaks a language spoken on Earth thousands of years ago. She's given you enough useful information to pique your interest and ours, but nothing so substantial that it provides us anything beyond that or prompts anything from her."

"Are you always this suspicious?"

"I'm not suspicious, I'm cautious."

"I suggest we go to the wrecked spaceship, so you can see how she lived and survived. Maybe then you'll have a little more compassion." James sat in the doorway so his legs dangled off the edge. An image of the roaring monster from last time biting them off flashed through his mind, and he gulped. Finally, he pushed forward and slid out, catching the edge with his hands, and let go.

He landed in the muddy quagmire with an ugly smack and was immediately greeted by the musty stench he remembered all too well. He stood, stepped to the side, and looked at the bushes rustling in the wind, their thorny, ash-covered branches growing like abscesses from the drab landscape of browns.

A *splat* from behind startled him and he wheeled around, his heart pounding. The major had landed grace-fully and was wiping the mud from his hands as he looked around with wide eyes.

The sky was dirty gray and the clouds hung so low that James felt he could almost touch them with outstretched hands. It smelled of decay, mustiness, and rotten eggs, suggesting a not insignificant amount of sulfur in the atmosphere. He tried to see which direction the clouds were moving, but they didn't shift, even though there was a light wind blowing. A flash of lightning twitched through the sky, recognizable as a flare on the horizon, briefly revealing something like texture in the patchy cotton blocking out the sky.

"You know the way, I hope?" Norton asked in a strained voice. "I'd really like to put something on."

That he can even think of clothes, James thought. He had almost forgotten how to breathe when he had rushed through the doorway and found himself in this place that was the definition of desolation. But it made a difference when you knew what you were up against rather than thrown unsuspectingly into an unprecedented situation.

"I think so," he finally replied, striving to sound confident.

He remembered they had walked in a direct line from the passageway to the south—though he now arbitrarily defined the teleporter as north. The light had already disappeared and the mighty ellipsoid stood black and with no unevenness in the twilight, but its flatter front was still clearly visible, and as soon as they reached the stone teeth, he would be able to find the spaceship, he was sure.

They set off, wading through the mire. He saved his strength this time, which gave Norton time to get used to the surroundings and sort himself out. Even if the officer didn't show it, James was sure he wasn't simply ignoring the significance of all this and was dealing with a plethora of thoughts all screaming for attention in his head at the same time.

The march was as exhausting as he remembered it. Several times he got minor scratches when he became careless and got too close to any of the bushes. The wind increased the further they got from the teleporter, which seemed to sit in a large, natural hollow, something he hadn't noticed last time. It also explained why it was more strenuous to walk in one direction than the other.

It was easy to lose track of time in the monotony of this environment, there was little variety in the landscape and a minute felt like an endless hour. He frequently looked back at Norton, who was always two steps behind him, looking around with narrowed eyes, as if paranoid. Every time James turned around he was obviously trying hard to pretend he didn't notice. Whether it was because he was ashamed of his nakedness or something else, James didn't know.

When they reached the monolithic rock formations that stretched northward, jutting from the rocky ground like curved fangs, he wouldn't have been surprised if it had a couple hours for them to get there.

He located the wreckage of the spaceship by accident when he paused to examine a large fang. It rose at least thirty meters into the air and measured about three meters across at its base. It was made of gray granite or something similar. At first, it was merely a large shadow that startled him and caused him to retreat behind the wall formed by the rock. But after a careful glance around the edge, he realized the shadow was not moving, so it couldn't be the monster he had heard before.

"Are you all right?" Norton asked whispering, scanning their surroundings like a hawk.

"Yes. I think I found the spaceship," James replied and cautiously continued west.

It was still half a kilometer away and they struggled through the forest of bizarre monoliths, carefully skirting the sharpest stones that had earned him several bloody scrapes on his feet.

The wreck looked like an Air Force turboprop plane with a bulky belly and large, broken-off wings that must have once been triangles extending from the center of the fuselage to the tail. The cockpit—or at least the part James thought must have been the cockpit—was buried deep in a mountain of debris created during the crash. The hull was marked with deep gashes and covered in mold.

"The entrance is up ahead." James started forward but sensed the major was not following him. He turned around and saw the officer standing next to a small monolith, staring at the strange ship, which seemed familiar and yet mysterious enough to have come from a science fiction movie, or if one added the dark craters and holes, perhaps from a horror flick. "Are you all right?"

Norton cleared his throat and snapped out of his preoccupation. "Yes. Definitely a flying object, maybe an orbital shuttle."

"Or a plane?"

"No. Delta wings are only efficient for very specific applications and speeds. Also, there are no engines on the wings. If they were inside the fuselage it would be difficult to control the vehicle for use in normal air traffic unless it was a rocket engine."

James got the impression that Norton was trying to release some of his tension by talking shop, so swallowed his impatience.

"I understand," he said, nodding. "Can you tell from the damage what might have happened?"

"That's not hard," the major replied, surprising James. He pointed at one of the holes near the front that looked like someone had dropped a bomb of black liquid on it. "See how the front part is about the size of a medicine ball and the damage behind it has widened and eaten through the hull in strips? That's classic impact damage from a massive, possibly kinetic, projectile impacting at high velocity in relation to the target. The projectile hits and the damage is minimal compared to the area of the hull, but the weakened structure causes pressure and relative wind which come into play and rip toward the rear. That's what you see there. Another way to shoot down aircraft is with fragmentation missile, which don't impact directly but explode in front of or below the target. The fragments inside the missile shred the fuselage and cause the vehicle to crash."

"So, this spaceship or plane—whichever—was shot down?" asked James, shuddering.

"I can't say with one hundred percent certainty, but if I

were called in as an expert after a crash, my primary theory would have been that it was down."

James held his breath and looked around, the sweat on his palms suddenly cold. The towering monoliths were suddenly menacing, and the few bushes that remained felt like eerie watchers.

"We should go in," he suggested, leading the way without waiting for a response. When he had set off with Nasaku to the teleporter, they had not closed the curtain behind them or else the storm had torn it from its hooks because the dark spot under the wing was merely shadow not cloth. Cautiously, he stuck his head inside and waited until his eyes adjusted to the twilight, which was several shades darker than outside. It looked as chaotic as he remembered, with blankets and scraps of cloth everywhere, small and large boxes with rounded corners, and empty packages between. Rocks and sand covered floor with small drifts.

"This is her lair?" Norton asked, who had entered behind him and was looking around. James had momentarily forgotten they were still both stark naked. The heat inside the wreckage caused a sheen of sweat to cover their skin and was easy to get used to.

"This is it, yes." James said, nodding and looking around.

He remembered the interior of the spaceship—or at least this part of it, which was certainly not the entire interior—as being much smaller and more cramped. That was probably due to his fear and confusion last time, after all, he had tried to take this place in, but had only noticed a fraction of what he was seeing now.

There were drawings on the few section of the wall not destroyed or covered in mold and lichen. They showed a woman with three children and a group of other stick figures. Others were marked with symbols or letters that could only be made out because they had been scratched into the metallic material.

Norton walked over to a stack of three boxes, pulled at the remains of a blanket that lay on top, and wrapped it around his hips before opening the top box. James stepped up next to him and looked at a collection of injectors, one of which Nasaku had given him when the abscess had formed on his hand.

"Is that—"

"Yes. That's where she got the drug she gave me." James pointed to an ugly red stain under the sheen of sweat on Norton's forearm.

"The injector looked the same, you mean."

"Yes." The major was right, of course. There could be a variety of small vials for the injector containing any number of chemicals. "I guess you'll need one of those soon."

Norton waved him off. "Nah. It's just a skin irritation, nothing I'm playing Russian roulette with alien drugs over."

"But we haven't been here very long. The reactions seem to happen very quickly."

"We should search the other crates. Start over there," Norton ordered, and James nodded. He would have loved to have possessed the officer's clarity and determination.

He walked over to one of the piles of fabric and rifled through it until he found something he could tie around his waist as an improvised skirt. He tore up a blue sheet with symbols vaguely resembling stars, barely recognizable from the dirt, into a dozen strips and wrapped one of them around each of his feet to protect his bruised soles from the rocks. He stuffed the rest into a small bag Nasaku seemed to have improvised. He also found a jacket that smelled disgustingly of mildew and spotted with burgundy stains that reminded him unpleasantly of old blood. He put that on as well and made a concerted effort to ignore the acrid stench. Only then did he set about trying to open one of the smaller boxes, which he could not do because it had no visible closure. He was about to ask Norton, who was rummaging through the longer containers behind him, when his eyes fell on something on the far wall, where there was a hole the size of a head.

James approached it as if spellbound, feeling like a moth that could not resist the urge to fly toward a flame. Hastily, he used his hands to wipe the sticky patina from the pleasantly cool metal and gradually uncovered writing that was faded but was clearly recognizable as such. The letters looked like a mixture of Far Eastern characters and Arabic, connected by short ticks and dashes. It made no sense, but only in the sense that he was looking at a language he didn't know, just as he might have in Central Asia or Africa. What he wouldn't have given to have a smartphone or camera to document it and present it to linguists back home who would have set about deciphering it.

"Did you find anything?" Norton asked over the clatter and thump from him rummaging in the boxes.

"Yes, there's something written on the wall here," James replied, adding unnecessarily, "But I can't read it."

"What about the boxes?"

"Locked, I think." James went up on tiptoe and peered through the hole in the wall. He waited with trembling calves until his pupils dilated to the maximum. He could could make out little in the darkness of the new room since there were no holes in the hull to let in the sparse light from outside, but what little fell past his head through the hole was enough to create reflections. James could make out long, bizarrely shaped metal objects, though he was sure the light and shadow were playing tricks on his eyes and his imagination was sparked. If pressed, he would have guessed that was looking at weapons.

He stepped back and looked at the hole from a distance. It was not round, but diamond-shaped and sharp-edged, with edges that curved inward. Deep nicks, rough and uneven, marred it on the right and left. James thought of Nasaku's improvised axe and swung it with his right hand as if he were hacking at the wall.

"What are you doing?" Norton's voice snapped him out of his musings and he lowered his hand. He turned and shook his head.

"Nothing, it's fine."

"Did you discover anything?"

"No," James lied. The last thing he needed was a soldier who heard the word "weapon" and felt nothing but a tickle in his trigger finger. That wasn't what they were here for, and he didn't want to imagine what could happen if the major mentioned weapons they had found in a wrecked spaceship when they returned. Besides, there was still a chance he misinterpreted the few outlines and reflections he had seen. It could have been anything, and that wasn't enough to raise the interest of a professional warrior. "How about you?"

He turned and walked back toward Norton to remove any urge to take a greater interest in the hole in the wall.

"Most of these are injectors like you described," the soldier said, pointing to two dozen neatly lined up plastic vials. Next to them in the box was a pile of others that were paler. "These are the full ones; the others are the empty ones."

Norton looked in the box standing open next to it. It was

full of devices James thought might have come from a futurist's drawing board.

"I don't know what these are."

Together they stared for a while at what lay before them: strange cubes of what might be plastic, or something else entirely, with round and square connectors and partially torn cables. There were small disks with matte undersides and long pistons with conical caps, but they could not be moved.

"No buttons, levers, or anything else to interact with."

"Maybe those who built all this are using their machines and equipment in different ways," James suggested. "But I can't think of anything to use it for."

"That would be something our scientists could figure out," Norton said firmly.

"So, you're in favor of bringing them here?"

"Of course. This is amazing. But we should be careful and make sure the arrival goes as smoothly as possible."

16

James and Norton improvised large bags out of two stained blankets into which they put some of the empty injectors and some of the full ones, along with as much cloth as they could find. They made more strips from the thinnest material they could find and wound them up before stowing those away as well. In the hustle and bustle of the cave Nasaku had created for herself, they found another axe, consisting of a hard branch and a triangular, sharpened sliver of metal set into a notch and held by some kind of wire, and a knife, also sharpened from a piece of metal. James handed Norton the axe and took the knife.

With all this, he felt like a burglar desecrating Nasaku's private space and wondered more than once if he was making a mistake—at least a moral one. This woman had lost her children and been stranded all alone in such a terrible place, possibly light-years from her home, not knowing if she would ever be rescued. This wreck, which had become her home, had offered her protection, and now they had come along and were taking everything apart to make the arrival of subsequent colleagues a little easier.

When they finally made their way back to the teleporter, it was darker outside and the clouds seemed to have receded a bit. At least the dark gray mass above them did not look as if it would crush them. The curved and jagged monoliths seemed to point the way for them, as if they were guiding them north with frozen gestures.

Norton remained silent as they walked with the sacks over their shoulders over the stony ground, which was now less onerous with the cloth strips around their feet.

"What are you thinking about?" James asked.

"Nasaku's story."

"What of it?"

"It makes no sense to me," the major said.

"Why not?"

"Let's go through it: She comes here, apparently unaware of what it's like on this side of the teleporter. Otherwise, I'm sure she would have preferred to stay at home. But she brings her children with her?"

"Maybe there were a lot like them," James said.

"Then where are they? Why did only she survive? A single woman hiding in a wreck? And I still don't understand about the children. Who brings children to a world like this?"

"Well, we don't know how long they live. Maybe their civilization is so advanced that they live for centuries. That's not even a stretch of the imagination for us these days. It's quite conceivable scientifically. So, they could be thinking in longer time frames." James skirted one of the gnarled bushes that looked like it was flapping its thorns at him in the wind. "It might be that something catastrophic occurred here after she arrived with her children as settlers, or something like that."

"It's possible, yes," Norton admitted but didn't sound

convinced. "Then where are the others? There should at least be the remains of dwellings or graves. Machinery, too—"

"Like a flying machine?" James made a gesture with the knife in his hand, which he felt was somewhat paradoxical in retrospect. "All I'm saying is that they must have been here for some time. Nasaku and her people, I mean. As far as we know, the teleporter doesn't teleport objects, and even if it did, it's unlikely to be anything the size of that starship. So, they were here long enough to build it themselves, and without any tools they could bring with them. That must have taken centuries. After all, you come through naked and without anything. Just to mine and refine the metals— without tools. It's like trying to start a civilization from scratch, which took us millennia."

"With our current knowledge, it would be much faster. Also, objects can be teleported, as we saw with the implants in Nasaku's body. Perhaps they are connected to her brain and contain detailed instructions. But that remains to be seen, even then it doesn't make sense to me," the major insisted. "Why is she the only one left? Why is there nothing else for miles around, except ugly plants that seem trapped in endless death and a bizarre landscape?"

"Maybe a natural disaster? That gray stuff on the ground and bushes looks like ash and it smells like sulfur. What if a supervolcano erupted?"

"That may be so, but then why didn't they go back? If there was an expedition here, why did they wait?"

"They evacuated when something happened on this side and everyone went back, one by one—that takes time when only one person can travel at a time. Nasaku and her kids might have been last, and then something else happened that broke the connection."

"Two disasters at the same time on two planets?" Norton snorted in disbelief.

"Unlikely, but how many unlikely things have happened?"

"Then why did her children die here? Children would be the first to be evacuated, wouldn't they?"

"*We* would evacuate children first," James corrected him. "Their culture may have produced very different priorities. Maybe they live in a caste system that prioritizes certain groups of people regardless of age."

"Such a society would scare me."

"That doesn't seem like a logical argument to me."

"I get the impression that you have to go to great lengths to justify this Nasaku's story, yet it has more holes than swiss cheese," Norton said. "I'm not trying to ridicule her, I'm just saying we need more information and should proceed with caution. This first contact is different than any of us imagined, but that shouldn't make us sloppy and forget our common sense."

"I guess you're right," James admitted with a reluctance he couldn't deny. He *wanted* to believe Nasaku, wanted to help her. He felt she meant well, but the major's logic could not be dismissed, and "I have a good feeling about this" was hardly a convincing argument. Not wanting to get into a deeper that discussion, he changed the subject. "I imagined the initial contact differently, too. I immediately thought of aliens when I first saw the teleporter and imagined scrawny little men with big heads."

"We have all been shaped by the imagination of filmmakers. Whether it's tentacled creatures, bugs, spider monsters, or little green men, I'm sure all of that and a whole lot more has been floating around in the heads of those working on the project."

"But certainly not us," James amended. "Nasaku, as it is, could live on Earth and no one would notice."

He thought about his words and the idea creeped him out. What if there had been aliens among them for a long time, who simply didn't stand out because they looked just like humans? Maybe *were* humans.

"I've thought of that, too. The only question is whether both sides are right."

"Both sides?"

"Those who imagined alien beings and those who see Nasaku as a human from another planet," Norton said. He shifted the sack on his back from one shoulder to the other. "They could both be right."

"You mean that Nasaku and their kind look like humans but are not really humans?"

"Let me answer with a question: How likely do you think it is that in several places in our galaxy, people just like you and me have evolved?"

"When you put it that way, not very likely. Evolution has made us what we are today, and that took millions of years. We are specialized exactly for the planet we live on; we would be different if the gravitational pull was a little different, or the atmospheric composition, or the intensity of the sun's rays, or the fauna. There are visual differences between people in Asia and Africa or Europe because they evolved based on the climate of different continents," James reflected aloud. "But it's also not impossible that there are multiple Earths that are similar enough, right?"

"And then, by chance, people like you and me came into being on each of them?" James glanced sideways at the major and he could tell from the latter's expression exactly what he thought of this notion. He couldn't blame him, it sounded absurd.

"But there may be a rationale that we can't see yet. That's always been your argument about everything concerning the teleporter," he said.

"Yes, and that's why I came here with you. Probably none of what you or I think is true. Even more reason for us to cautiously look for answers ourselves rather than hoping to find them from others."

"Just stop it. We'll agree on something in the end."

They walked on in silence and soon came to the edge of the stone forest, where the rock teeth were smaller and no longer towered over them like skyscrapers. The wind picked up and the darkness increased. Then James heard what he had been secretly dreading since he'd last been in this godforsaken place, the eerie roaring that seemed to come from nowhere. It was a hoarse sound that made him think of a toothy mouth, an primal animalistic scream, deep and raspy at the same time.

"What's that?" Norton asked alarmed, stopping and standing rooted to the spot.

Reflexively, they stood back-to-back and staggered as their bags bumped against each other. Silently they looked around, squinting, trying to differentiate the movement of the bushes in the wind from something else, something dangerous.

"The monster," James whispered.

"What?"

"I don't know what it is, but it was here last time, too, just significantly closer."

"Well, we shouldn't wait to find out," the officer decided and started walking again, much faster this time. The wind rustling through the knotty bushes pressing against the wet ground spurred them to haste. James's brain sent a flood of adrenaline into his system that made all his hair stand on end and left him tingling with goosebumps.

It was happening again. The monster was chasing them with its terrible roar and they had to run for their lives. They fled from the invisible danger on their heels as it got louder, more urgent. They left the stone forest and James knew they wouldn't make it this time. The roars became a bloodcurdling shriek that made his knees tremble.

"We're not going to make it!" he yelled over the nightmarish noise, reflexively looking over his shoulder. A formidable shadow was approaching from the east, running diagonally to intercept them. "We must turn left!"

Norton nodded breathlessly and they turned west, turned around, and headed for a particularly sharp and curved fang. Another deafening roar sounded just before reached the rocks, so close that James didn't dare look over his shoulder. They reached the base of the monolith and dropped their bags as if on an unspoken command, and the major clasped his hands to help him up with a robber's ladder.

James didn't argue, pressed his mud-smeared foot onto the officer's palms and climbed the jagged surface of the stone formation until it sloped enough for him to hold on. He broke the little finger of his right hand when it got caught in a crack and he refused to let go of his knife. He cried out but didn't stop and immediately turned around to help Norton. He had stuffed the axe into his belt and pulled himself up with amazing dexterity, until James was able to reach under his armpits and help him up.

Then the monster was *there*, just a shadow. A paw swept past out of nowhere and tore Norton's improvised skirt to shreds. For a moment, James thought the soldier had been injured, but apparently he had been lucky and only the fabric had been damaged.

The monster had four legs and two arms, a short, stout torso with brown, scarred skin which was steaming slightly. An arrow-shaped head sat atop a long neck that protruded between muscular shoulders. Its mouth was filled with several rows of razor-sharp teeth that shone as if made of metal. But the most frightening thing about the nightmare creature, besides its frighteningly human arms and hands with six-fingered claws, was that it had no eyes and no ears.

"Shit, that was close," James panted as they climbed toward the top of the rocky outcrop, which was so curved that it was almost level. "What the... what the hell is that?"

"I don't know, but it almost caught us," Norton said, breathing heavily.

The monster gave a guttural growl and prowled around the foot of the rock, its head held low, snuffling. James swallowed and looked at the many scars on its back. They were so numerous that it was impossible to tell where one scar ended and another began. Some rose from its skin, others penetrated deeply, some were rounded, others had frayed edges, and some were elongated as if from deep cuts. Its metal teeth made a strange clacking, as if it were grinding razor blades. An indefinable fear of falling from the monolith and being torn to pieces and eaten within seconds by this infernal creature overcame him. He felt like vomiting.

"Apparently, not everything here is dead after all," Norton grumbled, baring his teeth, clearly frustrated as he glanced at his axe, now lying in the muddy ground at the base of the monolith, lost along with his makeshift skirt. It shined brilliantly as if to punctuate that it was out of reach.

"What do we do now?" James asked, his voice high-pitched from fear. He was having trouble forming coherent words because of the lump in his throat. "That thing can't climb, can it?"

"If we could do it, it certainly can."

James looked at the creature. Each of its four powerful legs had three long toes which ended in claws. They were curved, not unlike the rock they were sitting on like two prey animals, and they appeared to be of the same material as its sharp teeth. He wanted the major to assure him they were safe up here, but he knew how ridiculous that was.

"Now, listen to me very carefully, James," Norton said urgently. All the muscles in the wiry man's body were tensed, moving like eels under the dirty skin glistening with sweat.

Why did he call me James? he thought in panic. *He never does that!*

"This thing is going to come up here, do you understand?" the major asked. How was he so calm and collected? "When that happens, and it *will* happen, I want you to be focus and do exactly what say, is that clear?"

James nodded more out of reflex than understanding what Norton was trying to tell him as they crouched on that narrow piece of warm rock, constantly in danger of plummeting twenty feet or more and being eaten by an alien creature. Norton was so composed that James became more frightened because it merely made the hopelessness finality of the situation more certain to him.

His gaze drifted and he noticed the clouds had dissipated in a large area above them that was not as circular as it had been when he had escaped with Nasaku. It was as if the gray masses had been torn apart like cotton balls. Stars twinkled in the firmament, and in the center, the shattered moon with its debris and fragments, which became smaller as they spread out from the open semicircle, the largest pieces like a string of pearls. The light it gave off was enough to see farther than before. He saw the stone forest reached as far as the eye could see. No, not as far as the eye could see, as far as his gaze could see until it met a black wall, higher than the teeth, that looked as if had been created out of material darkness. The wall was extremely far away, certainly several miles, but it stretched from horizon to horizon interrupted only a slight bulge.

"A wall?" he whispered in disbelief.

"Did you get that?" Norton roared, and James nodded lamely. The old soldier's voice had changed, and he wheeled around.

James was horrified to see the monster had started climbing toward them. Its jaws snapped closer, and it gave off a strange scent of ozone.

The major crouched and jumped. James, like a silent participant in a theatrical performance, watched as he flew over the creature's head, which snapped at him. It struck him, which was clear from the blood splatter that erupted in front of his eyes. Norton was knocked off course, but he still crashed into the monster's scarred back, bounced off with a muffled scream, and then landed wetly in the mud below.

James feverishly tried to remember what the officer had told him to do. Everything had happened so fast and his head was spinning. What was he supposed to do? His arms and legs felt like someone had filled them with lead. He only saw the razor-sharp teeth, turning. The creature's neck twisted unnaturally toward Norton, lying on his back below him, breathing heavily and staring upward. He wasn't moving.

Suddenly, James regained his composure and the knuckles of his right hand, which had closed tightly around the knife, popped and turned white.

It's going to eat him, he thought, and followed his instincts. He leapt forward, feet first and slid down the slope of the monolith. Gravity caught him and accelerated him downward. The creature jerked its head around, but whipped up by adrenaline James screamed, reached up, and jammed the knife into the monster's flesh. He couldn't see it, but a warm liquid splashed over him as he slid down and under the torso, between its legs grasping the rock. He didn't let go, keeping his hand tight around the knife and tensing every muscle in his arm to counter the resistance. He landed, feet first next to Norton and the weapon was wrenched from his grip as the creature spun around and let out a long, drawn-out screech.

James fell into the mud, right next to the major. The axe gleamed uselessly between them, as if taunting him. He jerked his gaze upward as the monster leapt toward him, staggered slightly, and a gush of white liquid poured from its torso onto the ground. It threw back its eyeless head, opened its mouth, its many rows of sharp metal teeth making horrible clicking noises, like a cobra preparing to strike. James gazed into the pitch-black maw that gave him a glimpse into a soulless infinity just before his certain death.

The teeth sprang forward as he waited for his legs to obey him so he could give in to his panic and run away, but he could not take his eyes off the shining death. There nothing in his head, only him and the metal dentures.

With an incoherent cry, he flung his right hand to his side, grabbed the axe, and jerked it up to smash the creature's head, but he was too slow and too weak. He was unable to extend his arm, so the weapon landed between him and the monster's mouth.

That probably saved his life.

The monster swallowed it along with it his arm up to the

base of his shoulder. There was a gurgling noise and the wedge-shaped head jerked back. There was an ugly crunch and James's shoulder exploded in pain. He saw his upper arm with its exposed flesh moving away and simply disappear in a cloud of blood.

He stared, horrified, at the red pulp that had been his shoulder, spouting copious amounts of blood. Suddenly, the pain was gone, no more than a memory. Instead, he felt a dull, cold sensation spread from the wound, muffled by sluggishness of his mind, as if he was slowly moving away from himself.

He found himself in a place that was much quieter, more distant, as if none of this concerned him. Yet he knew what had to be done. With mechanical precision, he got up and went to the two bags they had dropped. He opened one and took out two pieces of cloth, fumbled one into a kind of pillow and pressed it to where his arm had been. The other he wrapped as tightly as possible around his torso and neck to keep pressure against the wound.

Next he turned to Norton, who was still lying motionless on his back but following him with his eyes.

"Y-you have to go," Norton said, his voice thin. It sounded like wilted leaves carried away by the wind.

"*We* have to go," James corrected him calmly and walked over to the soldier. The way he was lying, sunk several inches into the quagmire even here at the edge of the stone forest, he must have shattered his spine. "You're paralyzed, I think."

"Get out of here, quick! The creature—it ran away, but I don't think it will stay away for long."

"What creature?" asked James lamely.

Something stirred in his mind. He barely made out his surroundings, he knew it was Norton lying there, that his right arm had somehow disappeared, and that his entire right side was numb, as if someone had softened him with a meat tenderizer. The emptiness in his head was filled by a block between his nearly dried-up thinking and his body.

"Listen," the major gasped with great effort. "You're in shock. You'll bleed out in half an hour or sooner, even with your improvised bandages. I can't feel my hands or feet, and I can't move. If you go to the teleporter now, you might be able to make it before you pass out. Just go back to the big black ellipsoid. Do you understand what I'm saying?"

James thought. It was infinitely exhausting. Finally, he nodded and squatted next to Norton.

"What are you doing?"

James grabbed one of the paraplegic's useless arms and wrapped it around his shoulder so he could hold his wrist with his remaining hand. Then he crouched and pulled the old soldier onto his shoulders and back.

"A-are you crazy?" Norton asked weakly, close to his ear. "We're b-both going to die."

"Maybe," James agreed and put one foot in front of the other. He could see the teleporter—a dark bump on the horizon—because of the better visibility, so he moved toward it. His legs burned with each step and made them protest, but he knew what he had to do. He had to get them both to the teleporter so they could get out of here. Yes, he had to do that because this place was bad.

"Let g-g-go of me," Norton demanded. "You m-must report b-back."

James ignored him and just kept walking. His body refused to send him signals beyond the burning in his legs and the feeling that he was merely an observer witnessing from afar, which came in handy. He knew what was right now, and he knew he had to get back to that black bump and carry the weight on his back. The world was suddenly so simple, and he found that quite delightful.

He walked on and on, unperturbed by Norton's feeble objections and warnings about some creature. Seen from a distance, he could have been mistaken for a walker who had discovered slowness for himself.

The numbness lasted for what felt like an eternity, during which James waded through the fetid mire like an empty shell, watching himself.

Suddenly, the teleporter had grown into a large ellipsoid, protruding from the otherwise flat landscape like the foreign body it was. Its matte surface seemed to soak up every photon in the environment and not release it again. It likely would have stood out from the landscape even in complete darkness.

Pain exploded in James's shoulder and spread in hot waves that nearly knocked him unconscious. He was hot and cold at the same time, and sweat poured out of his skin. Memories of the fight with the creature returned. He saw the horrible razor teeth snapping at him, the flexing muscles of the monster straining to devour him, his arm sinking into the maw and being torn off as effortlessly as if it were made of old newspaper. Blood everywhere, a mist of red, sudden pain rolling over him. Norton lying defenseless beside him, motionless, though outwardly appearing uninjured.

James collapsed to his knees and gasped. The pain, fueled by fear and panic, almost robbed him of his sanity. His entire world consisted of nothing else.

"Breathe," someone somewhere whispered. Maybe it was Norton. "Breathe. In and out."

James clung to the voice, trying not to look at his injured shoulder stump, and concentrated on breathing in and then breathing out, slow and controlled. It didn't dispel the chaos in his head, but it gave him a path through it, a guidepost with which he could use to move away from the madness. Most of him wanted to drop and surrender, not put in the effort he needed. This part wanted to give up and not face the mountain of pain and fear whose slopes surrounded him and wanted to remove his path of a way out.

"Concentrate on my voice and your breathing," Norton ordered, somehow giving his thin voice military emphasis. "You're going to let go of me now, and then you're going to go into the teleporter. You will sit on the seat and close your eyes. When you get to the other side, everything will be fine. Then you will go to Pavar and tell her everything."

James allowed himself three more breaths, then screamed against the torment and got to his knees. He adjusted the officer's weight and staggered briefly, almost losing consciousness as a wave of renewed agony ran through his body. Again, the major spoke, but James just kept screaming and running, concentrating on tension in his shaking legs and staring grimly at the teleporter growing larger before them. Somewhere, far away, an eerie roar could be heard, but he blocked it out along with the rest of this dead world. He didn't let it distract him from what he had to do.

Finally, standing in front of a black wall, he leaned Norton against the cold surface of the teleporter before groping in the mire in front of it with his remaining hand. Two meters above them, the passageway emerged, a rectangle of pure light that looked so spotless and pure that it could not have contrasted more starkly with the fetid muck under which the bleak landscape was suffocating. James felt like a Stone Age man, a savage trying to climb a complicated rocket.

It took what felt like an eternity before his fingers finally found what they were looking for. They grasped a piece of wood and he pulled hard until the crude ladder came sucking out of the mire. Drops of thick mud dripped from the uneven supports and rungs as he awkwardly tried to set it so the top reached the light opening and remained steady.

Then he tried to hoist Norton back onto his shoulders. The officer looked absent, his eyes half-closed, his mouth slack. A thin thread of saliva hung from the corner of his mouth and ran down his bare chest, which was covered with scrapes and dried mud. It looked like he wasn't getting enough air, but he still had a pulse. Awkwardly, James fought to get his companion slung over his shoulder, but no matter what he tried wouldn't work to get him safely up the ladder. Even without the extra weight, it was difficult for him to climb safely with just one hand.

The creature's howls were getting closer.

He had only one choice: Again, he set Norton against the teleporter's hull, then muttered an apology before dislocating—and presumably breaking—his shoulders with short kicks. Next, James unwound the lengths of cloth from his feet and tied the major's arms together in front of his chest. As he did so, they stuck out at an unhealthy angle, but it allowed him to secure them so they wouldn't cut off the major's air as he was carried.

Norton muttered something unintelligible as James struggled upward, rung after rung. It took several eternities, during which the pain caused by the officer's extra weight grew worse, but eventually, he reached the edge of the passage. Now he hung there, his knees shaking and the ladder swaying ominously. He had to let go of the top rung to pull himself inside the teleporter, but that hand was the only thing keeping them from tumbling backward. His field of vision was severely limited by the strain and pain and flickering black at the edges.

After a few breaths, he gathered his strength and courage and plunged his remaining hand through the light, searching with his fingers for support as he teetered backward, gasping in relief when he found along the edge of the passageway. Slow as a turtle, he pulled himself and Norton through the glare, pushing with his feet, rung by rung.

The interior was cold and he shivered as he lifted Norton's limp but heavy arms over his head. They laid briefly on their backs, side by side, gazing into the endless blackness that formed the ceiling above them.

"We'll make it, Major," he rasped, finally getting to his feet. His head was buzzing as he searched for the correct seat, which should have been easy since only one had a glowing green light, but in his current state, where everything blurry was and felt far away, he found it difficult. Like a drunk, he staggered to each seat and squinted at the headrests. H breathed a sigh of relief when he thought he saw the little green light. He removed his clothes and hung them over the armrest before returning to Norton and slipping his arm under the major's armpit to pull him along and lift him onto the seat.

His strength was almost at an end and he felt unconsciousness creeping up on him like a predator, ready to attack at any moment. But it wasn't just unconsciousness. From the copious amounts of blood clinging to the right side of his body and still running down his side, the last of his life was draining out of him and he knew death was approaching. Still, he proceeded methodically, draping Norton's forearms on the induction strips and managing something like a smile, which probably looked bizarre.

"I don't know how this even works," he said weakly. "I

wonder if your body is still on the other side, and if you'll go back into it like I did last time. Anyway, I guess I'll be in the other chair because only one can be in the departure seat at a time, huh? I guess I'll be a clone then. But then what about my real body?"

Norton looked like he wanted to say something, but he only blinked and his lips trembled without producing any sound.

"See you on the other side." James reached out and closed the officer's eyes with outstretched fingers. Nothing happened. It wasn't until he lightly slapped the man and his head slumped to the side that James knew he was either dead or already home. But the body was still there, just as his own had been the last time he crossed over. Why, then, had Nasaku's body not been here when he had arrived with Norton a few hours ago? Where had it gone?

The dull feeling in his head, as if he were under too much pressure, eliminated any attempt to think about it or come to a logical conclusion, so he pulled the body out of the seat and dragged it into the funnel the center of the tele-porter room then staggered back. Halfway there, he fell and skinned his knees. His vision went black and a high-pitched whine arose in his ears.

Groaning, he struggled to his feet, barely able to distinguish light from dark, and scrambled toward the seat, which he thought was the right one because of the darker tint on one side, and pulled himself groaning up onto the armrest. Every breath was painful and nothing could penetrate it.

His eyes closed for the last time and he slumped over, the last of his blood, what was keeping him upright, ran onto the seat.

17

James opened his eyes and heard an agitated roar. It surged up and down, up and down, and seemed somehow to correspond to his feelings. It created a vague urgency that manifested itself as a tingle on his skin and turmoil in his stomach. He wanted to jump up, to scream, to run, to get rid of his energy, which was not born of an excess of vitality, but of something he could not name.

Major Norton was in front of him, surrounded by men and women in white protective suits. At first glance, James was startled by them because they looked like alien astronauts. Only when a face pushed in front of him, hidden behind a face shield, did he flinch. He gradually realized he was not dead or on another alien world, but home, on Earth, deep beneath Wyoming.

"James! James!" The face belonged to Mila, so beautiful and smooth.

He pushed her aside and stood so abruptly that two figures, one on his right and one on his left, whom he had not noticed, flinched back.

"James, don't!" Mila pleaded, but he paid no attention to

her. He looked at Norton, just an arm's length away. He looked exhausted and, unlike him, he was not stark naked but dressed in the bodysuit he was wearing when they had prepared for the teleport. The officer's eyes were open and moist. When he saw James, he swallowed and nodded, his nostrils quivering. He raised one hand and moved his fingers as if trying to wave.

James sighed with relief, then grabbed at his naked body, looked at both uninjured arms, and sank back onto the seat where he had woken up. All strength left him, flowing out of him like water

"Take it easy!" It was Mette, standing on his other side. She took the white hood and hard hat off her head and gave him a rosy smile, yet she looked like she was at a funeral. "Stay calm. You're safe; that's all that matters."

"What's wrong?" he asked. He was confused and felt a growing pressure behind his eyes and swelling in his chest.

Mila approached him again while removing her helmet. At least a dozen people were running around in protective clothing, half were gathered around a stretcher, which was then carried with some haste to the passage.

"What's with them?" James started crying as the pressure continued. The nightmare from which he had escaped at the last second was over and yet the images of Norton's broken body, of the horrible monster that had nearly killed them, of his amputation and how he had dragged the major's naked body into the hopper like a piece of meat, would not let him go. Just seeing Norton alive and breathing was the most beautiful and terrible thing at the same time. It proved to him it had been a genuine, real, and unchangeable experience, and there was a chance that life could give him such a ghastly experience again. A part of him had secretly wished he would never wake up again.

And yet, it felt good to see familiar faces and to cry and sob. He was neither embarrassed nor uncomfortable. It was one of the most vulnerable moments in his life and his body simply took control, snatching it from him, gently yet firmly.

Mila held his right hand and looked sympathetic, as did Mette, though she seemed much more frightened.

"We are very sorry. I can only imagine what this must be like," the Russian murmured, gently squeezing his shoulder... the shoulder that, just a few seconds ago, had been a mangled chunk of torn flesh.

He looked directly into her eyes. Although she was blurry, he did not blink away the tears.

"But you don't even know what happened," he said, sniffling, confused. Mila exchanged a glance with Mette and looked uncertain.

Then it dawned on him what they meant. He had awakened in the other seat, the one meant for the clone. He was naked, not wearing his bodysuit worn during the teleport. Where was his body? His *real* body?

He jerked his head to the side and stared at the stretcher being transported through the glare of the passageway with two white figures blocking his view. If that was his real body and he was a clone, then who was *he*? He was himself, wasn't he? James Hamilton? His "self" felt the same as always; even the feel of his fingers nervously rubbing together was exactly as he was used to.

"I—" he stammered and swallowed. "What... what about him? About *me*?"

Mila and Mette exchanged a glance.

"Hey, talk to me!"

"You... your body went into a coma after your... transition," Mila started. "The major put you in the other seat as we discussed and then went in after you. Captain Miller

239

came in after the magnetic field settled back down, as Pavar ordered, and put your body in an induced coma here because we didn't know what the return would be like with two people. We didn't even know in what order you would come back. The whole thing was rushed and stupid, I think. We—"

"Mila!" he interrupted her a little more sharply than he intended. He heard a quiver in his voice. "Am I—is my— that is, my body, is it... dead?"

"I don't know. Your return announced itself with a significant magnetic surge and the instruments failed, as expected. That's why they have to get you upstairs to the clinic as fast as possible. They're doing their best, I'm sure. I'm so sorry, James!"

"It's all right," he said reflexively.

But nothing was all right. What did it mean? If his body died, was he dead and alive at the same time? Should he mourn for himself, or was it all the same because he was still alive, just in another shell?

A shell artificially created by an alien artifact, he told himself. Mette and Mila exchanged worried glances, and despite his inner turmoil, he knew exactly what they were thinking.

"I mean it," he said, wiping tears from his cheeks. "What can I do or say now? This is all an experiment, field research, and we learn from our mistakes."

"But we shouldn't have been so sloppy," Mila said, shaking her head. "We were chosen for our special expertise, and we didn't even think about things that were so obvious."

He briefly looked around at the crowded teleporter, which was still teeming with people. "It's impossible against the backdrop of this thing. You can't expect to function the same way you do at home, in college, or anywhere else. All of you have barely slept in weeks and have been under tremendous pressure."

"Still, we have to be more careful," the Russian insisted, looking him firmly in the eye. "If the doctors can keep your body—your original body, I mean—alive, then you can go back and we'll exchange your clone and the original, then everything should be back to normal."

"No!" He nearly shouted and all the people in the teleporter turned to look at him. He cleared his throat and lowered his voice. "I'm sorry, but I... I can't go back."

"What on earth happened there?" Mette asked sympathetically.

"The dean would like to know that, too." Captain Miller stepped in front of James and was preparing his right arm to draw blood. "I have her in my ear right now, and we shouldn't waste any time."

"Can't you see he's not in the best shape?" Mila glared at the doctor.

"I'll know in a few hours." The officer pointed to the vial in his right hand, which was rapidly filling with dark blood.

"I guess it doesn't occur to you that there are things that cannot be seen in the blood, does it?"

"Listen, if he needs psychological support, he'll get it. But as long as he's able to participate in a debriefing—and though I see signs of a strong emotional reaction, he's not a state of shock or anything like that—he can do just that."

Mila turned to him, ignoring the staff physician. "James, you don't have to do this."

"Yes, I do." She shook her head as though she didn't understand, and he took her hand and squeezed it. "We saw some things on the other side that might be important."

Mila and Mette looked at each other, and he could tell

they were barely holding back a barrage of questions. He wanted to explain what he meant, but Captain Miller beat him to it.

"Like this!" he said, pulling the cannula out of the crook of James's arm and passing it, along with two full vials of blood, to his nurse, who carried it all off in a surgical tray.

Norton straightened and stood examining his bare feet. There was a whole world of relief and disbelief in his gaze, probably because his toes were moving. Who could claim to have experienced paraplegia and then return to a healthy body? However, he didn't seem to think it was a good feeling, aside from the relief.

A woman came up to James and pressed a pile of clothes into his hand. He realized he had been sitting there naked since his return—and in front of Mila, although the materials researcher didn't seem to mind. He was suddenly uncomfortable, so he quickly got dressed, gratefully declined Mila's offers to help him, and then stood.

His clone body felt supple and vital, just as it had on the other planet, only without the horrible climate and stench that had constantly made him uncomfortable. Nothing was different from normal; his fingers obeyed as usual, his feet, now in military boots, tingled slightly, and the shallow pain in his lumbar spine that he had been carrying around since a disk surgery five years ago was also still there.

"Come on," Norton said, and for a moment it looked like he was going to tap James on the shoulder but decided against it at the last moment. An awkward silence ensued, ending when the officer cleared his throat and gestured toward the doorway. "We shouldn't keep Pavar waiting."

"I—"

"The best thing we can do right now is focus and move on. What happened, happened and we survived it," the major said sticking his chin out. "I've served in two wartime deployments and I've been through a lot, Mr. Hamilton. What you've been through no one should have to go through, but you're not the first and only one, do you understand? Just move on, live your normally and let it bring you back and ground you. I know you don't feel like it at all, but just pretend. Keep at it until it becomes normal."

James was too surprised by the older man's torrent of words to respond, so he simply followed him, lost in thought, forgetting about Mila and Mette for the moment. He walked, dreamlike, down the ramp into the cave, where there was more bustle than last time. White figures surrounded the teleporter with outstretched probes while others made notes on clipboards or rummaged through boxes of olive-colored plastic, clearly military issue, lined up against the walls.

In the airlock, they were disinfected and had to wait silently for five minutes until the door was opened into the underground complex, they went directly to the elevators. A soldier came running over to them and held out a uniform and boots to the major, who quickly put them. Then they got in the elevator and went up to Pavar's office.

"There you are." The dean greeted them and beckoned them to the two chairs in front of her desk, which, despite its imposing size and the many files on it, seemed lost in the small room. Kowalski sat at his own desk against the wall, surrounded by half a dozen displays, and acknowledged their entrance with only a breif sideways glance.

"You gave us quite a scare," Pavar said as she signed some document and set it aside to look at them. "Because of the magnetic field, I mean. We didn't expect you back after only three hours. What happened?"

"I can confirm what Mr. Hamilton reported to us."

Norton took the lead, and James had the feeling he was doing him a favor. Perhaps he thought he needed a little more time to collect himself. "I saw the crashed flying object, the stone forest, the dying landscape, and Nasaku's camp..."

James stopped listening when Pavar stopped the officer and asked him to tell her chronologically what had happened. On one hand, he didn't know how he would react if he heard it again. On the other, he was thinking about his real body receiving desperate measures to keep it alive in one of the nearby buildings. He just couldn't get it out of his head that there were two of him now, or maybe just one if his original died. Shouldn't someone be there to mourn him? But that would be absurd. Wouldn't it?

"Mr. Hamilton?" He could tell from Pavar's tone this was not the first time she had addressed him.

"Yes, ma'am?"

"Are you okay?" When he looked up, he saw she was worried. He hadn't thought the politician was capable of such a facial expression. "That sounds terrible, what you went through. And the way you saved the major, that was... *heroic.*"

She nodded approvingly, and for a few moments the only sound was the click of the keys from Kowalski's nimble fingers, who was presumably taking minutes.

"I don't say it often," she went on, "but maybe I was wrong about you."

"Um, thanks," he said.

"Is there anything you would like to add to the major's remarks?"

"No," he replied hastily, without even knowing exactly what Norton had said. "Although..."

"Yes?" Pavar leaned forward, her elbows propped on the tabletop, hands clasped in front of her pointed chin.

"When we were sitting on the stone tooth, the sky cleared up and I saw something on the horizon. It looked like a dark wall."

"A dark *wall*?" The dean looked at Norton, but he shook his head.

"Yes, it looked like a dark wall stretching across the horizon—in every direction."

"Are you sure? I'm sure you were very scared and under some stress with this creature eager to climb up to you two."

"I didn't imagine it!" he insisted.

"But it's conceivable that a panic reaction may have set in under the circumstances?"

"Yes, it's possible," Norton admitted. "At times like that, it's very easy to see something—"

"I didn't imagine it," James repeated, but shrugged when the two looked at him.

"We... will look into it, at the next opportunity." Pavar didn't sound like she believed him, but he gladly accepted the offer to stop talking about it. Another expedition would have to seek its own answers.

Without me, he thought.

"Good. What we're going to do now is interview Nasaku again. The polygraph has arrived, and with the new information you've brought back—about the writing on the wall, for example—I'm sure we'll get a lot more out of the interview. I want you both to write down the symbols as best you can, understand?" The dean waited until they both nodded. "Good. Norton, do you see yourself able to participate in the interview?"

"Yes, ma'am," the officer said after a moment's hesitation.

"I will also—" James started but was interrupted.

"You're going to get some rest. You have done enough, Mr. Hamilton. I have the utmost respect for what you did for the major, and with your dedication to this project, you deserve a little rest."

He wanted to object, but she nipped it in the bud with a raised index finger.

"Good, it is decided. I have requested a specialist to meet you in your quarters in one hour. His name is Dr. Cunningham."

"A psychiatrist?"

"Yes," Pavar confirmed.

"I don't need—"

"You don't need a doctor?" The dean snorted. "You're sitting across from me right now in a clone body while the survival of your real one is being fought for. I can't even imagine what that must feel like. And all this against the backdrop of the horror story that Norton just described to me from your mission on *Prime*."

"Prime?" James asked.

"The current internal code name for the planet you discovered." She waved it off. "You may think everything is fine, but it's not. Talk to Cunningham. If he certifies that you are fit for duty, I will trust his judgment. But until then, I am committed to the protection of my employees, and I am ordering you to rest and recuperate."

The phone on her desk rang with an intrusive electronic whine. Pavar lifted a finger and picked up the receiver.

"Yes?" She listened in silence, then her eyes widened. *"What?"*

James shared an alarmed glance with Norton and winced when the dean jumped up and pressed a red button to the far right of her desk.

A loud alarm howled.

"What's going on?" Norton shouted over the deafening noise.

"It's Nasaku," Pavar said, snapping her fingers toward Kowalski. "She's gone."

"Gone?"

"Yes, *gone*! Now mobilize your people! I want the entire base locked down! Get helicopters in the air; I don't care! She does not leave this facility, is that clear?"

"Of course, ma'am." Norton ran to the door, which was yanked open. Four soldiers entered. Two posted themselves against the wall and the other two followed the major.

"How is that possible?" Pavar asked angrily, pacing like a tiger behind her desk. "She was guarded!"

When no one answered her, she stared at Kowalski like a hawk on a mouse.

"She *was* guarded, wasn't she?"

"Uh, yes, ma'am, two guards, and her door was locked." Kowalski had a phone to each ear.

"Then how the hell did she get past them?" Pavar asked, apparently unmoved by the fact that her assistant was overwhelmed. On top of that, the noise of the alarm made it a challenge even to understand what she was saying.

"I don't know," Kowalski admitted meekly. Then he shouted into his phones, "No. I don't mean you. Send up the camera data."

The phone on Pavar's desk rang again, and she snatched the receiver as if she were trying to pull out a particularly persistent weed.

"Yes! What? That's impossible! Then make sure we find out how that happened! We're on a goddamn high-security Air Force base; there's no way some savage could trick you all!" She slammed the receiver back and snorted like a bull.

Her eyes fell on James and she growled, "She escaped via the elevator, right when the guard was changing. They saw her, but she was wearing the uniform of one of the soldiers who had been guarding her quarters."

"The elevator? It can only be used with a card and code since Nasaku is here," he mused aloud.

"Yes, she apparently managed this feat. How?"

"She must have known a code."

"You don't say? I know that, but how is that possible? She doesn't even speak our language, let alone our numbers."

James thought feverishly, then tensed.

"What?" Pavar asked, her eyes narrowed to slits.

"The translator, Ms. Eikes, she didn't have a working card, so you gave her a code as a substitute. When she came in, do you remember?" James asked. "1605 I think."

"No. 1604," she corrected him, and stared off into nothingness for a moment. "She couldn't have used that one, though, because she couldn't understand anything. That's why I spoke freely to Ms. Eikes."

"Then there's only one explanation."

Pavar did not react immediately, but he could see her working it out. The politician was thinking feverishly, playing out different scenarios, and it was obvious that she didn't like the conclusions.

"She understood us the whole time."

James swallowed hard.

"If she knows our language, a whole new set of problems and questions will arise." The dean's expression darkened. She grabbed the phone again and pressed a speed dial button. "Pavar here. If the target resists, I authorize the use of lethal force to prevent her from escaping the base."

"What?" James cried in horror before the receiver settled in its cradle. "You can't!"

"I not only can, Mr. Hamilton, I *must*! She has obviously lied to us and feels it necessary to run. Those are both bad signs. In addition, we now know even less than before about who or what we are dealing with. My responsibility is the safety of this facility, this country, and, yes, in this case, the world!"

18

"Disappeared, just like that?" Meeks asked, stunned, running his broad hands over his bald head. The mood in the leadership team's workroom was subdued. Around the table, James saw only horrified or frustrated expressions.

"Yes. I saw camera footage of her briefly taking out a guard who recognized her too late," he explained, shaking his head. "Then Pavar kicked me out and sent me down here."

"For now, none of us are allowed out of this room," Mila said, the bitter truth gnawing at them all since they had gathered two hours ago.

The hallways were full of soldiers, and all the entrances and exits were sealed off—not only to the former silo but also to the entire Air Force Base on the surface. It was hard to imagine, amid the tense silence, there beneath the many feet of earth, rock, and concrete, that a short elevator ride would have taken Nasaku into the daylight, where SUVs full of soldiers were speeding around, helicopters were hovering with searchlights, and loudspeakers barking orders cut through the night.

"They'll shoot her if they have to." All eyes fell on James. He nodded and pursed his lips. "I heard her give the order myself."

"Does she even have the authority to do that?" Falkenhagen demanded. The German looked unusually thoughtful. "I agree with the dean that Nasaku is a danger, after all, she obviously lied to us. But surely, we must not kill the first alien we come into contact with!"

"She looks like a human being to me," Smailov said.

"That may be, but she's not from here, that's for sure. We saw how her body was created in the teleporter. No one can tell me that it was just an East Frisian or someone else playing a trick on us."

"East Frisian?"

"Never mind." Falkenhagen waved it off, and his attractive face tightened as if he had bitten into a lemon. "Anyway, that would be a disaster for the future of the project. We'd have blood on our hands and whatever happened from there on would be built on something bad."

"He's right," Mila agreed and Mette nodded, while Meeks and Smailow brooded. "There must be something we can do!"

"To do that, we'd have to know how she thinks and what she's up to," Falkenhagen said. "But we don't know *anything* about her. We thought she didn't know our language, but either she learned very quickly or she's been leading us around by the nose for quite a while."

"She came here alone. That's a huge risk. I don't think she took all this on herself just to do... *what*, exactly?" Mila asked.

"Let's put ourselves in her shoes," Meeks suggested,

leaning his massive torso over the tabletop before looking at each of them in turn. "She was all alone on Prime, wasn't she?"

"And cut off from her home. She had no way back," Mila added.

"So, if we were in her shoes, stranded in the most horrible place you can imagine—the place where your children died and you were alone for who knows how long—and then suddenly the gate opens to a third world where people like you live, and clearly a highly developed world, what would you do?"

"It depends." James eyed Falkenhagen, who shrugged. "It depends on what background I have. Whether my own world has a similar technological level or higher. If not, a ten-year difference is enough. Someone from the jungles of Sumatra wouldn't be able to cope in a highly developed city like Singapore. If her homeland is underdeveloped, she won't understand anything here."

"I think we can rule that out if she knows how to use switchboards, key cards, elevators, how to sneak past cameras, and after"—Meeks glanced down at his wristwatch—"almost two hours, still hasn't been caught."

"All right, so let's assume—just for our hypothetical—that she knows technology at our level. What would we do in her place?"

"E.T.," Mila said and immediately had everyone's attention—including some confused looks.

"E.T.?" asked Smailov, as if she had lost her mind. "The ugly Steven Spielberg alien?"

"It wasn't ugly; it was *different*," his associate corrected him. "But E.T. was stranded and wanted—"

"Phone home!" James clapped his hands so loudly that the scientists were startled. "Of course!"

Silence fell before Meeks said, "She might want to send a signal, but to do that she first has to figure out Earth's relative position in the Milky Way. Then she'd have to send a signal strong enough to reach whoever she's trying to contact. But unless it's a neighboring star—which is pretty much out of the question because they're all quiet—it would take decades or centuries for the signal to reach her home."

"He's right," Smailov agreed. "It wouldn't be very practical."

"Maybe not. But would we think it through first, alone and stranded, surrounded by strangers who don't seem particularly friendly?" James said, shaking his head. "No. We'd want to break our chains and call home, at any cost."

Mila nodded. "I guess he's right. I would certainly go about it that way."

"Then we have to let Pavar know. She needs to alert all the observatories within range and have them protected by the police. Then the FBI or anyone else with leads who can look for her," Meeks said, looking to Smailov, who was nodding thoughtfully. "If she even made it off the base."

"They'll shoot her before she gets very far. I'm sure she found it awful on Prime," James said. It felt strange to speak of the dead planet as Prime. But it did feel good, in an absurd way, to be confronted with the problem Nasaku running away because it didn't give him any time to brood over what he'd gone through there with Norton, which would probably cost him several months of sleep. "But she's not going to get locked underground and hooked up to machines that are strange to her like a lab rat."

"You think she'd rather get shot?" Mette asked, her eyes wide.

"I'm afraid so," James said.

"Even if we wanted to do something, we can't do anything. The entire facility is on lockdown! There's only one thing we can do: let Pavar know our theory and hope she makes the right decisions," Meeks insisted.

"No, we can't!"

"She's a politician. She's going to do what hurts her the least, and that's to eliminate Nasaku," said Falkenhagen, of all people, jumping in to help James. "Without her, we're back to square one."

"No! We still haven't tried the other connections. Maybe we'll find a lot more out there,", Meeks said.

"It would be naïve to travel randomly instead of asking the person who knows about the teleporters! We must not let this advantage slip from our hands. She is not a danger just because she wants to contact her home. On the contrary, this contact could be in our interest! For decades we have hoped for contact with other intelligent civilizations, and now we have found one. One that is also very similar to us!" James became increasingly frustrated.

"He's right," said a new voice. It was Major Norton. He entered the room, looked over his shoulder, and then pushed the door closed until it locked. Everyone looked around uncertainly, and froze.

"Major!" James cleared his throat. "We were just discussing the current developments."

"I get it." The officer came and stood between Mila and Mette at the table, leaned forward on his fists, and eyed them each in turn. "I think you're all Pollyannas. Despite being chosen for your high IQs and scientific bravado, you're amazingly bad at assessing risk."

The silence in the room became more oppressive under the soldier's words of the hard facts. He seemed to rebuke them like a stern father.

"We just wanted to—" Meeks started, but Norton silenced him with a sharp gesture.

"*Naive* is what you were being. I don't think you realize what a danger this woman is, if she is one at all!"

"Did you overhear us?" James asked.

"Overhear?" Norton snorted. "I didn't need to. I heard you locking yourself in together, and all I had to do was put one and one together. What you did for me, Mr. Hamilton, I want you to know I will never forget, but I don't think you're seeing very clearly in this matter. You *want* Nasaku to be a friendly, protective alien who is also one of us. You *want* this first contact to go well. So you consciously or unconsciously ignore the risks and the big holes in her story."

"But we don't even *know* her whole story!"

"Exactly. We only have a handful of pieces of information, and even those are full of holes."

"This is a 'glass half empty or half full' thing!" James protested. "One could assume that we have too little information to say that these *holes* you speak of should alert us. But maybe it's the other way around, maybe we're interpreting the wrong meanings into these holes."

"The fact is," Norton countered, "we have an alien entity that somehow managed to escape one of the most secure Air Force bases in the world."

"She got away?" Mila asked, both surprised and delighted, earning a scowl from the officer.

"Yes, and since she's just *not* a little green man, it's going to be hard to catch her. But I'm sure *you'll* have an idea the FBI doesn't."

"The FBI?" Meeks looked as if he'd seen a ghost. "But—"

"The Air Force is not suited, nor legally authorized, to conduct a manhunt off military property, and because of the risk of flight across Wyoming's borders, Pavar has had to involve the FBI."

"They don't even know who they're dealing with!" Falkenhagen said.

"No, and that's why I'm coming to you. Nasaku has been passed off as a fugitive terrorist with the highest threat potential and the FBI has announced it won't do anything by halves." Norton paused to make sure everyone was paying attention and continued urgently, "So, we have the awkward situation of having an alien at large who is capable of considerably more than we thought and who might get shot at the first opportunity. We can't have that."

"Well, we finally agree on something," Mila grumbled.

The major ignored her and tapped the top of the aluminum table with an outstretched index finger as if trying to pierce it.

"Have you talked about how to find her and bring her back?"

Dismayed silence.

"It will not leave this room," Norton assured them.

"We did," James said, shrugging his shoulders as he received a few somber looks.

"Do it."

"What?"

"I said, 'Do it.' I'm delaying the changing of the guard at the southern freight elevator, where new supplies will be delivered in fifteen minutes. The base is no longer on lockdown since Nasaku *has* escaped. Since Pavar thinks you're stuck down here, she hasn't issued any orders to prevent you from leaving the base."

"Why are you doing this?" James asked, curious and voicing what was hanging unsaid.

"We need to interrogate Nasaku, and we need to do it

intensively to minimize the potential danger of future missions." Norton pursed his lips. "Also, I'm afraid that this thing could pose a problem for the continuation of the project if it goes wrong. The president is not at all pleased with what's been happening. It wasn't easy to convince him to put the alien machine into operation in the first place."

"Your country can't just get out of this without giving us the teleporter," Smailov objected.

"We're certainly not going to hand it over to the Kremlin or Brussels, you can be sure of that."

"Then we're going to have a problem."

"And for that very reason," Norton said, "you must find Nasaku and bring her back here. Do you understand?"

The major had not lied to them. Via the freight elevator— whose camera had an 'unforeseen malfunction'—they entered a small warehouse normally guarded by four soldiers. They were standing outside smoking when their small group walked by. As promised by Norton, a dark SUV was waiting in a nearby parking lot.

The sprawling facility was surrounded by large meadows and had two north-south runways hemmed in by flat barracks and hangars that provided a restrained glow in the darkness of the early morning. Helicopters continually took off and landed, roaring and flashing red lights against the clear starry sky. Night time lighting, a secret exit, hushed atmosphere, and the search for an escaped alien in the American backcountry. For James, this made him feel like he was the protagonist in a Steven Spielberg film.

Meeks got behind the wheel of the SUV after they found the keys behind the sun visor as promised. James sat next to him in the front, while Mila, Mette, Falkenhagen, and Smailow sat on the two rear benches.

Getting off the compound was also easier than they anticipated, as they merely had to show their Air Force-issued IDs identifying them as civilian advisors and they were let out. The lights from Cheyenne illuminated the horizon like a beacon, but Meeks turned onto a country road heading vaguely west.

"Looks like you have a plan," James remarked.

"There's only one real observatory in Wyoming, and that's WIRO, the Wyoming Infrared Observatory," the husky engineer explained. "It's on top of Mount Jelm, eighty miles to the west, south of Albany."

"Somebody knows their stuff."

"I'm from Fort Collins, Colorado. I took a class trip there once when I was a teenager."

"I see." James kept glancing in the rearview and side mirrors because he couldn't shake the feeling they were being followed. More to distract himself, he said, "At the risk of asking a rather stupid question, we're quite sure Nasaku needs a telescope, yes?"

Meeks nodded. "Of course."

"And, uh, what for? I understand the part about looking at the stars to determine her position, but that still doesn't do her any good to send a message, does it? After all, a telescope is for looking, not transmitting."

"That's true in principle, but with telescopes, you can also transmit," Meeks said, turning west at a deserted intersection onto Interstate 80, where traffic was light. The red taillights that suddenly surrounded them were a strange, melancholy reminder there was still a normal world out here as they were exploring underground for the stars—a thought that once struck him as surreal and very far away.

"Parabolic mirrors are, strictly speaking, excellent for focusing a radio signal on a specific point, i.e., sending it in exactly one direction with high intensity. This, by the way, is how you keep in touch with very distant space probes like Cassini and Co."

"I didn't know that," James said, summing up his ignorance, and with it, demonstrated the big difference between him and the others in the vehicle.

"I have a question," Smailov said changing the subject. The cosmonaut had been quiet so far and, unlike usual, had stayed in the background. "If we arrive at the observatory *and* we get lucky and Nasaku is there, what then?"

"We'll talk to her and..." Mila trailed off in frustration.

"Exactly. As far as I know, none of us have learned Sumerian in the last few hours. So, we can't talk to her even if she wanted to."

"She knows English," James said. "She must have learned it pretty quickly or she wouldn't have known Anosha Eikes's code."

"She learned our language in just one day?" Falkenhagen said, incredulous. "No one can do that."

"Well, she must have. After all, not only did she pull the elevator trick out of a hat, but she also snuck off a military base that was sealed off. If we find her on Mount Jelm, that's confirmation that she knows our language. How else would she even be able to figure out where the observatory is?"

"And that's what worries me," Smailov said. "We should be very, very careful. If we confront her, it could become a problem. But we *have* to talk to her. She has already lied to us once and could do it again. I think the major is absolutely right when he says we are naive."

"I know some of you don't want to hear this, but Adrian is right," Meeks said. "We need to be vigilant and not look through rose-colored glasses, pre-determining that she means well and is the poor lost loner with the hard fate. I mean, it all sounds like the most pitiful story you can come up with. A woman stranded alone in hell, children dead, no way back home."

"I had the same conversation with Norton," James grumbled. "When we were at Nasaku's hideout."

"And he's right. We're a team and need to pull together, that's the most important thing right now," Smailov said. "That's why I didn't go against you guys. But I ask you: Pay attention to these facts when the time comes."

"We will," Mila promised.

"We *have* to," Meeks corrected her.

19

WIRO was operated by the University of Wyoming and had been scanning the sky with a two-point-three-meter mirror since the late seventies. The drive took a full two hours, despite it being only eighty miles away. They left the interstate to the south, where the slopes of mighty Mount Jelm rose three thousand feet into the sky. They drove along small, winding country roads surrounded by dense coniferous forests that just added to the darkness. Soon there were only the lone headlights of their car and dense forest rushing past at their edges. James was reminded uncomfortably of one of those *X-Files* episodes in which Mulder and Scully would investigate eerie phenomena in the most remote regions of rural USA—always at night in coniferous forests, of course. Small towns and houses no longer existed here. They spiraled up the increasingly barren slopes of Jelm in seemingly endless twists and turns. There were trees here, but they alternated with open spaces and slopes overgrown with shrubs, all illuminated by the moonlight. When they reached an altitude of about two and a half thousand meters, James could see white patches along the edges of the dirt road, which turned out to be snow.

Soon they rounded the southern flank of the ridge and the road stretched in front of them. The lights of Laramie could be seen to the east, and beyond it the much larger city of Cheyenne. James even thought he could make out the Francis E. Warren Air Force Base. The contrast between the brightly lit plains in the distance and the absolute darkness on and around the mountain created a stab of loneliness in his chest he couldn't quite explain.

"There it is!" Mila exclaimed. She leaned forward between the driver and passenger seats, her index finger extended.

James saw it too, a bright matte dome, its white base protruding like a pimple against the equally white snow of the slope and the dark night sky. The observatory sat to the left of the road, apparently accessible only by a gravel path that traversed the last twenty or thirty feet of elevation to the summit in a long loop. Several cars were parked in a lot in front of it.

"It's open," Meeks said, and sure enough, a large crack in the dome stood open like the maw of a hungry fish. "It must have started already."

"I guess we're about to find out." Mila said as they pulled into the parking lot.

"Don't any of you still think it's funny that Norton would just let us go off on our own to bring Nasaku back?" Falkenhagen asked. Mette snorted, annoyed.

"And now it starts again. Are you scared?"

"I am afraid, yes, and I am not ashamed of it. It just seems very naive of the otherwise cautious major."

"He knows he can trust me," James replied, thinking

back to how he had carried the paraplegic Norton while his own shoulder was a squishy red mass.

"Trust you?"

"Yes." He said no more and the German fortunately had no opportunity to follow up, as Mette and Mila had already opened the doors and were getting out.

He and Meeks did likewise, and they all stood shivering in the cold air pulling on their jackets. James finally led the way and headed for the door, through which a warm light was shining. Three other cars were parked in the small asphalt lot. Two were nondescript, small Asian models parked side by side. The third was a large GMC with tinted windows, the kind he would associate with the FBI or other government agency, that was parked crossways, the driver's door half open, and one turn signal on.

"Someone must have been in a hurry," he muttered and cautiously poked his head through the open door.

The inside of the observatory was what he had expected from the outside. Not a huge facility, a small round, more intimate room that couldn't have accommodated the four cars in the parking lot side by side. The telescope itself was a yellow machine in the center of a gray steel structure on top of which was the parabolic mirror. A small platform below formed the rotating mount and base for the control instruments, but these were apparently not used. Along the circular walls under the gray domed roof, which was open with a large gap, were several cabinets, a server, and two desks. At one of them sat Nasaku, tapping the keys at an insane speed. In front of the other were three bound and gagged figures in colorful down jackets, staring, frightened at the woman who had assaulted them. She was still wearing her gray Air Force training clothes but strangely did not appear cold, although James was already chilled even with his thick clothes.

"Nasaku!" he said, stepping through the doorway and out of the wind that blew across the mountaintop.

The whole situation was surreal. Her head jerked to look at him and the others pushed through the door behind him. He had imagined something else without knowing exactly what. But ascending a mountain to a small observatory, as if on a school trip, and seeing her sitting there as if it were a mundane occurrence had not been part of it.

Her eyes narrowed to slits like a predator targeting its prey. He raised his hands placatingly.

"We are unarmed and mean you no harm." He looked to the right and left, and the others did the same, although Smailov hesitated.

"We have to put all our cards on the table now," Mila whispered, voicing what he had been thinking.

"I understand that you're lonely and want nothing more than to contact your home. I would want the same after all you've been through," he said.

"I thought I had more time," she replied in perfect English so free of accent he felt as if she had slapped him. She turned back to the screen, and her fingers flew even more rapidly over the keys.

"What do you mean?" he inquired cautiously, slowly walking toward her, timidly at first, but more confidently when she remained relaxed. The sound of engines and the roar of distant rotors came from outside.

"They'll be here soon," Smailov called from the door. He didn't sound surprised, and neither was James.

"Nasaku, please. I know you haven't been honest with us, but I refuse to believe that you've just been using us and are up to something evil. I've built my whole career on people skills, and I hope they won't let me down now, when it matters more than ever before."

"Your people skills can't work on me, James Hamilton."

James swallowed before saying his next words. "Because you're not human, are you?"

"That's correct. But it's not what you think."

"Then what is it? I really want to understand."

"I am synthetic. The last of my kind, made by the Atlanteans," Nasaku replied. The engine sounds were so close that the hairs on the back of his neck stood on end.

"Atlanteans? You're a robot?"

"Yes and no; I'm synthetic." She hit Enter and seemed relieved as she pulled a USB drive from the rather aged computer under the desk and walked toward him. His instincts told him to back away, but he didn't. The others also stayed where they were.

"Come on, guys, we've got to buy them some time!" Smailov, of all people, shouted from the doorway, frantically waving the others over. Outside, he could make out the first cones of light from vehicles rushing up.

"Wait." They stopped and Nasaku tossed the USB stick to the Russian. "This will help you."

Smailov caught it and merely nodded before running outside. Mila stayed behind for a second and shouted, "Hurry!"

Nasaku returned to the computer and typed something in. The telescope mirror shifted to face west with it the open section of the observatory dome above them.

"Come with me!" James said impatiently as he realized what she was doing and climbed onto the platform under the mirror. Outside, voices could be heard. The alien followed him with an amazing jump and landed with a crash beside him, making the metal plate tremble under his feet. Before he could recover from the shock, she was already climbing the steel rods of the support structure like a gecko and reaching out a hand to him. James grabbed it without hesitation and was amazed when she effortlessly pulled him up to her.

Together they worked their way to the edge of the open roof. The voices behind them became louder and mixed with harsh shouts and orders that only policemen or soldiers could give.

"We don't have much time," he groaned, but she didn't answer. Instead, she jumped outside, landed on the steel of the dome, and slid out of sight. After a muttered "Shit!" he leapt and did the same. The impact nearly took his breath away, but he was already sliding down the curvature and then he was falling, arms flailing, into a pile of snow so wet and cold it took away the last of his breath. However, it wasn't just the air in his lungs that disappeared, but all sound and the twilight of the starry night. By the time he realized he was completely submerged in a pile of snow, two strong hands grabbed him by the shoulders and yanked him back out. Nasaku wasted no time and ran. A quick glance back showed James an artificial terminator line above the observatory dome and irregular blue light spreading across them like a magical substance.

He knew they were doomed to fail, that they were in the last stretch of a hopeless endeavor, but Nasaku had to know that, too, and that's why he decided to follow the path he had chosen to the end.

So, they ran down the slope, avoiding trees and listening to the rush of adrenaline in his ears, watching their breath form long clouds in front of their mouths. They rounded a small slope and Nasaku huddled under the small ledge that offered some protection and could not be seen from above.

"My time is almost up," she said, breathing heavily. James was still struggling to catch his breath. "In a minute, the police will be here and delaying it won't help the cause."

"What... what cause?"

"Just listen to me. I deceived you so I could gain access to your planet. I had a hunch that you were the youngest, but now I have proof."

"The youngest?" he asked, confused. "I don't understand what you're talking about."

"It doesn't matter. There's no way back for me to do it myself; that's why you have to do it," she said fervently, gripping his shoulders so tight it almost hurt. Her small eyes fixed on his. It was impossible for him to break away from her gaze. "You trust me and that's good, but I need to ask for more. For your world and mine."

"Which one is your world? That horrible planet you were stranded on?"

"I wasn't stranded there. The death zone is my area of operations."

"Death zone? Area of operations?" James's head was spinning. He felt like he was in the middle of a horse race riding a lame donkey.

"The Death Zone was the last protective wall of the Atlanteans who created me, but it has not stopped the First Children of the Elders. It is bordered by a seemingly insurmountable wall," Nasaku explained as the barks of dogs and shouts of men rang out. They sounded harsh in the cold air.

"The wall!" he breathed. "I saw it."

"Good. It was built to stop the First Children, hostile creatures who are driven by fear and seek to destroy anything that frightens them. You have to get past the wall and put the data I extracted there, but you can only do that if you can convince the gatekeeper that you're not one of the First Children!"

"Nasaku, I don't understand." James was almost pleading. The FBI officers were very close. He expected them to come running past the rock and corner them at any second, barking dogs with drool flying from their jaws.

"You'll understand. Listen." She pulled him even closer until their noses were almost touching. He noticed that her breath gave off no scent and her eyes were a deep green. "In the darkness among the stars lurks an ancient danger."

"The First Children of the Elders."

"Yes. They will find you, it's just a matter of time. There is a way to restore the other teleport links, but for that, the Atlanteans need help that only you can give them. Go back to Al'antis and find the Temple of Heaven. There you must deposit what I am about to give you. You will discover everything else when the time comes."

"There's an outcrop up ahead!" shouted someone.

"For what—"

"Shh!"

Nasaku pulled a pistol from her belt and thrust it into his hand. James gasped, suddenly afraid. But she didn't hesitate as she pulled out a knife with the Air Force emblem and jammed it into her sternum and sliced upward with no apparent reaction. Then she stuck her free hand into the wound and pulled out a bloodstained piece of metal that looked like an onyx-colored marble.

"Shit!" He cursed when he saw all the blood running from her chest and hand without her seeming to notice and felt a wave of nausea rise within him. Perplexed and horrified, he looked at the gun in his hand, which she grabbed and held with the barrel pointed at her wound.

"Now you're going to kill me, James Hamilton."

"What? *No!*"

"Yes, you must."

"I hear something!" someone shouted, and a dog barked so loud it could have been next to his ear.

They had only seconds left.

"You need to trust. My job is done." She slipped the marble into his pocket. "Go and help my creators, then my service will be complete. I trusted you; now you must trust me one last time. It is the only way."

I have so many questions, he thought, trying to sort out his racing thoughts and failing miserably.

Fueled by adrenaline, they raced through his cerebral convolutions like a hurricane, chasing question after question, so fast he couldn't grasp them and only caught vague impressions. He saw the wall before him, a distant black structure from his memory, replaced by a wall of concrete hundreds of meters high that his imagination created. Nasaku as a robot, as a clone, as a hologram, as a ghost. Her words repeated endlessly, forward and backward, all at the same time and so fragmented that it made even less sense than it already did.

"There you are!" someone shouted triumphantly. A whistle sounded, then another, and more.

"Now, or all is lost!" Nasaku hissed, drawing the blade of her knife across his right arm.

James pulled the trigger. Whether it was the twitch of his muscles, now cut just above the elbow, the shock of the cut, or the figures in blue jackets with 'FBI' written on them running around the edges of the ledge, he couldn't tell, but he saw Nasaku's chest burst open and a gush of hot blood sprayed his face.

He stared in disbelief at the shattered body of the now-dead woman lying before him and then at the pistol in his trembling hand, a fine curl of smoke rising from the barrel.

"FBI! Drop the gun!"

Blinking, he looked into the glare of a half dozen flashlights pointed directly at him.

Pull yourself together, he told himself. But his heart was beating frantically and an enormous lump in his throat threatened to cut off his air. *You've been in worse situations!*

"I got her!" James shouted, dropping the gun and raising his hands and then intertwining his fingers on top of his head.

"Don't move!"

In the dim light, two figures, no more than moving shadows, knelt beside Nasaku's corpse; others pulled back the dogs that wanted to snap at James.

"Make way!" growled a voice he recognized. Major Norton pushed through the group of federal police officers. "Mr. Hamilton, are you unharmed?"

James was urprised that the concern in the officer's voice sounded genuine.

"She got me, I think, on the arm," he muttered.

"Get a paramedic, damn it!" Norton hissed at one of the FBI agents. "What happened?"

"She tried to take me hostage, but I was able to get to her gun," James lied, looking at his shaking hands which were covered in red blood. "I—I'm sorry, I just didn't know what to do."

It probably helped his credibility that he was completely serious about the last part, and he didn't have to add the tremor in his voice.

"Mr. Hamilton, that's your name?" asked one of the officers who stepped behind him. Only now did he notice that several pistols were pointed at him.

"Yes," he replied lamely. "James Hamilton."

Cold metal wrapped around his left wrist, followed by a metallic *clack*, then his arm was pulled behind his back, and the same was repeated on the other side.

"James Hamilton, you are under arrest for the murder of a person of as yet unknown identity. Anything you say can and will be used against you in a court of law. You have the right to an attorney if you do not have one—"

"You're not to say a word until your lawyer gets here, understand?" Norton said over the FBI agent's legal litany as he roughly dragged James to his feet. His colleagues used plastic bags and rubber gloves to secure the murder weapon. It was getting more crowded all around them, and a helicopter he had not noticed until now hovered overhead with a powerful spotlight. The area under the ledge was illuminated as bright as day, and Nasaku's body was clearly visible. He swallowed hard.

"Mr. Hamilton! Did you get that?" Norton prompted.

He nodded weakly. "Yes. You'll provide the lawyer. Don't call anyone. It won't take long."

20

James sat at a simple metal table, his wrist and ankle cuffs connected by a chain and attached, between his wrists, to a massive ring protruding from the tabletop. There were no windows or furnishings in the room except for the table, two cameras mounted to the ceiling, and two chairs.

The drive from Mount Jelm to the Cheyenne Police Department, where he was taken into custody at the main station while the FBI and state police presumably jockeyed for authority and priority to grill him, was unspectacular.

A man and a woman had led him to the vehicles, three of which were parked haphazardly in the parking lot in front of the observatory. Mila, Mette, Smailow, Falkenhagen, and Meeks stood by their car and gave him pitiful and frightened looks as they were held back by several officers questioning them. He couldn't blame them; he had to look like a butcher.

No one spoke to him during the drive—presumably, the officers had been muzzled. After all, they were dealing with a murderer whom the Air Force had an interest, which was odd enough, and the murdered person had likely been a headache. If a victim's identity could not be determined, alarm bells usually rang at the Department of Homeland Security and the intelligence agencies were called in to investigate terrorist backgrounds.

So, the two-hour drive dragged almost endlessly, and he tormented himself with thoughts of what he had done. Again and again, he went through what he had experienced in the last minutes with Nasaku, pondered her words and began to worry that he remembered some of it wrongly and his memories had deceived him. Feverishly, he repeated some parts over and over, only to be plagued by the impression it was all wrong and not true. How much could one wrong word matter in this case? But most of all, could there have been another solution? Why had Nasaku been so convinced she had no alternate way out, that she couldn't go back? And why had she not shown even a hint of fear or regret before she died?

"Mr. Hamilton," someone said, and he looked up wearily. A middle-aged man in a blue suit and brown tie entered the room, tossed a file on the table, and sat across from him. His hair was fastidiously coiffed, his beard trimmed, his eyes were as blue as the sea and as stern as the teachers he remembered least fondly from his high school. "My name is special agent Dougherty. Good morning."

"Good morning."

"You're not much of a talker, are you?"

James did not answer. Not only were Norton's words still echoing in his head, but he knew enough about how this was likely going to work to stay silent. His last job had brought him into contact with such proceedings more than once. Twice he had even been present for interrogations at CIA black sites.

"All right. You have the right to a lawyer, but it will take a long time, so we'll pass the time a little. You've already got new clothes, and I see you've had a chance to wash. All the victim's blood on your jacket and face must have been unpleasant," the agent continued.

"I'd like a glass of water."

"Ah, he can talk after all. You know what?"

"Yes, you'll bring me one if I offer you something," James guessed. "My thirst isn't that strong."

"I'm not that old-fashioned." Dougherty winked at him as if they were just two buddies chatting.

He seemed to have rehearsed his game a lot and had plenty of experience. He waved and the door opened. A policeman set a bottle of water with a straw in front of him. James leaned over, sucked on it, and emptied half the bottle before leaning back.

"Thank you."

"Gladly. I'm not here to force you to confess or anything like that. You could destroy the case because I talk to you without your lawyer present, and I don't want that. But there's one thing I'm just dying to know: How does someone who shows up on the State Department payroll with the cryptic title of Advisor for Security-Intensive Foreign Intervention end up in Wyoming shooting an unknown woman who doesn't show up in any database?" Dougherty raised a brow and sighed. "It just doesn't add up for me. Then the Air Force tried to hijack it, and the State Department refers all inquiries directly to the White House."

James's expression remained cool and a mask of calm. What had happened in Al'antis, as Nasaku had called her home planet, had been traumatic. Without the excitement and drama that immediately followed, he probably could have been committed to a psychiatric ward to process it all and not lose his mind. Also, the events of the last few hours had created a knot in his stomach that just wouldn't relax. But a situation like this was something in his wheelhouse and, ironically, it helped him to not go crazy, to become calm and collected.

"A man with restraint, I respect that. I even envy that. But when someone kills a woman, I get really angry," Dougherty said, and he could see the anger in the agent's blue eyes. Could he blame him?

"My name is James Hamilton. I did not consent to this interview, and, for the record, I am again requesting legal counsel," he said, pointedly looking into the camera hanging in the right-hand corner behind the FBI agent.

Dougherty grinned mirthlessly and leaned back in his chair.

"That may take some time, Mr. Hamilton. And as I said, I don't want to interrogate you, but it is also within my authority to interrogate you."

"And I have the right to refuse to testify since there is no acute danger to others," James said.

"That's right."

"You know what I think?"

"No, but I'd like to know."

"Well, listen carefully: I think my legal counsel is already on the way, and whoever it is has brought sweat to your brow, and you fear you'll never see me again when the time comes." James shook his head. "Surely, this is an act of desperation, not a tactically reasoned move."

Dougherty was silent long enough to confirm his guess, though he didn't need it. Just as the agent was about to reply, the door opened and two men in Air Force uniforms entered. They were tall, their hair cropped short, and they wore cuffs marked "MP," for military police, around their arms.

"We'll take it from here," one of them said to the special agent, who nodded, pursed his lips, and clicked his tongue.

"Could I see your IDs, please?"

"No, they were already checked at the entrance. This is our suspect," the other soldier said. "Your authority ends here."

The soldier extended a hand while the other rested casually on the holster of his pistol. "The keys, please."

The FBI agent snorted and reached slowly and deliberately into his pocket, pulled out three keys, one of which he offered and was snatched out of his hand.

"You're taking him with you? Just like that?" Dougherty wanted to know.

"Just like that," the soldier confirmed as he freed James from the shackles, leaving red welts on his wrists.

Slowly, James rubbed them as if it would help with the pain. The other MP pulled a letter from the breast pocket of his uniform and handed it to the special agent, who opened it and skimmed it.

"This bears the seal of the secretary of state's office. You've got to be kidding me."

"No, we're not, sir. Please remove yourself from this room."

Dougherty's jaw muscles began to tense visibly, but he finally straightened his tie, glared at the two MPs, and then walked past them without a word.

"Please follow us, Mr. Hamilton," an MP said to James as his leg irons fell to the floor and he was finally free.

Walking between the two uniformed men, he felt like a lanky teenager being escorted by his big brothers after being called before the principal. Throughout the corridors of the police station, they were met with puzzled looks, officers peered through the doors, and it was dead silent except for the many ringing phones.

They stopped at a small counter between two uncomfortable-looking wooden benches. A bulky officer in a dark blue uniform asked his name and then placed a small plastic tray containing his belongings at the time of his arrest on the counter, the two sides of which were divided by a metal grille.

"A pack of handkerchiefs, Dixie brand, a pair of underwear, Levi jeans, a pair of cotton socks, a lined United States Air Force jacket," the policeman droned, placing each item, one by one, next to the tray until he took out the last item. The dark marble Nasaku had slipped him. "And a marble."

"A personal memento of my ex-fiancée," James explained, shrugging. The officer merely raised an eyebrow before packing everything back into the plastic box and having him sign that all his belongings had been returned to him.

Outside the columned rotunda, a black GMC SUV with tinted windows waited between two military police Humvees with the Air Force eagle on the doors.

He was taken to the SUV and he got into the back, where Jeena Pavar was waiting for him. The dean was dressed in a tight blue pantsuit and had a large stack of files on her lap, which she pointedly worked on without looking up as he sat next to her.

The leather creaked slightly, an unpleasant sound. He saw the major sitting next to the driver, nodding at him but he looked serious. After a second glance, James saw out of the corner of his eye that Norton was making a small gesture he had almost missed: he clenched his left fist very briefly.

What does that mean? That she's mad? Or that he's mad? Or that I should be tough when the starts?

The small convoy started to move.

"You're free," Pavar stated after a few minutes, during which James had joined the silence and said nothing. She placed the last file next to her. A small pile had formed between them, then fixed him with her bird-of-prey gaze.

"Yes. Thank you."

"You now have until we arrive at the base to convince me not to let you disappear into a CIA hole that you will never crawl out of." Her voice was extremely calm and collected, something he understood. "It's a very short drive."

"Go ahead and do it. I understand," he responded, though he would have preferred to babble like a waterfall. Nasaku had put her trust in him, and the urgency of her words had only been surpassed by her ultimate sacrifice. He had to honor that sacrifice, and to keep from losing his mind knowing he had murdered the first alien they had contacted. "But I had to choose between my good and the good of my fellow man."

Pavar frowned. Good. He had reacted differently than she expected, and her being thrown off her game was already helping. It was like he had driven a spike through her thick skin. Now he had to inject the poison before she pulled it out.

"Explain," she prompted.

"Nasaku tried to escape and had—"

"Taken you hostage. You've already explained that to the officers on the ground." Pavar waved it off. "I'm not buying it. This woman was crafty enough to escape a high-security facility, and God knows how. No offense, but she certainly wasn't tied up in a knot by you."

"Right. I wasn't done yet. She wanted me to shoot her

and make it look like we had fought. That's why she cut my arm." He raised his right arm, which was in a sling and stitched and bandaged above the elbow.

Now he had really thrown her off her game. She blinked, surprised. It was so brief that he had to give her credit, but it did not escape him.

"My guess is that she wanted to be returned to the base. Most certainly she expected they wouldn't just hand her over to the authorities, but would instead lock her up underground or, at best, send her back through the teleporter," he continued, shaking his head and snorting. "But that meant whatever she had done was complete and she wanted to go back now. It would be to our detriment, I was sure. She had been a danger and I didn't want to see her win."

"A late insight."

Now it's time to go all out, he thought. "When Major Norton visited us in the science leadership's work area, I knew that I—we—had been given another chance to save this project. If Nasaku had disappeared... that would have been a disaster. An alien with unknown abilities who had led us around by the nose. I figured *you* had sent Norton to us. He wouldn't betray you, much less his oath as an officer, but I took the hint and knew we were in the unique position of not being scary to Nasaku, we would look weak in her eyes and not cause her to flee right away. She would use us or kill us effortlessly, of that, I had no doubt."

Pavar's expression remained unmoved. So, he knew he had hit the mark.

"It made sense to me, in the end, to take advantage of being underestimated and take her out the moment the opportunity presented itself."

"You killed a valuable prisoner."

"I neutralized a threat to protect the project. It certainly wasn't the only one of its kind," he lied. "The most important thing, in my mind, was to preserve the integrity of our project and our deployment."

So you keep your post, he translated inwardly, knowing full well that she would easily understand his insinuations.

"Who knows what else she would have done?" he added.

"Now we've lost our only source who knows more about the teleporter and a possible teleporter network," Pavar replied darkly. "A source that knew our language and was therefore much more valuable than we thought. Now we have nothing."

"I imagine the White House was already breathing down your neck about a possible danger to the public. That my firing was forced by the State Department and not the president's office tells me I didn't underestimate your wisdom."

"I can't stand flattery."

James shrugged. "Just an observation. They didn't pass it all the way to the top but waited to see if the problem could be resolved before the president pulled the rip cord."

The dean remained silent and examined him with narrowed eyes.

"Besides, we are not empty-handed. We were able to convince her that we were helping her. She left us a USB drive that should contain stolen observatory data. Smailov has it and will hand over the data to you."

Now Pavar seemed surprised, and some of the grimace around her eyes dissipated—a barely noticeable change, but enough for James to feel a little hopeful.

"Take care of it," she ordered Norton, who nodded mutely. To James, she said, "We'll see what we can find on that flash drive."

If it's useful and your story checks out, this could turn out well for you, he translated to himself.

"The most important thing is that the project continues, that we don't have discord among the participating nations, and that our leadership is not constantly being replaced. I may not have always agreed with what you decided, but no leader will make everyone happy all the time. That's not their job. They have to hold it all together and make sure it moves forward, which is the top priority. This teleporter is a once-in-a-lifetime opportunity that we can't give away lightly," he said in a sort of closing argument that seemed a bit heavy handed to him but considering he had just been freed from prison for murdering someone, it was like an admission that he had had no choice and he felt had done the right thing. "Nasaku was too much of a risk to all that."

Pavar looked thoughtful as they arrived at the main gate of Francis E. Warren Air Force Base, showed their IDs, and were admitted. They made the trip to the main building, the former mock frontage that now served as the entrance to the missile silo and the dean's office, without their escort of MP vehicles.

"What happens now?" he asked.

"You and the leadership team stay in your work area and compile all the information in the central database. I want to create a comprehensive compendium on the teleporter, which will include with everything we've been able to gather so far."

So, she being pressured by the secretary of state. He's in on it and wants something in return for his favor today, James thought. *Information is power, and power is everything in Washington.*

"In the meantime, I'm going to check out what's going on with that drive you were talking about."

She wants to wait and see if my story is nailed down.

"I understand," he said.

Pavar turned to Norton as they got out the vehicle and walked through the cold dawn toward the entrance, in front of which now stood a half dozen soldiers in combat fatigues. "Major, I want you to be part of this."

"Shouldn't I—"

"No, you were on the other side too, and every detail could be important. Besides, I want your signature at the end under the reports, if you know what I'm saying."

"Of course." The officer nodded to the soldiers, who saluted at his arrival and held the doors open.

21

J ames went straight to the management team's work area. Four soldiers stood guard—an unmistakable sign that a significantly different wind was blowing through the concrete corridors of the silo and that Pavar was concerned for her own neck. He was met by a wave of rejection. Smailov gave him a look that would have sent him running under other circumstances, and Meeks and Falkenhagen scowled. Even Mila looked glum.

"You *killed* her?" the cosmonaut asked in a quavering voice. "When I said to be careful, I didn't mean to *murder* her!"

"What the hell has gotten into you, man?" Meeks added, snorting contemptuously. "And then you tell Pavar that Adrian's USB drive came from Nasaku? Do you care so much about your own damn skin that you can't even show a hint of backbone?"

"That you even dare to come back here at all," Falkenhagen added, his German accent sounding sharper than usual. "We believed you—despite our reservations—and started to trust Nasaku on *your* initiative. And this is how you repay us? By stabbing us in the back to get your own head out of the noose?"

"Are you done?" James looked around, waiting, enduring the mixture of reluctance and frustration that stood like a wall between him and the team. "This room isn't under video surveillance, is it?"

Meeks frowned. "What?"

"After each teleporter event the cameras have to be replaced because the magnetic field destroys them. The last few times, the work areas were the last to be refitted, after the cave and hallways. Have the technicians been here yet?"

"No," Mila said. "Why?"

"I lied to Pavar."

Now he had their undivided attention. Mette, who seemed a little less hunched than usual, looked at him, her mouth twitching. The rest just seemed confused.

"Nasaku asked me to shoot her."

"She *asked* you?" Smailov said incredulously.

"Yes. And I'll tell you exactly what she told me. She said that the Atlanteans created her and that she was the last of her kind. The wall I saw last time does exist. She called the area in it the 'death zone' and where I found her, her 'area of operations.' I believe she lived there to protect her people, or rather her creators."

Falkenhagen raised an eyebrow. "The *Atlanteans*."

"Yes. She also spoke of a gatekeeper and that only those who are not among the First Children can cross the wall. By this, she obviously meant the enemies of the Atlanteans."

"The enemies? So, someone did this to their planet?" Mila asked.

"You don't believe him, do you?" Smailov roared.

"I'm listening to him," she returned coolly. "Which is what we should all be doing."

"We've done this before, and—"

"And what's the downside of just keeping your mouth shut?"

Her Russian colleague glared at her but remained silent, crossing his strong arms in front of his chest.

"I think so. She also spoke of 'elders' and said that we were the youngest. Or the last?" James rubbed his aching temples. "It... it all happened very quickly. She wanted us to go back because she couldn't. She wants us to go over the wall and deposit something that she gave me in the 'temple of heaven.'" He pulled the marble from his pocket and held it between his thumb and forefinger for all to see. Then he placed it in the center of the table. All eyes rested on it as if transfixed. "She said that we can restore the teleporter connections; there is a way. I know this is all very confusing, I feel the same way, but that's what she said."

"If you hadn't murdered her, we could have asked *her*," Smailov growled.

"Hey!" James shouted angrily, glaring hard at the Russian. "It wasn't you who had to go through this shit! You know I was on her side. It was *my* idea to trust her, and I thank all of you—especially you and Meeks—for relenting despite your misgivings. But why would I want to kill her? I'm not a murderer, and I certainly didn't want to do what I did, but *she* wanted it. I could see that she saw no other way out, and I understand it. What would have happened to her? She would have been trapped in the ten square meters of her prison down here and would have been questioned every day. And who knows what experiments would have been done on her? So, she served us a story on a silver platter with which we could use Norton's ruse of enlisting us in his search and secretly following us to keep Pavar's and his confidence. She got Pavar's head out of the noose with her death and probably saved the whole project. We should not destroy her sacrifice now by our misguided frustration!"

Smailov's mouth twitched and his jaw muscles stood out. James could see he was struggling for -control, but finally, the cosmonaut in him seemed to gain the upper hand and he took a deep breath before gesturing with something like a nod.

"Atlanteans," Mette said as if to break the tension. "That's interesting. She really spoke of her *creators* as Atlanteans?"

"Yes. Strange, isn't it? She couldn't possibly have meant Atlantis?" Smailov asked.

"She called it Al'antis," James said.

Mette rubbed her chin and glanced around.

James went to the only empty chair, waited a moment, and was relieved when no one dismissed him. Finally, he sat and breathed an inward sigh of relief.

"I am not a historian and certainly not a mythologist, but Al'antis sounds more Arabic than ancient Greek," the Dane continued.

"Atlas was a Greek Titan," Falkenhagen said. "He was a tragic figure doomed to carry the heavens on his shoulders for all eternity. I learned ancient Greek in school."

"Maybe they call themselves Al'anter rather than Atlanteans, and Nasaku merely said Atlanteans so we'd draw the connection," Mila suggested. "Atlantis is a supposed extinct advanced civilization that fought ancient Athens, long before Jesus was born. An allegory that today is more likely to be Plato's invention, meant to highlight the glory of the ideal Athens he would have liked to see. If myths always held a kernel of truth, it could be that the teleporter was already active three thousand years ago or more and that there was contact between Al'antis and Earth.

According to the myths, Atlantis was destroyed and sank into the sea. The teleporter was under the ocean floor in Venezuela."

"A false connection possibly," Meeks objected. "Besides, it must have taken the teleporter hundreds of thousands of years to get that deep underground. The tectonic movements required to achieve that feat would take extremely long periods of time."

"Yes, I know, but it also offers a parallel. Prime was apparently destroyed as well, and the fact that Nasaku mastered Sumerian is an indication that they or their civilization have been to Earth before—and a very long time ago."

"Or very recently because she also knew English."

"I think she learned it here," James said.

"In such a short time?" Meeks shook his head.

"Well, she also knew how to drive, use computers, and deceive us. But since the teleporter was demonstrably buried long enough to not allow contact with us, there must be a much simpler explanation. She's extremely intelligent. Perhaps a robot. She said she was 'synthetic.'"

"Mhm," the engineer intoned, scratching the back of his head.

"Back to Atlantis," Falkenhagen said. "Perhaps there was indeed contact, although I can't explain it based on the location of the teleporter. Then the question is why ancient Greece would make Atlantis out of Al'antis even before its writing was invented. After all, Atlantis must have been a legend even in Plato's time. Sure, it sounds very similar, so it could be mere falsification by oral reproduction. Or else something was made that fitted the world view of that time."

"Perhaps the Al'anter of Prime were seen as tragic beings who had to bear a heavy burden like Atlas, and so the name was adjusted accordingly," Mila suggested. "Everything James and Norton have told us points to a tragic fate, and the end of Atlantis has been handed down. Could it be that it was destroyed for so long and our ancestors knew it?"

"The only way we're going to find out is to go to Al'antis ourselves and do what Nasaku asked us to do." James put all his determination he into his expression as the others stared at him.

"We're all supposed to go?" Falkenhagen asked, sounding uncomfortable with the idea.

"Yes. We should at least suggest it to Pavar."

"I would have thought you would never want to go there again." Mila said, eyeing him.

"That's right. And this time soldiers should come with us, as many as possible. I think we'll need them if we want to reach this Temple Of Heaven."

"Even if she let us all go there, we'd still have to get over that wall you told us about, and then what?" Falkenhagen said.

"Then that will help us." He pointed to the marble in the center of the table. "Dr. Smailov, you said it yourself during the trip to the observatory: We decided to take a path. Finding out whether it was the right one can only be done if we follow it consistently to the end and don't veer away. Has anything changed in that regard?"

The cosmonaut was silent a moment, but then shook his head. "No."

"Then we should stick to it. With a well-planned expedition, we can make it, I'm sure of it."

The conversation went on for many hours. Arguments for and against a large group being sent through the teleporter went back and forth. First, there was the danger of insufficient biomass stored on the other side, and the first through would have to make sure to get enough of it, which wouldn't be easy. After all, only so much compacted organic material existed in the form of the monster, and James felt nauseated at the mere thought of it.

Next, there was the concern that the military might take control of the mission and make stupid, short-sighted decisions. Falkenhagen pointed to the apparently toxic environment, recalling James's abscess, which had appeared the second time around in Norton, and therefore probably pointed to environmental influences and not individual genetics.

In the end, however, they were sure action had to be taken, at to least follow up on Nasaku's statements, even though several around the table still found it hard to believe what she had said. James couldn't blame them, it seemed absurd to him, too, but it had been the same with the teleporter. If he hadn't seen and used it, he would have dismissed Norton's stories on the flight from Kenya to the US as the fantasies of a madman.

The conversation ended only when the door was unlocked and Norton entered. James quickly dropped the marble in his pocket before turning to the major, who motioned to the guards outside to let him enter alone. Only when the door was locked again did he join them at the table. His face was as hard as stone.

"What happened?" James asked. Something had happened and it was clear from the officer's posture that was not a trifle.

"We have a problem."

"Another one?" Meeks asked laconically.

"A definitive problem. NASA analyzed the data Nasaku downloaded from WIRO," Norton said. "It was a fifteen-minute image of a star system 34 light-years from Earth that we didn't know about. Before you ask, yes, obviously we don't know as much about the universe as we think.

"The problem is that this is a system with a sunlike central star and seven planets, one of which appears to have the same mass as Earth and may be in the habitable zone. Orbiting this planet and two others are large structures that are causing headaches for the eggheads in Houston. That's only the second-worst news, though."

"And how is that a problem?" Mila asked.

"It would be a sensation to say the least, but the problem is that Nasaku sent a signal just seconds before arrived on Mount Jelm. We're trying to decode that right now. The NSA's best cryptographers are currently on it, but it could take months, maybe years or decades."

"She sent a message to a possibly inhabited system? That's..." James swallowed, unsure if the pounding of his heart was due to fear or amazement.

"That's a risk. At best, it says 'hello, we're here'—and that's dangerous enough. We don't know anything about the targeting of this message, so we don't know what danger we'll face from detection."

James said, "What if it's Al'a"—Falkenhagen's eyes grew wide—"uh, Prime? That would be the best-case scenario, wouldn't it?"

Norton didn't seem to notice his near mistake or at least he didn't let on.

"We think that's impossible. Why would she come here to send a message back to the place she was determined to escape, for a signal that won't get there for another thirty-four years?"

An ancient danger lurks in the darkness between the stars. Nasaku's warning went through his mind as a wild discussion broke out around him. Could she have meant *this* darkness between the stars? A place that the space agencies hadn't yet discovered, not near their solar system, but relatively close in cosmic terms. But why would she send a message there of all places and thus betray the Earth?

"They've known about us for a long time," he said aloud, and the conversation around the table fell silent. "Our radio signals should be there by now. We've been sending radio signals into space for well over eighty years—albeit unintentionally." He froze. "Major, you just said there was worse news."

"Yes." Norton took a deep breath. "The telescope images —infrared images from WIRO—show other objects, and they're not in the system christened LP-3445. At first, it was thought they were pixel errors in the data analysis. But comparison images have already been taken, and the James Webb telescope has already been realigned to check them optically. No errors. We are talking about a total of six hundred smaller objects—possibly more. The NASA people have said that they are only the ones between us and the central star of LP-3445; anything outside that range would not be visible to us because it doesn't account for any brightness shifts."

"Smaller objects," Smailov said. "You mean spaceships?"

"We don't know, but the possibility exists, yes. The president has ordered this as NASA's top priority to try to find out if they are approaching Earth."

In the darkness between stars lurks an ancient danger.

Somber silence filled the room like a viscous, invisible mass was making it difficult to breathe.

"Until then, all teleport activity is suspended. Pavar just issued the order; it came directly from the president."

"What?" Meeks gasped, and even the usually controlled Smailov blinked in surprise.

"We can't do that, Nasaku has—" James swallowed.

"What?" Norton asked, glaring at him. "What's wrong with her?"

"I—we have to go back, Major!"

"Oh yeah, why?"

When James said nothing, his gaze became even more intense. James wouldn't have been surprised if lasers suddenly shot out of them and burned him to a pile of cinders.

"Suddenly not so talkative? That's what I thought! Pack all your things. They've already begun clearing the plant and tonight the cave will be filled with concrete."

"*WHAT?*" they all shouted simultaneously.

"You can't!"

"Who allowed this?"

"Have they gone crazy?"

"You can't do that at all!" Mila's angry voice stuck out of the confusion. "Our government will never agree to this! This is not an American project!"

"*Your government* already knows. Russia, China, and the EU have already been briefed on NASA's data and are one hundred percent involved. This is a potential global problem and the president has ordered full transparency," Norton hissed, unusually charged with emotion. Something was wrong, was different, but James didn't know what it was. "The teleporter is shut down until further notice."

"But it's our only link to *out there*!" Mette gestured toward the sky, which was made of unplastered gray concrete matching the tense mood.

"This is exactly why the presidents of our countries have decided to pull the plug until we know more. One less risk is one less problem at this point, and I agree with the politicians for once."

"This was Pavar's idea, wasn't it? She recommended it," James growled.

"Yes. Based on the information she has, it was the right decision," Norton said, very coolly. Again, he appraised him with that piercing gaze, holding something back with difficulty. "This is not a discussion. Pack your things and be at the elevator in thirty minutes. I will remind you that you are not to steal any documents or items from this facility. Only your personal belongings from your quarters. Everything else will be taken care of by the Air Force."

"It can't be over," James whispered. The others also looked dismayed.

"What was that?"

"Nothing."

"All right, let's go! That's an order! The ramp to the teleporter is about to come down and be evacuated through the freight elevator."

Norton turned on his heel and stomped out. While the door was ajar, James glimpsed one of the soldiers still standing guard there. He looked rattled. *I wonder if he was listening to the tirade.*

It was dead silent except for the creak of one of the aluminum chairs.

"The ramp," Mila finally said, just as Falkenhagen was about to stand up, shoulders drooping. "We have to do it *now*."

"Do what?" the German asked.

"You know very well *what*."

22

"If we do that there's no way back; you realize that don't you?" Falkenhagen asked, his face pale. He had jumped up when the others at the table had stood, holding both hands before him as if he could magically stop them.

"I do," Mila replied already on her way to the door.

"Norton said they're going to concrete over the whole cave! If that monster James told us about comes, then—"

"Then there's no escape." Smailov, who was standing at at Mila's side, pressed an ear to the cold plastic door and listened.

"Justus, we don't have time, and we have to decide now. Either we leave and forget that there was ever a possibility of discovering alien worlds and what Nasaku and those tele-porters were all about, or we leave *this* behind," Meeks said forcefully, pointing to the raw concrete surrounding them. "I'm afraid of that, but I'd be even more afraid of sitting in a rocking chair on my porch twenty years from now thinking I could have found something big, a new truth about the cosmos. That's what we became scientists for, after all."

"I promised her," James said more to himself. "But it's

easy for me to say that because there's nothing keeping me here except my fear of the most horrible place I've ever been."

"Think about our bodies! If we really use the teleporter, they—*we*—will be left behind, and then we have to hope they get us to the hospital in time and put us in a coma. What if we can't get back for ten years and they've turned off the devices?"

"I don't think we're coming back," James said.

"But..." The astrophysicist blinked as if he had something in his eye and staggered back. "But..."

"Make up your mind, Justus!" Meeks urged. He was was quite pale but had jutted his chin out.

"How are we even going to do this? I mean, we're not just going to walk into the cave and get started."

Smailov replied, "I'll check outside and see if there are still four guards. We'll go out and through the airlock if there are. We'll say that we have to get equipment from inside the teleporter. If there are fewer, I'll draw them in here and we'll overwhelm them. I'm sure we can do more if we have two uniforms."

"But the major has forbidden us to bring equipment. We're only supposed to pack personal things," Falkenhagen said.

"I doubt his men know that, especially since there is sure to be a flurry of activity."

"We'll soon see," Mila said, nodding to her compatriot.

"When I lure them in, you'll have to overpower them quickly and turn off their radios if they have any. Everyone ready?"

Falkenhagen shook his head and swallowed. "No, but do it."

The cosmonaut nodded and waited until the group had positioned themselves then he pointed at Mette.

"Lie down on the floor in front of the table."

The Dane followed his instructions without hesitation and pretended to be unconscious. Only then did Smailov push down the handle and walk out. James saw only the strange white gray door and heard muffled voices.

"Emergency... immediately..."

It was only one soldier who came in and ran to Mette, not two or even four. After a moment where no one stirred, they simultaneously lunged at the tall man in combat fatigues and they went down in a tangle of arms and legs. James crashed painfully onto his side but got ahold of the radio and snatched it from the Velcro shoulder strap holding it in place. The others wrestled behind him, and he crawled a meter away from the commotion. Unable to find the correct button with his fingers trembling with adrenaline, he finally threw it as hard as he could against the wall.

"The other one ran off to get medics," Smailov called out as the others tied and gagged the soldier. "We'll just run to the airlock and hurry. Hopefully, by the time they return, we'll have a few minutes' head start."

"Let's go then!" James shooed the others out, rushing after the Russian into the large corridor where they turned left, and the airlock waited some distance away.

Dozens of footsteps echoed under the curved ceiling, their echoes lost among the many plastic pipes and conduits under which men and women were running with boxes and rolling containers toward the elevators. At the end stood a sergeant yelling orders, obviously busy trying to bring order to the chaos. James had not known so many people were on duty down here. And now everyone was on emergency status, and James felt as if he had been thrown into a Cold War nightmare, when this place had been under the constant threat of a nuclear war. When soldiers were trained to receive orders from the Pentagon at any moment for a first strike or a retaliatory strike, to send out the nuclear arsenal and in effect, destroy the earth.

"Get in there, get in there, get in there!" Smailov hissed. When they reached the airlock he pulled it open. He ushered them in one by one when a shout echoed over the din in the hallway.

"Hey! No one else is allowed in there!"

James didn't need to look to know it was the NCO. He quickly slipped past Smailov and exhaled with relief as the cosmonaut immediately followed him, locking the airlock and pointing to the suspended protective suits.

"Everybody get them on!"

"But we don't have time!" Meeks objected.

"It's all about the disguise. We won't be recognized, and if there's any tidying up to do in there, they'll all look like that, and at least we won't be noticed right away!" Mette said, pulling a suit off the rack. The six of them practically filled every square inch of the tiny room, and it was difficult to even get their feet through the legs. Then, before he got around to zipping up the suit, loud thumping could be heard at the door.

"Open up!" said a muffled voice bellowing through the thick polymer door. For a breathless moment, the group froze, then quickly resumed even more frenzied.

"I'm triggering the disinfection," Mila said.

"But we can't breathe that stuff, it—" Falkenhagen started to object.

"Because it's unhealthy?" she asked, snorting as her fist crashed down on the red button. James held his breath and put on his helmet and hood before he had his upper body in the white plastic cover. Mila and Meeks had already put their hands on the locking wheel, no longer struggling with their boots, so James let them go, too, after finding no way to bend down past Smailow's back and Mette's waist to slip them on.

The hissing died away and the dense fog subsided. Ahead of them, he saw a brighter area. The two scientists in front of him started running, and he suddenly had room. He followed them with his head down. Like a volatile liquid, they burst into the cave, where, to everyone's surprise, there was no one. It was empty except for the ramp still leading to the teleporter, jet black and dull between the four columns, an eerie constant covered with a thin layer of frozen water crystals. A few overturned rolling aluminum containers and tables lay to either side, surrounded by sheets of paper and abandoned files.

James had expected another mess, personnel frantically moving the last remnants of equipment out of the cavern and opening the hatches that covered the chamber from the intercontinental ballistic missile tubes above. Soon hundreds of tons of liquid concrete would flow downward, suffocating everything like a bad memory. It was hard to imagine and yet would soon be a reality, for he did not believe Pavar was someone whose mind could be changed too quickly. And if the president had already made his decision, there was no turning back anyway.

"Come on, to the ramp!" Smailov urged them to hurry up and shooed them like a bunch of headless chickens before him to the white frame made of hardened plastic polymers.

"*Halt!*" barked a harsh voice just as they reached the bottom of the ramp. Time stopped as they froze. Mila was at the very front, one foot already on the ramp. James nearly collided with her. A handful of soldiers came running out of the airlock on the other side, dressed in spotless camouflage uniforms, helmets, and armored vests. They fanned out and pointed their pistols at them.

"We don't want to cause any trouble," the cosmonaut said, but his rolling Russian accent probably didn't make it any better for the infantrymen.

"We just want to get into the teleporter," Meeks said. "Look, fellas, we're not going to cause any trouble or hurt anybody. We're just going to go up there and get out of here, all right?"

"Negative!" yelled one soldier, a compact Latino with a stern look on his face. "Step back from the ramp and lace your hands behind your head. This area is off-limits to all personnel."

"We don't have time," Mila cursed and stepped forward.

"Last and only warning!" the soldier shouted, and James saw his pistol swing toward the Russian woman. Instinctively, he stepped beside her, so he was in the line of fire instead of her. He raised his arms and stared at the gunmen.

"James!" she whispered. "Don't!"

"I'm exactly where I want to be," he replied in a firm voice.

"We have no choice," Meeks said. "I hope you don't feel the need to shoot unarmed civilians because we have to go into that teleporter."

"I said, last warning. One more step and we open fire. Everyone step back and clasp your hands behind your head. *Now!*"

One of the soldiers grabbed the radio on his chest with one hand and began speaking into it.

"Damn it!" Meeks cursed.

"There is only one way," Smailov said, his face grim.

"No!" James yelled, but it was already too late. He sensed Mila's movements before he saw her like a shadow out of the corner of his eye. She sprinted up the ramp, amazingly fast and nimble. Tense and paralyzed, he watched her go, his heart leaping as the brilliant light of the passageway appeared, spilling its golden glow into the huge concrete cavern.

The first shot rang out. Then another.

Horrified, James watched as Mila ducked her head, only two steps from the light. He started to breathe a sigh of relief when she apparently managed to dodge the shot, but then red blood exploded from her left shoulder and she was thrown to the side. He was afraid she would fall off the ramp, but she barely caught herself on the railing, and was hit in the thigh. Her pain-filled screams hit him in the gut. He wanted to go to her, but someone was holding him back.

"Don't!"

It tore at his heart to see the Russian woman trying to pull herself forward. The blood seemed to glow on her white suit—so much blood.

Groaning, she scrambled on. More shots thundered through the cavern, echoing off the walls. Each one made him wince violently and struggle harder against whoever was holding him back with fingers like steel cables.

Mila crawled through the light, but not before she was hit in the lower leg. Then her foot was gone. Silence fell. The smell of gunpowder hung in the air.

"*You damn pigs!*" James shouted at the soldiers, who now pointed their pistols at him and his companions again.

"We have a Code 101," one of the men said into his radio, and again the airlock opened. More uniforms came running in, raising pistols and assault rifles, aiming at them.

"On the floor! Go!"

They were going to storm the teleporter. It was over.

"Don't!" boomed a new voice. Major Norton stepped through the other airlock, the one which James and the team had also comet through, without protective clothing.

"Lower your weapons; that's an order!" he barked at his men.

"Sir, we have orders directly from the dean not to let anyone near the teleporter," replied a tall soldier, his cheek pressed against the butt of his assault rifle. It was aimed at James—at least he thought he was.

"We don't shoot fucking civilians here. Do you understand that?"

James suddenly felt a tingle on his tongue and blinked in confusion.

"Mila!" he gasped. *She's alive!*

The magnetic field suddenly gained strength. Dozens of weapons were snatched from the hands of the soldiers and hurtled toward the teleporter, hitting the hull with dull thuds and sticking there. Some of the men cried out, writhing over broken index fingers, others had held on so tightly they had been pulled forward for a bit.

"Now!" Smailov shouted, but James already on his way, running as fast as he could up the ramp and jumping through the passage.

Mila was lying on the seat that led to Prime, Al'antis. She was covered with blood and did not move, a white figure covered with red flowers. He rushed to her and touched her face. It was cold and her eyes were closed. Two fingers on her neck told him she no longer had a pulse.

"Please, make it," he pleaded, wiping the tears from his cheeks with the back of his hand. Sniffling, he pulled her from the seat with help from Meeks, who suddenly appeared beside him. It seemed sacrilegious to him to handle her body so roughly, but it was now merely a ruined fleshy shell. He considered dragging her into the hopper, but he would not have had the heart to do so. Instead, they placed her on one of the other chairs. Meeks shoved him into the Prime seat and ripped the hood and helmet off his head while he pulled up his sleeves so he could rest his forearms on the induction strip.

"You next," the engineer said. His eyes were red, and his voice trembled slightly. He presented a horrifying sight, that of a man who had just seen something he should never have seen, which hit James especially hard because Meeks, with his size and bearishness, normally radiated a fatherly quality, now lost, at least for the moment.

Mette and Falkenhagen arrived, running to them sweating and with widened eyes. Smailov was the last, breathing heavily. He wheeled around when Norton appeared behind him. The Russian punched him in the stomach with his fist, and the major doubled over, gasping for air. James thought he would fall or attack Smailov, but instead, he merely raised an arm and pointed through the light behind him.

"The... ramp..." he groaned. "Knock... it... over!"

The cosmonaut seemed to consider briefly whether to give Norton the rest, but he finally knelt on the floor, and half of his torso disappeared into the light barrier before returning. James thought he heard screams and a distant *clang*.

The major, meanwhile, pulled himself up enough to sit against the teleporter's honeycomb wall, drawing rattling breaths into his lungs.

"That should buy you enough time," he moaned.

"Your people shot Mila!" Smailov growled, beside

himself with anger. "I swear to you, if she didn't make it over, then—"

"I tried to stop them."

"You put us in this position in the first place!"

"What was I supposed to do? This project is under civilian control in the form of Ms. Pavar. I didn't give those instructions. I can only help you get through before everything is cemented in," the major replied.

"They used us to find Nasaku," James said with a bitterness that surprised himself.

"I used all of you to *protect* Nasaku. Would you have preferred the FBI had discovered her first? I don't know what she told you, but I hope it was all worth it."

A thought flashed through James's mind. He released his right arm from the induction strip, unzipped his protective suit, and reached into his pants pocket. He breathed a sigh of relief as he held the dark marble between his fingers.

"This must be the only way," he grumbled, taking it into his mouth and swallowing it.

"Hurry up, man! I'm trying to buy you some time, and I hope I can make sure that sense comes to Washington regarding this project," Norton said, holding his stomach with both hands. "But it would be better if you're prepared to be on your own and without back-up. It could take months, years at worst once a new administration is sworn in, for anything to change. Considering there may be an alien fleet headed for Earth, they could also bury the teleporter completely. You should know that."

"We all know that," Meeks said, and not even Falkenhagen protested.

"Let's go!"

"Our bodies—" Mette started.

"I'll do what I can," Norton assured her, waving at them impatiently.

James didn't need to be told twice and put his right arm back on the strip.

Please, Mila, let me see you when I get to the other side, he thought. He became anxious thinking about opening his eyes and waking up alone in the teleporter room on Prime. But there was no way back, and the only way to find out was to close his eyes now. He looked at Meeks.

"Hurry up, no false cautiousness with my body." He swallowed. "It's just a clone anyway."

He waited for the nod from the engineer and then lowered his eyelids and exhaled one last time.

23

James opened his eyes slowly and carefully. They felt a little heavier than he was used to waking up on Prime, but he pushed himself, and tore them open halfway, and saw a naked Mila standing in front of him. Her blond hair fell in waves to her shoulders and half covered her shapely breasts. Her body was amazingly toned and—his cheeks were getting hot, so he blinked a few times, looked her in the face, and jumped out of his seat to hug her. He didn't care that he was naked himself and felt a twinge of fear she might feel his pleasure in more ways than one.

"You did it," he said, blowing her hair out of his mouth. She returned the hug.

"Yeah, I wasn't sure, it was..." She swallowed. He felt her against his shoulder before they broke away from each other. "I thought I was dead, James. I must have passed out on the seat in our teleporter, but just made it."

"The main thing is that it worked." He gave her another squeeze, just in case, to make sure she was real and he wasn't imagining it. "That was really a heroic thing you did!"

"I did what was necessary."

"Don't ever do that again, all right?" He gave her a serious look, and she gave a strained laugh.

"I guess I can't, James, but thank you for caring, I..." She faltered and cleared her throat before pointing to a body. He hadn't even noticed it in the excitement.

The corpse was *him*, covered in abscesses and white fuzz that looked like fungal lichen had settled over his mouth and nose like spider webs. The remains of his last clone made him blanch. His right arm missing, his body was covered with blood, and lying in a huge pool of it. The oozing skin was a pale lime, and on his shoulders and neck were deep scrapes and welts impressed into the flesh where he had wrapped Norton's arms around him to climb the ladder.

"Oh, James," Mila whispered, squeezing his hand. "I can only imagine what you've been through. This is... this..."

"It's all right," he said. "It was just a body, after all."

She seemed to notice that he was pulling himself together and looked pained.

"Where's Norton's clone?"

"I dragged it into the hopper before I followed him."

"That was smart," she replied, looking out of the corner of her eye at his battered corpse. "And brave."

"It was horrible, Mila," he whispered, trying not to look. "But the worst part is the idea of having filled out so many bodies. I see my own death before my eyes and yet, somehow, I live. There's another *me* back home on Earth, either in a coma in an Air Force ICU, or already in a morgue. It seems so—"

"Worthless?"

"Interchangeable." He nodded. "A shell of flesh and bone to be discarded and recreated."

"I understand."

"Yes, now you understand, and for that I am very sorry."

"It's all right, I guess. Honestly, I don't know. Oh, here comes the next one!"

He turned around and saw the mercurylike milk spreading across the seat he had just used, flowing together from several invisible glands to gradually form a body. Although it took just a minute, the process now seemed to be in slow motion.

"Did you all make it into the teleporter?" Mila asked, and he nodded.

"Yes. Norton tried to order the soldiers to stop firing, but they didn't listen."

"What?"

"Yes, it seems that Pavar has issued an order over his head. Either she doesn't fully trust him anymore, or she's afraid for her position. Politicians like her become control freaks when things might land on their heads."

"You're probably right about that. Is he coming...?"

"No. He wants to stay behind and try to influence what happens around the project as much as he can. I think he wanted us to do this."

"Mhm," Mila intoned and nodded. "The speech he gave us about the evacuation? The reference to the ramp being taken down soon? I thought that was a little strange. Who would have thought that a military man would end up being the most sensible?"

"Yeah, who would have thought?" They reached forward as Mette opened her eyes and looked around in disbelief. They pulled her out of the seat as gently as possible, yet insistently, before maneuvering her into the opposite seat, careful not to put her arms on the induction strips.

"It's all right, Mette," Mila said gently.

"Mila!" The confusion faded from the Dane's eyes and was replaced by genuine joy and relief. "You're alive!"

"Yeah, I guess so. I guess you can't say that about my body on the other side?"

Mette's expression darkened, and compassion spread across her face before she shook her head almost imperceptibly.

Mila nodded. "It's okay; I was expecting it. At least I'm still alive."

She pronounced the word "I" in a strange, drawn-out manner as if it was difficult for her to get it over her tongue. On impulse, James grabbed her hand and squeezed it. She did not let go and nodded gratefully, which warmed his heart in all the excitement.

"Could have at least taken off a few pounds for me," Mette muttered, feeling her soft, bulging belly.

"Don't worry, this place will take care of it," he replied, wishing he was joking.

Next was Meeks, which was evident early on from the size and dimensions of the clone. The engineer narrowed his eyes in confusion and smiled a moment later in relief when his eyes fell on Mila. He hugged her, too, and then let them put him behind the outer row of seats to stand next to Mette like a schoolboy. They talked in hushed tones while James and Mila took care of the new arrivals.

Falkenhagen, with his muscular body that seemed to have no fat at and whose tanned skin was evident early in his clone's buildup, climbed out of his seat somewhat awkwardly and looked around like Alice in Wonderland. Amazed, he let them lead him to the side.

"You were right," he said as if surprised. "This is another teleporter. I'm not dreaming, am I?"

"No," James assured him, shaking his head. "I'm pretty sure, at least."

The German gasped in fright when he saw James's body, startling Meeks and Mette, who had ignored it until then. James and Mila turned back to the seat and waited for the "milk," while horror filled three voices behind them. He did not come. The glands remained closed.

"Where is he?" Mila whispered, looking over her shoulder at the others who had begun talking in hushed tones.

"I don't know. Maybe he got held up."

"Held up? You think Norton didn't have his back?"

Tense, James shrugged. Then his gaze fell past the back-rest to the dark funnel beyond.

"Or there's not enough biomass," he said, walking over to his body lying next to the outside seat where Mila must have dragged it after she arrived. He carelessly shooed the others away and grabbed his own ankles. They were cold and felt wet and far too soft. He concentrated on his task, groaning as he maneuvered the body along with Mila's help. The others watched, their faces pale and bewildered as they dragged the dead flesh to the hopper and pushed it between the backs of the seats. One of his legs, which were surprisingly heavy, broke with a sickening *crack*.

It took only a few heartbeats before the funnel made a smacking sound and his corpse slowly dissolved into a squishy red-gray mush that was sucked downward with a bubbling gurgle.

Violent nausea rose in James as he saw his own face amid the rapid decomposition process. It seemed to give him a reproachful look, the mouth agape in a silent scream held back by the dense white fibers. Then it cracked and crunched, and the head was pulled into the funnel.

His self-control broke and he fell forward on his trembling hands, vomiting and spitting out acrid stomach acid, as there was nothing else he could throw up.

Cold beads of sweat broke out on his skin and made him shiver. Mila, just as horrified, sat behind him, wrapping her arms and legs around him. She pulled his head back to her shoulder and held him tight.

"It's all right, James. It's okay."

Spasmodically, trying to calm his racing heartbeat and the much too rapid rise and fall of his breath, he barely noticed Smailov rising from the inner seat and being greeted by the others with hushed voices. Slowly he calmed down and let Mila's nearness ground him as he waited for the trembling in his limbs to subside.

"Thank you," Smailov said after a while, during which James hardly noticed anything around him. The Russian knelt in front of him and put a hand on his shoulder.

"It's all right, doctor," he said weakly.

"Adrian. My name is Adrian."

"Thank you."

"And I'm Justus," Falkenhagen said, standing behind everyone and eyeing him with a mixture of compassion and amazement.

"I am and always will be Meeks, just so we're clear," the American said, struggling to grin. He actually got James to crack something like a smile—or at least attempt to pull one off.

Everyone seemed confused. He could tell they didn't know how to handle the situation. True, they had known what would happen on an intellectual level—they would leave their bodies behind and waking up in new ones, exact replicas made by an alien machine on an alien planet. Experiencing it for themselves, however, was an entirely different matter.

He remembered how, in his mid-twenties, he had once been given a skydive as a birthday present. Because of his fear of heights, he had prepared for it for weeks, learning how to behave while hanging in front of the professional jumper's chest. When the time had come, and the airplane door had opened, all that knowledge was gone, and there was only him, the air, and the fear. Except this situation, here and now, was more comparable to jumping *without* a parachute because there was no way back. Shortly, the silo would be cemented in and thus sealed. When, or if, that should change, it could take years, which they all knew.

But how could they *understand*? How could they understand a situation like this? Being cut off from everything they knew, having their backs to the wall, and only able to flee forward. That they didn't seem to notice they were all standing around naked was another indication that their minds were on completely different things.

We need to keep moving so we don't have time to think about what we're doing, James thought. He tried to get up. Mila was slow to disengage from him. She and Adrian helped him to his feet.

"Thanks," he muttered, and turned to the glaring light behind him. "We should get going."

One by one, they nodded.

"Before we go out there, I need to explain a few things to you. It's really not pleasant out there. It's hot and smelly, and the monster I told you about... except for Adrian, you've all seen what it can do. Everything looks and smells like death. Be careful with your feet, don't touch the bushes, even if the layer of ash on them looks soft, you'll cut yourself on the thorns, and every scratch will turn into a festering abscess. We tried to bring strips of cloth and medicine from Nasaku's hiding place last time, but the monster... The things are now in a place I don't know that I can find again." James looked everyone in the eye to add emphasis to his words. "We're going straight to the downed spaceship because there are weapons there."

"Weapons?" Meeks asked incredulously. "But you never said anything about that! And neither did Norton."

"I didn't want the military to usurp the mission and go berserk at the mention of weapons, especially at what could be advanced technology. Who knows what the consequences would have been for Prime and Earth?"

The team nodded in agreement.

"I can't be sure they're weapons either because I couldn't see much, but we should at least check them out if we want to make it to the wall."

"Agreed," Adrian said.

"Take some of the fabric and wrap it around your feet. It's more important than your shame," James explained, seeing the first red cheeks and bashful looks. He gestured to the scraps of cloth near the seat, soaked with his clotted blood. "Trust me."

Reluctantly at first, then with a sudden determination, they set about wrapping their feet in the fabric. Only Mila stayed behind and knelt next to him.

"Are you really okay?"

"It's okay. None of you are better off, I think, but we have to live with that now because we have to *survive*."

"What about the marble Nasaku gave you?"

A shock ran through his limbs like electricity.

"I guess we'll find out soon enough. I just hope she knew it had to work. Otherwise, she wouldn't have given it to me and told me to bring them here. Also, we saw the implants in her body on the X-rays. So, the teleporter must be able to create objects as well."

"At least as long as they are part of the body."

James nodded. "You should take some of that stuff, too."

"What about you?" She glanced at the others. "Doesn't look like there's enough for everyone."

"I'll be fine. I'm reasonably familiar with the terrain, after all, and last time hardly anything happened," he lied, relieved when she nodded after a brief hesitation and went to join the rest of the team.

He took advantage of the moment alone. He turned around and with stiff limbs covered the two steps to the exit and slowly stuck his head through. The ladder was where they had left it—a little crooked, but the top rung still touched the edge. He lifted it with one hand and noticed that the branches that made up the end on the right and left were neatly trimmed as if by a precision laser. He let go of them and pulled back, looking at the glaring light and shuddering.

"Everyone ready?" he asked when Mila finally wrapped the last piece of cloth around her foot. The group was engrossed in quiet conversation. It was obvious from their faces that many thoughts were racing through their heads. There was a heaviness about them he felt inside, but they were making the effort and staying in control, which was the most important thing. "All right, let's go. There's a ladder. Be careful and crawl out backward. I'll go first and hold it."

Without waiting for their responses, he led the way and climbed through the light until his feet found a the first top run. Gently, he worked his way down, careful not to cause the ladder to sway. Once he was all the way out, it suddenly became warmer, though not as hot as it had been away from the teleporter. The stench of decay and sulfur was almost like recognition, and the horror of his escape with Norton on his back struck him in disconnected images. He closed his eyes for a moment and took a deep breath, stepping his feet into the ankle-deep mire and grabbing the ladder with both hands to hold it steady. There was something soothing about the mere touch of the rough wood.

Justus was the first to come out, and he was clearly more adept at it than he had felt. He landed in the swamp next to him and wrinkled his nose, then took the left side of the ladder in both hands. James did the same on the right side until the others had come out too. They then placed the ladder in the mud until it was no longer visible.

Mila looked up into the cloudy sky, and the others looked around uneasily. He gave them a moment to get used to their surroundings.

"You weren't exaggerating," Mette whispered.

"Let's get going," he suggested, adding in his mind, *before the monster notices us.*

When no one stirred, he started forward, walking in a straight line from the front of the teleporter toward its south. It was a little darker than last time, probably evening, or else the cloud cover was even thicker than usual, letting less light through. After a few hundred yards walking silently in single file with smacking footsteps and gurgling mud, a gray snow set in. James reached out and caught some of the flakes. They didn't melt, even though it was so hot. He smelled them and swallowed.

Ashes, he thought. *It's ash!*

The others murmured, but the sounds soon died away as the ground became rockier and the first foothills of the stone forest began. Now they had to concentrate so as not to slash their feet on the sharp-edged stones, but at the same time, he couldn't blame them for marveling at the impressive rock formations—perhaps the only thing in this godfor-saken place that radiated something like a bizarre aesthetic.

"They look like the giant claws of a monster that was buried here and frozen when it tried to break free," Adrian said reverently. His voice was quieter than expected. James turned and saw that the group had stopped and was looking around, wide-eyed, among the huge rock formations.

"I've never seen anything like it." Mette reached out and touched the rough rock. "How can rock bend like this? It's not like it was shaped and abraded like this by the wind."

"Maybe it's an ancient work of art?" Mila suggested.

"A work of art in this environment?"

"That's why ancient. Who knows what this place used to be."

"I'm sorry," James interrupted. "We have to keep moving!"

To his relief, no one objected, and they quickly detached themselves from the sight of the teeth—now that he had heard the comparison with the claws of an animal, he felt this image was more apt.

They made it to Nasaku's lair without any more stops, and more importantly, without the creature's howls. All the way there, everyone was silent, thinking, but as they slipped past the opening into the darkness of the cavernous room, they broke the silence.

"*This* is where she lived?" Mette asked, looking around in the twilight. Fine dust motes danced in the warm air, which provided enough buoyancy to lift the ubiquitous dirt —or let it trickle slowly from the ceiling.

"Is it a plane or a spaceship?"

"Where did all this damage come from?" Mila stroked one of the walls. "The material shows signs of abrasion, hard to tell how long it's been exposed to wind and weather, but things flying in the air or even in space shouldn't get holes that quickly."

"Norton wrote in his report that he believed a force of arms brought it down," Meeks replied, rummaging among the blankets James and the major had left behind to hang one of them around his neck.

"We don't have much time," James reminded them, and walked over to the hole in the wall. He almost felt guilty for not giving them time to get used to their new surroundings and process what they were seeing—after all, he knew all about it, and they didn't. Still, every minute the monster didn't hear them counted. Besides, the environment was toxic enough to cause abscesses to break out and trigger who knows what else in their bodies. So, the sooner they got to the drugs he and Norton had left behind when they escaped, the better. He had considered not looking for them, but the wall looked far away, and he could already see the first red spots appearing on the back of his hand, So, time was a scarce resource on Prime.

"The hole is here!"

He stood against the wall and rapped his knuckles on the cold metal next to the spot Nasaku had tried to pry open with her tools. "Norton and I took an axe and a knife last time. But I think there were others here, the light is pretty bad."

"This is hardened material," Meeks said, rapping his knuckles against the wall.

"Hardened?"

"Steel and other ferrous materials can gain increased mechanical resistance by changing their microstructures," Mila explained.

"What kind of structures?"

"The microstructure, the arrangement of its components. Mostly you do it industrially using heat and then quenching." The materials researcher ran her hands over the wall, which she gradually began to free from patina and lichen.

"If the spaceship really was shot down and the weapons are stored behind this wall," Justus said, helping her clean up the area just as Adrian and Mette were, "it makes sense if it was built entirely of composites. Where's the door?"

"There is no door," James replied, who had stepped back to give the scientists room, feeling useless as they exchanged ideas.

"Of course, there is," Meeks snorted. "Ever flown in an airplane where one area was inaccessible? It's hard to get in an out from the outside during the flight, after all."

James said nothing but wanted to hit his forehead with one hand. He had been too frightened the last few times or had seen the shelter more as a cave than a spaceship, which had prevented him from thinking clearly. In any case, he was glad they were there now. The group seemed completely in their element, exposing the wall and, with it, a lot of bumps and a ripple that went straight through the entire wall.

"What is it?"

"A deformation, that's good," Mila replied absently, directing Mette further to the left, where a straight shadow could be seen, now that his eyes had adjusted to the darkness.

"A deformation?"

"Yes, when metals like these deform plastically, for example, from a hard impact like a crash," Mette explained, "dislocations move in the structure. A perturbation of the periodicity of the crystal lattice that makes it up, simply put."

"I get it."

"A weak spot," Justus translated, emitting a triumphant sound as his fingers found a depression in the shadow line close to the wave. "This could work."

"Puncture and pry," Mila said. The rest of the team nodded, then turned away from the wall as if on silent command and systematically ransacked the lair.

James stood amid the ensuing chaos and watched as they gathered various items, like splinters, sticks, fragments of the blown open hull that looked almost pointed and sturdy, and fist-sized rocks. Everything that was sharp-edged, they finally hammered lengthwise into the depression along the edge of the deformation until a metallic screech was heard. Then they became even more motivated to work.

A few hours later, during which, helped by a shard, he had cut skirts from two blankets—one of which he took away from Meeks—and two bands so Mila and Mette could cover their breasts, which they had done.

Using a metal rod that had previously held the curtain over the door, they pried open the weakened wall structure and created a gap that eventually grew larger from bottom to top, through which a particularly slender person could climb.

24

"I'm going in," Mila decided, who was slightly taller than Mette, but noticeably slimmer and smaller than the men.

"No!" Everyone looked at James, who rose from the box where he had been working on the fabric and distributed the results to the others. "I'll go first; we don't know if it's dangerous there."

"It's just a room."

"We're not taking any chances," he insisted. "I've been watching you guys, and I'm sure you're more useful here than I am."

They wanted to contradict him, but he waved them off and pushed his way forward until he was standing in front of the opening in the wall. It looked like a folded-down lapel, except that it pointed in the wrong direction. More light than before now fell into the darkness, a bright, trapezoidal glow that illuminated an uneven floor. Several cracks ran lengthwise through the gleaming metal as if a monster with huge claws had torn it open. James carefully climbed through the sharp-edged cleft, moving slowly to avoid cutting himself until he finally stood on the other side. There was considerably less dust here, and the air was cooler, although a steady stream of warm moisture followed him. To the left were the oblong objects he had spied through the hole the last time. He eyed them thoughtfully, contemplating the bright shine, and did not move while the others tossed questions after him.

"What's wrong?"

He startled. It was Mila, who was suddenly standing next to him and eyeing him with a furrowed brow.

"I was just thinking."

"Now?"

"Yes. Nasaku apparently tried to punch a hole in the wall. Why would she have done that other than to get in here?"

"I see. You wonder why she didn't come up with the same idea we did, after all, she was pretty smart," she said.

James nodded. "Smart enough to learn English, escape from a high-security facility, learn to drive, and use a computer in an observatory in a matter of hours. So why didn't she pry the wall open herself?"

"It was quite a bit of work, even for five of us."

"She had all the time in the world."

"Hmm. Maybe she wasn't interested in guns." Mila shrugged.

"There's still the monster out there. And she always had an axe and a knife with her," he countered.

"The axe and knife are tools. She could have used them to cut cloth when her shoes needed mending or to build things like the ladder. The axe might even have served as a kind of climbing hook she could use to get into the teleporter without taking the ladder." Mila sensed he wasn't convinced. "When you were first here, did she use her tools as weapons to intimidate you?"

"No, I don't think so." He shook his head and tried to remember. "But that's not proof that she didn't need weapons."

"It's possible she found a way to avoid the creature or knew its sleeping hours."

"It's possible. But she was worried when we heard it and made me hurry."

"That also makes sense. After all, you didn't know how to act and she couldn't very well explain it to you." Mila went to the left wall and James followed her. There was a built-in cabinet that merged into the wall forming one piece. Inside were six items that took considerable effort to remove from the pincerlike holders.

"These are clearly rifles," he muttered, surprised. He grasped the handle with one hand and placed the other under the barrel. It was slightly shorter and wider than a normal assault rifle, but it had a muzzle and a trigger. Undoubtedly a weapon, albeit very light.

Mila checked deftly her own. She pointed the front end toward the ground and pulled the trigger. A sudden flash blinded them both and they cried out. Dirt and metal shards sprayed up.

"Shit!" he yelled.

"They obviously work," Mila commented dryly.

"Can you give me a heads-up next time?"

"I honestly didn't expect them to work. I haven't been able to find a reloading mechanism yet."

"Maybe they work off a high-capacity battery or some other power source. Was that even a projectile?"

"I don't know."

"Are you all right in there?" Adrian asked anxiously.

"Yeah, all good!" James called back, walking to the opening to pass his rifle through. "Watch out, they're loaded."

He released the others from their holders and handed them out until there was only one left. Mila nudged him and pointed to the other side of the room. He could just make out the dark outline of some kind of framework that covered that entire area of the spaceship.

"Do you see that?" she asked, but he shook his head. She walked to the opening to Nasaku's hiding place and said something he couldn't hear. Someone handed her a piece of metal, which she polished using her improvised skirt until it shone. She then positioned herself in the center of the faint area of light and turned the metal so it reflected light on the armature.

James turned to it and recoiled. What he had thought was a black wall turned out to be a row of figures. At first, he thought they were alive and rushing toward him, but that was merely an optical illusion. There were six humanoid outlines clad in armor that looked familiar and yet very alien. Dark slats stretched across the limbs and came together in a suit that appeared to be made of a single piece and looked like rubber. The helmets were conical, with a dark band where the wearers' eyes should have been, but he saw only nostrils and bits of skeleton behind a transparent visor.

"Damn..." he said and swallowed.

"They've obviously been dead a long time," Mila said, pressing the metal shard into his hand so he could provide light while she walked over to the bodies. They were stuck in holders on the wall much like their weapons, as if someone had planted them there. "No tissue residue left. I'm guessing at least a few decades, more likely centuries. You can already see bone abrasion, even though the skeleton is completely encased in this armor."

"With the hot, humid air, they should have decomposed by now, right?" James asked, controlling his breathing.

"Yes, actually. At least there are usually weak spots in any material after so long. Any kind of insect normally thrives in this climate, but apparently there's nothing here that will eat away at the bone."

"But then how did the meat come off the bones?"

"Microorganisms. Even if there's hardly anything crawling around there must be bacteria; after all, the bushes outside wouldn't survive without microorganisms. It's possible that the skulls behind these sensor bands will turn to dust if we touched them—although I can't be sure because of the humidity."

"Exactly six."

"Excuse me?" she asked, glancing over her shoulder at him.

"Six bodies, six guns." He pointed to the dead in their bulky suits and the now-empty gun cabinet across from them. "And there are exactly six of us, too. A strange coincidence, don't you think?"

"Yes, but irrelevant."

"Irrelevant? How can anything here be irrelevant."

"Quite simply because people always tend to see parallels in everything and interpret meaning into it because the brain is constantly looking for patterns. These are coincidences, false connections." Mila shrugged and grabbed one of the rigid suits by the shoulders and pulled on it with all her might. Nothing moved except a small avalanche of dust that blew toward her and triggered a violent coughing fit.

"Are you okay?"

"Yeah," she gasped hoarsely. "Those things are stuck like granite."

"Do you also think it's a mere coincidence that we find people here, of all places?" he asked laconically.

"No."

When she added nothing more, he sighed. "We shouldn't waste any time. Let's get going. The last two times, it's always cleared up at night. The clouds seem to cover the sky during the day; that's why, paradoxically, it gets lighter at night."

"Okay." Reluctantly, she broke away from the silent witnesses of a time gone by and returned to him. "I wish we had more time to investigate all this."

"We don't, though." He lowered the improvised mirror and gently took her hand in his. She looked up at him with an almost shy expression. He wanted to just stand there and sink into her big blue eyes, but instead he turned her hand over so she could see the abscess forming. It was already showing the first signs of pus blisters.

Startled, she blinked. "Oh, my goodness."

"Yes. We need to hurry and find the drugs," he said anxiously, and pushed her toward the four pairs of eyes gathered around the opening trying to see as much as possible, though he didn't think they could make out much with the dim scattered light.

They quickly explained to the team what they had found and, under Adrian's and Mila's instruction, familiarized themselves with the rifles, which functioned exactly like ones they knew from Earth. muzzle on target, fingers on the trigger—which was bent outward somewhat oddly— and the shock pad on the shoulder, though Mila assured them that the weapon hardly had any recoil and had fired an energy pulse rather than a kinetic projectile.

Somewhat clumsily, they each now carried a rifle in their hands, which seemed out of place except for the two Russians, especially since they all looked like dirty savages with their improvised loincloths and skirts made of half-torn fabric covered with dirt.

James poked his head out of the breach leading outside. He saw irregular holes already forming in the cloud cover, and the darkness was being dispelled by slowly penetrating moonlight.

It would have to do.

They set off on a direct path toward the teleporter, for which he merely had to lead them at a right angle from the wreckage of the spaceship. The torn-off delta wing served as a signpost. Even now, the monster was not to be heard. No eerie roaring, no hissing, and no gentle tremors in the rock beneath their feet. Still, James remained tense as a spring and tried to make as little noise as possible, which wasn't difficult with his wrapped feet. It was more difficult to get the team to remain silent because they constantly wanted to discuss what they had found in Nasaku's lair. He understood they wanted to distract themselves from the eerie landscape and the shattered moon that extended across the starry sky. They had also found evidence there were—or had been—people outside of Earth, which seemed to make them alternately nervous and pensive.

It was probably his anxiety that eventually caused them to relent and fall silent, and soon they were trotting, a silent procession through the stone forest with its rocky claws frozen in time.

Where did we turn left? James kept thinking until they

reached the edge of the morass, where the layer of mud and smelly biomass was several inches thick. *Too far.*

He headed toward his relative west, trying to block out the memories of the last time he had run through here, almost blind with adrenaline, Norton behind him.

How long? How long did we walk?

It was impossible to remember. If he barely had a rational sense of time now, he hadn't had it at all during their flight. He beckoned the others over and they fanned out, ten meters apart so they could keep a good eye on each other while simultaneously searching a larger area. Although Mila and Meeks plodded nearby to his right and left like shadowy figures, he felt more alone than before.

But it worked. After what felt like an eternity, Adrian shouted and ran to one of the large rock cliffs. Even at a distance, James recognized the huge white patch and the two brown piles that looked like closely spaced bushes but were actually the two bags he and Norton had left behind. Hastily, he grabbed one bag and shook it gently. Satisfied, he opened it and pulled out six of the filled injectors.

"Come on. This is the stuff Nasaku gave me for the abscesses. It worked quickly, and we shouldn't risk anything."

"Not risking anything?" Justus asked, wiping dust and sweat from his forehead with the back of his hand. "Injecting us with a foreign drug we know nothing about sounds pretty risky."

"I guess it's an antibiotic. Highly effective, if you ask me. After just a short time, my abscess had receded."

Adrian stepped forward and held out his arm. "There's no time for caution here."

The cosmonaut was right. Even worse than the others, his skin was covered with red petechiae and he had thick pustules on his face and stomach. James pressed the injector to his neck and triggered the button on the back. The Russian blinked briefly. He tossed the empty container away and repeated the procedure on Mila, Meeks, and Mette, and finally Justus, who took a deep breath before reluctantly presenting his neck.

They allowed themselves a short break, during which James walked a short distance away from the group and stuck a finger down his throat. At first, it didn't work because his gag reflex didn't kick in, but he kept doing it until his throat hurt and he tasted blood. Finally, he vomited up the dark marble in a gush of acrid stomach acid. He held it in his hand along with some bloody threads of mucus in relief. He wiped it off and returned to the others.

"Good. For the wall, we just go in any direction. I don't remember too well, but it looked like the teleporter was right in the middle, so we should stay away from the swamp and walk in one direction until we hit the wall," he suggested. The others nodded silently. James shouldered one of the bags, and Adrian took the second one with the cloth samples. Because of the heat, no one helped themselves to the many ribbons he and Norton had prepared .

They had just started moving when they heard a deep, drawn-out rumble. At first, he thought it was distant thunder, but James quickly realized it was his brain's refusal to recognize the true source: the monster. All his hopes that it was injured from their last encounter and had retreated were dashed away with that one angry sound.

"Oh, darn!" He gripped the assault rifle's handle a little tighter and held it against him like a drowning man clinging to a piece of flotsam before reluctantly grabbing the bag of medicines and slinging it over his shoulder. "We should get out of here."

"I think it came from the direction of the teleporter," Adrian said, squinting and looking in the appropriate direction. The black plain of the swamp seemed to absorb the pale moonlight, which created no reflections at all and made it hard to see anything.

"Then we should go in the opposite direction." Mila pointed to the west. Her head jerked back and forth. If she had been tense before, now she seemed electrified.

"Go!" James moved, settling into an easy run, even though a voice in the back of his head screamed at him to take flight and run as fast as he could. But he didn't let the adrenaline pulsing through his veins take over, instead focusing on steady breaths and precise strides to avoid falling with his load. They still had several miles to go, and they wouldn't make it if they exhausted themselves in the first few hundred yards.

This time they stayed close together, which probably wasn't very smart, but no one said anything, feeding off each other's proximity. The gurgling calls of the monster drove them on like a bow wave of ferocity, and every single thought of the gleaming metal teeth made James shudder. It still sounded far away, but it was undoubtedly getting closer.

The landscape soon changed. Though still rocky, it was now free of the large rocky crags. Round patches on the bare ground appeared glazed and looked slippery, but James's feet were already so bruised, the fabric so soaked in blood, that this paradoxically made it easier for him to keep his balance. He hardly felt the pain with all the excitement, even though he that he would have to pay the price once the adrenaline wore off—or the monster ate him.

"Do you see that?" Meeks gasped at last. The tall engineer seemed to consist primarily of sweat, which ran in rivers from his forehead, nose, and chin and coated his skin with a film of damp dirt.

James was about to reflexively say "No" but at that moment he saw it too: The wall.

It had been visible as a dark dividing line on the horizon for a while because it was a bit higher than they would have been expected the ground to be, and there also appeared to be some kind of door or port to the east, through which the dark blue night sky could be seen.

"What... is... that?" Mette asked breathlessly. The portly Dane looked fatigued. She had stopped as little as the rest, yet was barely stumbling along. Every other step looked as if she would lose her balance and fall.

"A damaged piece of wall?" Mila suggested, slowing down giving silent permission to the others, who seemed to have been merely waiting for a sign, to do the same. The whole group slowed their steps and struggled for air, panting. The air was thick enough to cut and hot enough to make James's lungs glow.

"Don't stop!" he admonished them. "If it's a breach... we should change direction. But never stop."

"James, I'm almost at the end of my rope," Mette whined.

"If you'd seen the monster, you'd find some." It came out sharp, which he didn't notice, and so they ran on in silence, driven by their loud panting. The glassy plain now looked like a huge skating rink, smooth enough that the moon's debris could be seen mirrored in it, and single passing wisps of clouds formed dull patches.

After a while, Adrian snapped James out of his trance of burning muscles, steady rushing breath, and adrenaline throbbing in his ears.

"I don't hear it anymore."

"What?"

"The monster. It's finally..." The cosmonaut paused and propped his hands on his knees. "It's been a long time since we've heard it."

It was true. He hadn't noticed, but now that he thought about it, he realized Adrian was right. There had been no roaring or hissing for a while now. Had the monster disappeared? Had it lost their scent?

"Maybe... it stays in the stone forest? Could be some kind of range," Meeks suggested. "Shit, what I wouldn't give for a drink of water."

James didn't answer. He let the others talk while he stared into the twilight with narrowed eyes. The forest of rocky crags was just visible as a distant stubbly field behind them. In front of the group, the wall loomed, a gigantic black barrier, perhaps a hundred yards high, and still a mile away, which seemed to him as far as a marathon. It was overwhelming, and under other circumstances he would have simply stood there in amazement that something so impressive could exist.

Just as he was about to turn back to the group, he looked one last time in the other direction, to where the teleporter stood somewhere in the distance.

Suddenly the glassy stone floor broke open a few dozen meters away. A fountain of shards and debris shot into the air like a geyser of sharp-edged shrapnel. Two powerful arms tipped with gleaming claws struck the edge and emitted an ugly screech as the monster pulled itself out of the hole. Eyeless and with its mouth open, its razorlike teeth glinting in the moonlight, its head swung around, snuffling, until it settled on James and their utterly debilitated group.

"Run!" Adrian yelled pointlessly, and no one needed to be told twice. They took off. James was right behind Mette, who tripped on a notch. Her right ankle cracked so loudly that it went through James's spine. She fell prone. Her rifle slipped from her hands and skidded across the slick ground like a metaphor of her dwindling luck.

The shock on everyone's faces said what he knew: there was no rescue for them.

Uncertain, James knelt beside the Dane, who began crying bitterly. She shooed the others away, sobbing, as they came to her. He looked at the monster, which was about to work its way out of the hole and rubble.

"Keep running!" he finally said to the team, pointing to the breach in the wall, well within reach and yet so far away. "Go!"

"No, we're not leaving her alone!" Mila protested.

"We aren't. I'm staying with her." As soon as the words left his mouth, a deep calm spread through him. That surprised him as much as what he had just decided to do without thinking about it. Still, it felt right.

"No! We fight!"

"We won't discuss it. I'm not leaving her alone..." *Die?* he thought, swallowing. "You're much more suited for all this than I am. The rifles probably won't do much to the monster. Besides, my feet won't carry me much further."

He pointed at his bloody toes peeking out of the equally bloody fabric. Then he took the marble and held it out to Mila. When she didn't take it, Adrian snatched it from his hand and gave him a look of respect.

"You are the bravest of us, and we need you the most," Mila whispered, her eyes filling with tears as the inevitability of what was to follow became apparent to her. She seemed to want to say much more, but her lips trembled uncontrollably.

Meeks and Justus looked agonized, unable to say

anything, and trembled when the creature let out a blood-curdling scream.

"*GO!*" James roared, shooing them away. Adrian grabbed Mila and dragged her along. Her hesitation quickly broke under the monster's roar, and he was immensely relieved when the four scientists ran away.

"James, no," Mette whimpered, lying on the ground, clutching her broken ankle.

"I'm right where I'm supposed to be. I can't run anymore, but I can walk this last road with you." He raised the rifle and looked at the approaching creature. With the stock against his shoulder, he leveled it and pulled the trigger. A flash burst from the muzzle and tore a piece of skin from the monster's flank, but James didn't see any blood, nor did he notice it slow down. Nodding, he threw the gun away and stood in front of the Dane so she wouldn't have to face the approaching horror.

"James, it's not too late—"

"Yes, it is," he interrupted her, staring at what was rushing toward them and would reach them in a few breaths.

"Is that the gatekeeper?"

Her question surprised him. "What?"

"You told us Nasaku said that we had to convince the gatekeeper that we were not one of those First Children to get past the wall. If she meant that one, then the others will..."

A loud roar tore the night apart.

"The gatekeeper. That comes from *portenarius*, meaning gatekeeper," he said, surprised by his sudden analytical calm, even though the knife-armed mouth was moments away from tearing him apart. The silence deepened, born of the knowledge that this was his end, and he became quite lucid. "It's the guardian of this place, just like her."

Nasaku had no weapons with her because she didn't need any, he thought. *She was not an enemy of the guardian. What if he protected this area from the enemies of this world? The First Children who destroyed it? They destroy anything that scares them, just like we do on Earth. Why didn't it pursue and kill Norton and me after we fought it?*

On impulse, he spread his arms and closed his eyes, anticipating the fatal bite.

But it did not come. When he opened his eyes, he was staring into the eyeless grimace of the beast, which sniffed at him, its two nostrils flaring from the top of its wedge-shaped head. Its mouth was slightly open and smelled of ozone and rusted metal. Like a gigantic shadow, it had built itself up in front of him, crouched and yet clearly larger than he was.

"James?" Mette asked behind him. She sounded uncertain but not panicked.

"We are not afraid," he answered without moving. "We are not afraid of you because we are not your enemy."

The monster retreated a short distance, then roared at him again with its mouth open, so loud that his ears rang. The teeth were barely a hand's width from him and he stared directly into the black hole that formed its throat which seemed to swallow every scrap of light from the environment. James remained steadfast, clenching his jaws and closing his eyes briefly until he heard another sniff and saw the creature was sniffing his left hand, the hand that had held the marble before Adrian grabbed it.

Slowly, the creature retreated, its claws scraping across the glasslike ground, the head tucked and shoulders hunched, before wheeling around and running in the direction where James suspected the teleporter was.

"What... what was that all about?" Mette asked.

"That was the guard who realized we are not a danger because we do not belong to the enemy but to his mistress."

"Nasaku," she breathed.

He nodded and turned to her.

"Come on."

"I can't."

"But I can carry you."

EPILOGUE

The view from the top of the wall bridge was breathtaking. James stood between Mila and Mette and held both their hands to confirm that he was really here.

Even before the monster had disappeared from view, he had carried the Dane piggyback, dismissing her pleas that he leave her behind as nonsense. Although his back and legs—nay, his entire body—ached, he got her to the base of the cleft in the wall, cut through the gigantic structure as if a giant's axe had struck it. At its highest point, it was still many stories higher than the glassy ground. The others had seen him, thanks to Mila, who had turned around further up the slope and stared at him in disbelief before running so frantically down the descent that his heart would have stopped if it hadn't been pounding so hard in his chest.

Stunned, the others fell over him like age-old friends or family members, embracing and hugging him—an outburst that would have been strange under other circumstances since they hardly knew each other. But nothing brougth people together like looking death in the eye.

They somehow managed to carry, pull, and heave Mette over the large fragments, even if it cost them precious energy. Her chapped lips and the dark circles under her eyes told of her impending dehydration. The Dane now sat on a column of rubble that reminded James of weathered concrete. Adrian, Meeks, and Justus, on the other side, were breathing heavily and kept rubbing fresh drops of sweat from their eyes and the tips of their noses.

"This is beautiful," Mila said from beside him, and he could only agree with her.

The land laid out before them was bathed in lush green, not exactly glowing in the moonlight but illuminated enough to suggest that it would resemble Earth's finest greenery in sunlight. The seemingly endless forest land-scape stretched to the horizon, and amid the green leaves glowed myriads of tiny blue fireflies—at least that's what he thought they were. Straight ahead was a river or gulf that narrowed like a funnel toward the wall, its black tides reflecting the fragmented glow of the moon. It ended a few miles ahead of them, splitting into dozens of smaller branches.

"You see that?" he asked, extending a hand to the northwest.

"Are those lights?" Meeks asked breathlessly.

"I think so."

"It could be a city," Mette commented.

James squinted and had to agree with her. He saw some-thing like evenly shaped towers, duller than the surrounding trees, and between them were scattered lights that illuminated the unnatural structures in warm yellow.

"Do you hear that?" he asked. No one answered, but they all smiled, which was answer enough for him. Birdsong could not be ignored once you hadn't heard any for a long time. Excited chatter, happy chirps, and complex melodies blended into a crescendo of life after coming from the most hostile place James had ever been.

"Sounds like we made it," Mila said softly, squeezing his hand.

"I see water; I see green vegetation, and I see and hear *life*," Meeks said.

"I see a whole planet we have to explore." Smailov peered into the night like a hawk. "We've stumbled forward along the path since we left, but now, finally, we can see it."

James nodded. "I see *hope*, and the birds singing can only mean that a new morning is dawning."

AFTERWORD

Dear Reader,

Stanley Kubrick did it in his film adaptation of *2001: A Space Odyssey* (and *The Sentinel*), Stephen Baxter did it with *Proxima*, MGM did it with *Stargate*, and more recently, Peterson did it with *Transport*. The subgenre of portal fiction has fascinated me for a very long time, and after enjoying (and in some cases adoring —*go SG1*!) all the aforementioned representatives as a whole, I wanted to write my own story with a portal to the stars. I hope you enjoyed this opening volume, even if it was set up a bit differently than my previous books with significantly less action and only one protagonist.

If you enjoyed this book, I would be very happy if you would leave a star rating or a short review on Amazon. This is the best way to help authors continue to write exciting books into the future. You can contact me directly at Joshua@joshuatcalvert.com —I answer every email!

If you subscribe to my newsletter, I'll regularly tell you a bit about myself, my writing, and the great themes of science fiction. Plus, as a thank you, you'll receive my e-book *Rift: The Transition* exclusively and for free. Sign up at www.joshuatcalvert.com.

Warm regards,
   Joshua T. Calvert

Made in United States
North Haven, CT
16 April 2023

35518295R00211